Envisions
PUBLISHING COMPANY

AUTOGRAPH PAGE

To be used exclusively to recognize that special King or
Queen for their support

i

7/09 15⁰⁰

This is a work of fiction. Any references or similarities to actual events, locales, real people, living or dead are intended to give the novel a sense of reality. Any similarity in other names, characters, places and incidents is entirely coincidental.

Envisions
PUBLISHING COMPANY

Envisions Publishing, LLC
P.O. Box 83008
Conyers, GA 30013

ISBN: 978-0-9706102-2-5

First Printing September 2008
Printed in the United States of America

10 9 8 7 6 5 4 3 2 1

Submit Wholesale Orders to:
Envisions Publishing, LLC
P.O. Box 83008
Attn: Shipping Department
Conyers, GA 30013

Preacherman Blues is dedicated to the Creator. Whether you call Him God, ALLAH, Jehovah, Yahweh, or the Most High, He knows when you're speaking to Him. So as not to offend, I'll use the One or the Creator. The word *the* signifies His oneness. We must realize that it's about Oneness, the Oneness that ties everything, inanimate and animate, together. Without Him nothing is possible. So, in closing, I want everyone who reads these words to take a moment and pray for wisdom freedom, and strength, and then pray the same for someone you don't even know. Next, stop letting Man and the Media lead you. Follow God and you won't go wrong.

Enjoy PREACHERMAN BLUES, family

Love and Life

Jihad

APPRECIATION PAGES

There are so many wonderful Kings and Queens that helped make PREACHERMAN BLUES a reality, and I may miss a few but please, family, chalk it up to my tired and exhausted mind.

First and foremost I give thanks to the Creator, for without You nothing is possible.

I took a lot of flack for not mentioning family in my last book MVP as I'm sure I'll miss family and friends with Preacherman Blues. Please fam, chalk it up to my mind not my heart. I'll start with Mom, always have to start with the woman that gave me life and light. My younger brother Andre' Frazier his wife Katrina Renee Frazier, My superwoman sister La-Shl Frazier; my nieces; Ja-Queitz, Sadaka, Luscious, Ja-mease, La Meeka, Ronnie, and Shommie; my nephews: I-Keitz, and Billy; and my sister, Karen.

Thanks, Maurice, my friend, brother, and Publisher, for believing in me enough to take that buyout from FORD, packing up and moving down to the ATL. Thanks, Reshonda

Tate Billingsley, for all your input and trash talk. Without you as a friend I'd be lost. *Oh yeah and I'm still waiting on my role in your new movie*. Thanks, Thomas Long, for your friendship and always having my back. Thanks, Kevin Elliott, for schooling me and being down. Thanks, Travis Hunter, for always giving me that extra push. Thanks, Letonya Shaw for that revolutionary Christian spirit that you bless me with everytime I speak to you. Thanks, Victoria Christopher Murray, for all your input, support, and most important your friendship. Thanks, Kim, for being my proof reading eyes. Thanks, S. James Guitard, for taking me to school, and giving me so much invaluable game. Thanks so much Zane for everything. A very special thanks to my co-publisher, Bridget Robinson for making this book happen.

Thanks, James B. Sims, my editor; you are the man. And for those who haven't read his book *In Rare Form* (the bible on how to write a novel from start to finish) log on to amazon.com to purchase *In Rare Form* by Cordless Sims. Thanks Keith for weaving your magic with the cover and all the publicity material. Very special thanks to RJ publications and Richard Jeanty for all you've done.

Thanks Pam Hunter of *Wake Up Publicity*, wakeuppub@hotmail.com. Girl, you are off the chain. Thanks for being so much more than a publicist.

And I'd like to give a very special thanks to Barrack Obama. If a man with the name of Barrack Obama can get past the hate so can a man name with the name Jihad.

Special thanks to the queens of J.O.W. book club in the ATL. T.C. and RAWSISTAZ, you've supported my books since day one. Thank you. Thank you so much, Nova Wade, Gloria Withers, and the other queens of *Changing Chapterz* book club in Philly. Thanks to all the queens of *Turning Pages* book club in Oakland. Thanks to Shunda Leigh and all the Queens of *Circle of Sisters* book club, the ATL chapter. Thanks Lenda, and the Queens of *Mo' Better View* book club. And thanks to all the book clubs that have supported me in the past, and please keep on supporting.

And I give a very special thanks to the Kings and Queens living behind America's prison walls.

And, as usual, I'll save the most important thank-you last. Every King and Queen who reads my work, if it weren't for you I would've given up long ago. I read and answer every e-mail and it is you who inspire me to keep writing. When others tell me to write real hardcore street fiction, baby momma drama or something closely related to infidelity mainstream fiction, it is your words that keep my eyes on the prize, and true to the creating of uplifting, conscious, real-life stories. Thank you and keep the **e-mails, the guestbook, and Amazon.com reviews flowing.**

Buy any of Jihad's books online or at a 30% discount and learn where he'll be signing or speaking at www.jihadwrites.com and please tell others what you think by posting a review on www.amazon.com or signing Jihad's guestbook at www.jihadwrites.com. Or you can purchase any of his books at any store where books are sold.

Love and Life

Jihad

PREACHERMAN BLUES

"Whoever controls the images, controls your self-esteem, self-respect, and self-development. Whoever controls the history, controls the vision."

Dr. Leonard Jeffries

PROLOGUE

"**F**ifty dollars?" The sing-song voice had all but disappeared. "Negro…" The same fingernail that ran up the length of TJ's arm a minute ago was now threatening to stab him in the chest. "You really thought I was gon' open my legs for your old crusty behind for fifty damn dollars?"

TJ looked around the small church, knowing good and well they were the only ones there. Suddenly, he grabbed her arm and pulled her "kiss close". In a low, guttural tone, he replied, "A deal is a deal. I gave you twenty the first time for nothing. The second time I gave you thirty so your momma could get your lights turned back on. And both times you promised that you'd come back to play."

"Ouch. You're hurting me," she whined.

He released her arm.

"No more games, Pastor Money, I swear. I just need one more tiny favor, and I promise I'm all yours," she said, licking her bright red lipstick stained lips.

TJ crossed his arms and legs, trying to prevent Tracy from seeing the bulge emerging from the crotch of his gray slacks.

"Aunt Carmen ain't got no money, and she tired of getting slapped around by her husband, Ray. She need sixty dollars to buy a gun so he can't come get her when she move in with us. I swear to God—"

"Don't swear," TJ interrupted her.

"Promise to God, cross my heart, hope to die, stick a brick in my eye–you give me that money right now and I'll be back in twenty."

Tracy's small chest heaved and her little nipples threatened to break through the tight cotton wife-beater she wore.

With his eyes still glued to her chest, he reached inside the small bank bag with the day's tithes and offerings. "I'm going into God's pocket for you, little lady. You can take it or leave it, but I'm tellin' you, if you don't make good on your promise, I'll be around to collect what you owe God."

CHAPTER 1

Shortly after earning his Masters in Divinity, Percival had married his high school sweetheart, Maya Jackson, and they'd bought a small starter home near New Bethel in the Atlanta suburb of Lithonia.

It was a beautiful May day in 1985 and everything was going well until his mentor and spiritual leader, Pastor Garey, passed away in his sleep. Within hours of Pastor Garey's passing, Percival was told that he would be next to lead New Bethel.

"Maya, come on now!" Percival shouted in the direction of his and his wife's bedroom. "Woman, you gon' be late to your own funeral."

"No, I won't. Not if you have anything to do with it. Ain't like Pastor Garey got somewhere to be. Besides, his funeral is at one. It's only eleven-thirty!" Maya shouted from the bedroom.

"I know, Sweetie, but it's a plum mess outside. You know folks in Atlanta already drive like a blind man without no arms."

"Why don't you call Pastor Shady Long Dollar again?"

"Maya?"

Maya stood knee-high to a grasshopper, but she was a fiery woman with a loose tongue.

"Why are you so insistent that I call him by his real name, TJ Money? You know I'm just kidding," she said.

"No, you're not," Percival stated with a disapproving look on his face.

Maya had never liked TJ. She swore he was a phony. She just couldn't see what Percival saw in the man. TJ was his best friend, and had been since their college days. No one could convince him that TJ wasn't one-hundred percent devoted to spreading the word of God. Percival knew the man had his shortcomings, but he always reminded her that so had the Apostle Paul.

Maya walked into the kitchen wearing a black dress and silver hoop earrings. Her walk, talk, and everything about her put one in the mind of *Sofia*, Oprah's character in *The Color Purple*.

"I'm a little worried, Sweetie. This isn't like TJ."

"What do you mean? TJ's the stand-up king," Maya flatly stated.

"No, I mean he always returns my calls. And you have to admit, TJ hasn't missed Sunday dinner in a long time now."

A minute later, Maya and Percival were walking out the front door when a dark blue Chevrolet Caprice pulled into the driveway behind Percival's ten-year-old white Fleetwood.

Percival looked at the detectives getting out of the car. *Why do detectives look like undertakers?* he wondered. *And if a brotha took off running, how in the world did they figure they'd catch them wearing those shiny, round hush puppies? Especially in the rain.*

"Why you smiling?" Maya asked.

"No reason, just thinking." Percival handed Maya the umbrella. "Baby, take this, and go wait in the car. Whatever this is, it shouldn't take long," Percival said, turning toward the two men who were now on the doorstep.

"Percival Turner?" the taller of the two asked.

"Yes, Sir."

"Can you please come with us?"

"Come with you where?" He frowned. "And for what?"

"We need you to come downtown and answer some routine questions."

"Routine questions about what?"

"We're not at liberty to expound until we get downtown," the other detective explained.

"I'm on my way to preside over a funeral. I'd be glad to meet you afterwards."

"A funeral on a Monday?" the taller detective asked.

Before he could reply, the phone rang. "Hold on; let me get that," Percival said before turning and heading to the phone on the kitchen wall.

"Hello, Percival Turner speaking," Percival answered at the start of the third ring.

"Pastor Turner, my name is Marvin Taylor. I'm an attorney representing Pastor Terrell Joseph Money," the voice on the phone said.

"What happened?" Percival asked while instinctively massaging his temples.

"Pastor Money was accused of sexually assaulting a young girl last night. He told the authorities that, at the time the girl was molested, he was at your home having dinner, and afterwards, you helped him study for his doctoral dissertation."

Percival almost jumped out of his skin when he turned to see one of the detectives staring down his throat.

In a much brighter tone, Percival spoke into the receiver. "Yes, Ms. Bailey, the service is at one sharp."

"Huh? Who is Ms. Bai—"

"I would love to talk to you about your late husband, Ma'am, but I've got company and I have to get over to New Bethel," he said, before hanging up the phone.

"Mr. Turner, while you were on the phone, I made a call to my superior. He informed me that we could wait until after the funeral. So, if you're ready, we're prepared to escort you and your wife to the service," the taller detective said.

"I have a better idea," Percival said, picking up the phone. Seconds later, Deacon Perry answered. "Deacon? Percival Turner. I don't have time to explain." Percival shook his head. "No. No. No. I'm fine, but I have a family emergency and I need you to preside over the services. I know it's last minute; forgive me, but I have a dire emergency. Thank you. God bless." Percival hung up before the Deacon could say anything else.

"Maya!" Percival shouted after opening the front door.

"Baby, what's wrong?" Maya asked.

He held a hand over his chest. "Other than scaring the life outta me, nothing," he said.

"Sir, are you ready?" one of the detectives standing behind Percival asked.

"Ready for what?" Maya asked.

"Sweetie, I need you to represent me at Pastor Garey's homegoing services." He shot her a please don't ask look. "Please, Maya. I have to go downtown and answer some questions." He grabbed her hand. "Don't worry; I'll explain everything later."

*****

Were funerals held for prisoners executed by the state? Percival didn't know where this thought came from as he was escorted down a long hall that reminded him of the movie, *The Green Mile*, where prisoners walked down a narrow hall to the death chamber. At the end of the hall, a police officer opened a door and led him to a stainless steel seat behind a long, stainless steel table.

The gray concrete floor matched the walls, and the room smelled like disinfectant.

All types of questions and weird "good cop, bad cop" scenarios tap danced through his mind before a short black woman entered the interrogation room.

"Reverend Turner," she said, looking up from the clipboard she held in her hand, "I'm Detective Simone Lacy."

Percival stood up.

"No need to stand, Sir." She took a seat across from him.

He nodded, not sure what to say. He was still waiting for some big, evil-looking white cop with a cigarette dangling from one side of his mouth to enter.

"I want you to look at these," she said, pushing some photos toward him.

He shook his head as he went through them. "Good lord, what kind of monster would do something like this to a child?"

"That's what we're here to find out," she said.

His expression was grim, but the detective's face remained blank.

"See the marks on her neck?" she asked.

He nodded, too choked up to speak.

"They show signs of strangulation. She can't speak yet, due to her broken jaw and the windpipe fracture she's suffered."

No way in Harry Hell did TJ do this. No way.

"The young lady managed to write these two words on this piece of paper," Detective Lacy said, before pushing a sheet of notebook paper across the table.

Pastor Money.

Percival shook his head.

"If this were your daughter, what would you do if you knew who did this?" the detective asked.

Too shocked to speak, Percival just shook his head.

Detective Lacy tore off a piece of paper from the clipboard and pushed it toward Percival. "Reverend Turner," she put a hand over his, "I'm not going to threaten you with five years in prison for perjury or obstruction of justice. You're a man of God, and there's nothing the State can do that compares to what God can." She looked deep in his eyes, "I need you to write down where you were, who you were with, and what you were doing between the hours of nine and twelve last night." She kept a straight face while handing him a pen.

*****

The sun hit him like a ball of light after stepping out of the precinct double doors.

"Sir? Sir? Excuse me?" A butter-yellow Appalonia-looking sista' grabbed Percival's arm just as he made it to the last precinct step.

"Yes, Ma'am, can—"

"Tell me you didn't provide an alibi to Satan."

Seeing the pain on the angelic face that stood before him made him want to run back inside the precinct and tell the truth; on the other hand, he knew TJ hadn't done what the young girl alleged. For a moment he stood there, mouth open, dumbfounded.

"Why?" she cried, taking his silence for confirmation that Percival had indeed covered for his friend.

Slightly recovering from the sting of her words, he instinctively placed a hand on her shoulder.

Shaking her head she said, "She just turned sixteen Saturday. She's only a child. Why?"

Steam rose from the wet street as Percival looked across to the other side. An empty park bench was as good a place as any. "Let's take a walk."

"Why? Why? Why?" the woman repeated at an hysterical pitch, while she let Percival lead her away from the station.

A couple of minutes later they sat down on a damp, wooden park bench.

"I can't imagine how you must feel. What happened to your daughter was...was..." He shook his head—too choked up to continue. The woman's small hands seemed to melt in his as he placed them in his lap. "Father God—"

"Please, don't." Barely audibly, she interrupted. "No," she shook her head. "She went to church every Sunday, every Sunday. And look what church got her. Where was God last night? Still at church? Oh, no, that's right, he was forcing himself inside a child, a sixteen year-old baby."

"Ma'am?" Percival interrupted. Her hands were still hidden inside his.

"My sister's oldest child."

Percival squeezed her hand. "Ma'am?"

9

She looked up, her blood-shot, watery eyes penetrating to the core of his soul.

"God was there, but it was Satan who molested that child. God is who you and your family must now turn to, for wisdom and strength."

She jerked her hands from his comforting embrace. "Strength? Why the hell should I turn to God for strength when He wasn't strong enough to get that nigga off my niece last night? Where was God when you, a self-proclaimed man of God, was sitting in a room lying on Satan's behalf?" she asked.

Again, he was speechless.

"Please, Mr. Turner." Sliding off the bench to her knees, squeezing his ankles, she pleaded, "Please go back across the street and tell them the truth. Just tell them, please," she begged.

Percival reached down, gently grabbed the woman's wrists, and pulled her to her feet. They were standing close, her hands in his, his eyes looking into hers. Like a thirty-foot ocean wave, feelings of guilt and betrayal washed over him. "I-I can't do that. I really am sorry, Miss." His eyes pleaded with hers for understanding as a single tear ran down his face.

"Carmen. Carmen Lewis."

"Huh?"

She looked up. Her eyes were watery red. "My name is Carmen Lewis."

Their eyes locked and the electricity between them was undeniable. He was momentarily mesmerized by her innocence and beauty. Finally, he dropped his head and pulled away in hopes of breaking the spell that was beginning to consume him.

A minute went by without either of them speaking. For a moment, their souls were one, and that's what scared him.

"Mr. Turner?"

"Per—" He thought about what TJ had said about his name. But PC had never stuck. "Percival. Call me Percival, or Rev."

"Unlike that leach," she grabbed his hand, "I know you're a good man, and I know you'll do the right thing." She squeezed his hand, and this time he didn't break eye contact as they drew closer.

"Auntie! Auntie!" a little girl shouted as she ran their way. "Get your hands off my auntie." She kicked Percival.

"Ouch!" He grabbed his ankle.

"Meka!" Carmen shouted. She let go of him and grabbed the little girl. "I'm sorry, Rev. This is Tracy's little sister, Meka."

He bent down. "Hi Meka," he said.

Ignoring him, the young girl grabbed Carmen's hand. "Come on, Auntie, Mommy's waiting."

"Shemika Monique Brown, apologize to Reverend Turner right this minute."

She let go of Carmen's hand and crossed her arms.

"Young lady, don't make me take off my belt."

She just stood there.

Carmen pointed a finger at her. "Go back to the car. I'll deal with you later, young lady, and tell your mother I'm coming. Now, go on."

A second later ,the young girl took off running back through the park.

"I'm sorry, Rev. She's been through a lot."

He nodded. "I understand."

Turning to face him, Carmen said, "No, you really don't. You see," Carmen grabbed his hand, "two years ago, Meka was ten when she killed her father."

"What?"

"He'd been molesting her the summer she went to stay with him. One night while he was asleep, naked in her bed, in one swoop, she sliced his penis and one testicle off with a meat cleaver."

Percival cringed. "I am so, so sorry."

"She's only been home from Georgia Regional for a few months now."

"She was in a mental institution?"

Carmen nodded. "For two years."

What were the chances? Two sisters. Two men. Percival knew then that he had to help this woman and her family. There was just too much healing that had to be done, and he didn't care how many hospitals or doctors these girls spoke to, without God they would never be able to heal. He had to pray real hard.

He was still sitting on the park bench forty-minutes after Carmen left. Why couldn't he get her off his mind? Finally, he stood up and looked around before adjusting himself. He just wished the bulge in his pants had come from thinking about his wife.

Chapter 2

a little over three months had passed since the charges had been dismissed. TJ and PC were sitting in a U-haul, waiting for some of their frat brothers to arrive and help them set up folding chairs and the huge red circus tent for tomorrow night. TJ's old friend and college professor Drake Gardener had pulled some strings and gotten them the permits to hold their first revival in the Atlanta Braves' parking lot.

He dropped his head. "I'm sorry, TJ. I should've told you a month ago when it happened. It just seems that I've been on my knees ever since it happened. I haven't even seen or spoken to Carmen since that night. She was upset, as was I, but she understood that we couldn't see each other again. TJ, I love my wife. God knows I love Maya. I never meant for it to happen."

PC was so green, TJ thought. Still the country boy, he couldn't see that Carmen was just like her niece. Tracy was sixteen, but she had played a grown-up game and she had to be taught a grown-up lesson. No tellin' how much that gold-digger Carmen had gotten out of him.

"I know God has forgiven me, but I haven't forgiven myself because I'm still in love with her," he said.

"I thought you said you loved Maya."

"I did. I do. But I'm in love with Carmen," Percival said.

"Is this the real reason you stepped down after only two months of pastoring New Bethel?" TJ asked.

PC nodded in the affirmative.

TJ shook his head.

PC dropped his head. "I m telling you this, TJ, because I can't lead the revival. I'm not worthy. And tonight I'm going to tell Maya about Carmen."

"No, you're not." TJ reached over and grabbed PC's shoulders, forcing Percival to face him. "Listen to me, PC. Moses was a murderer. Samson was a murderer. Solomon was a fornicator. Paul was a liar and a thief. But what they all had in common was that they were worldly men chosen by the hand of God. And you're no different. Maya loves you and supports you; don't do this to her. Don't do this to me; and most of all don't do this to the people in need of God's wisdom."

As if he hadn't heard a word of what TJ had said, PC continued, "I know you've had it hard over the last few months, but, TJ, you're charismatic and a great preacher. Lead the revival; I'll be there to support you one hundred percent."

This was too big of an opportunity. TJ had paid off the two biggest radio personalities in Atlanta to mention the revival on the air. It cost him way too much time and money to secure the location, the seating, the tent— everything.

He shook his head. "I don't know. I just don't know," Percival said.

"What don't you know? Better yet, let me tell you what I know." TJ squeezed Percival's shoulder. "I know you're a God loving, God fearing, man. I know that our people are lost. I now that for lack of knowledge our people shall perish. And I don't know a better teacher, with the fire, venom and wisdom to save our people from perishing." He paused. "Man, you told me your whole life you've wanted to spread the Word, that you've wanted others to see and experience what you have."

"But—"

"But nothing," TJ interrupted. "Furthermore, the idiot reporter, whoever he was, had me looking like a rapist in the *Atlanta Journal*, and I wouldn't be surprised if that same reporter wasn't responsible for the story about Tracy's mother, Sharon, coming at me with a knife in the middle of my last church service." He shook his head. "No, you have to do this. It was only three months ago when that little con accused me of rape. Not nearly enough time has passed. True enough our people have short memories, but not that short," TJ said, sitting in the U-haul truck's passenger seat.

CHAPTER 3

*N*early nineteen years ago, on a gloomy day in mid August, TJ Money had convinced Percival Cleotis Turner to lead his first revival. Who would've thought the revival would've led to all this? TJ was still a high yellow, low-calorie mini-version of Al Sharpton with pork chop sideburns. Percival had filled out some during the past decade, but for the most part he was still a big ole country boy, with the exception of his speech. Maya had helped him dramatically improve his grammar. The Rick James soul-glow look PC had worn for so long had been recently replaced with a much more conservative, short haircut. His mustache-less goatee made him look like a jazz musician.

Five years ago, something happened that would change the course of his life forever.

*****

"Reverend? Reverend? Are you still there?"

"I'm sorry. I'm just so honored that you want to do a feature story on me in your magazine," Percival spoke into the phone.

"And modest, too," the feminine voice replied. "Come on, Reverend, you have the largest following in the state of Georgia. One World Faith AME seats over sixteen thousand, and a little birdie told me that you and Reverend Money are doing big things in real estate. These are the kind of success stories our readers want to hear."

"Well, thank you," he said.

"Looks like you're doing for Atlanta what the Bishop One Free and his One Free movement is doing for Chicago and other ghettoes in surrounding Midwestern cities," she said.

"I don't know a lot about the One Free movement, but I like what I see," he said.

"You didn't read the story we did on the One Free Movement last year?"

Embarrassed, he replied, "Sorry to say I missed it."

"No problem, I'll send it to you. Now I know you're a busy man and I'm not going to hold you, Reverend. I can't wait to meet you next week."

"It was and will be my pleasure. I hope to see you at the Million Family March in October," Percival replied.

After getting off the phone with the executive editor of *Black Enterprise Magazine*, Percival walked over to the picture window in his studio-apartment-sized church office and looked out at the stars. "Thank you, Lord. For all you've blessed me with—a beautiful wife, a wonderful son, the greatest best friend; and thank you for placing all the right people in my path."

Now, six years after opening the doors of the One World Faith AME megachurch, near the Atlanta Braves stadium, right around the corner from downtown Atlanta, PC and TJ were getting close to securing the land to build another megachurch on the South Side.

At ten-thirty, the sky was lit up with stars instead of the rockets that were shot out of bottles last night.

Thirty minutes later, Percival looked at his watch as he pulled his Bentley into one of the six garage bays at the Turner Estate. He decided not to turn on any lights as he made his way to the wraparound rear staircase. Before he knew it, he was in bed and dead to the world.

*****

Percival almost didn't hear the phone ringing.

He looked up. The numbers 4:22 flashing brightly on the clock beside the phone on the nightstand, hurt his eyes.

"Maya?"

Sound asleep, she didn't answer.

He blinked a few times before gently moving her arm from his chest.

Gotta be TJ at this time of morning. Thought I turned the ringer all the way down.

More ringing.

He reached out, grabbed the receiver, and placed it to his ear. "Hello?"

"Reverend Percival Cleotis Turner?" a deep voice inquired.

"Yes?"

"Sorry to call so late, but I've been informed that you're planning to attend and speak at the Muslim's Million Family March in October."

"Who's calling?"

"Let's just say I'm the governor of the AME church."

18

"Governor of—"

"I'm sure my information is in error," the man continued. "I just wanna hear it from you. I mean, surely a man of Christ would not participate in a heathenistic movement such as the Million Family March—especially a man that's about to become…" he paused, "the next AME bishop residing over all of northern Georgia."

"What does the March have to do with me becoming bishop?"

The man ignored Percival's question. "Well, that is, unless you decide to join the followers of that Farra con man."

"You mean the Honorable Minister Louis Farrakhan."

"Honorable? Ha!" the man shouted into the phone. "Minister of what? Lies and deception? Look, I'm not going to debate the issue. I just wanna know if you're with Christ or with them?"

"Always with Christ," Percival replied.

"Thank you. And good evening."

He couldn't sleep. With his hands behind his head, staring at the ceiling, he contemplated waking Maya, but thought better of it. Earlier, they'd had another argument. It was the same story.

Two months after the fact, Maya was still heated about him spending close to two hundred thousand on the Black Bentley Continental that was parked outside in their temperature-controlled, six-car garage.

Most women would be happy with the lavish lifestyle. "We don't need a new speed boat," she'd say. "Instead of buying a plane, set up another scholarship fund; open up another shelter," she'd say, as if he hadn't already done enough community outreach.

"What are you doing, Percival?"

He turned to where she lay. Her back was still turned away from him.

"Huh? I thought you were sleep."

"I was, until you woke me up moving around in the bed."

"I'm sorry, Sweetie. Go back to sleep," he said, while getting out of bed.

"What time is it?"

He looked over to the nightstand. "Quarter til five."

She said, "thank you," as if she were dismissing a child.

"The more money I make, the more you insist I give away," he muttered while leaving the bedroom.

"I heard that," she said.

Downstairs, sitting in a lounger in the library, he picked up the phone.

"Good morning, Sister Barbara," he said to TJ's second wife.

"Reverend Turner?"

"Uhh, yeah. I'm really sorry to call your home this early, but it's kind of important. Can I please speak with TJ?"

There was a momentary pause. "I thought he was with you."

"Yeah, well, he was. But, uh, we parted company and I thought he'd made it home by now."

"Reverend, you don't have to cover for him. I know. I've known for some time. But I love the man. I just pray he sees the error in his whorish ways. Try him on his cell phone. He won't answer my calls, but I'm sure he'll answer yours."

"Thank you, Barbara."

A minute later, he had TJ on the line. "Reverend, where are you?"

"PC, what's really goin' down, big dog?"

"You, if you don't change your ways. It's nearly six in the morning. Not only have you been out all night, but you didn't even tell me what you were up to."

"Uh, last time I checked, I was grown."

"You don't act like it. Phyliss divorced you because of the other women, and if you're not careful, Barbara will too. She may not know who they are, but she knows there are others," he said.

"So she knows; big deal! I could be doin' worse. I don't drink, get high, or smoke. I don't beat my wife. I'm a good provider and I take care of all aspects of home, if you know what I mean." He paused. "When the good Lord sees fit for me to change, I will. But you just remember, PC, as the song goes, *Please be patient with me, God is not through with me yet.*"

"God's not, but I'm getting pretty dog-gone fed up."

There was an uncomfortable moment of silence between the two.

Percival continued, "Look, Man, I don't wanna argue. Right now, I have a dilemma that I need your advice on."

"Baby, is you comin' back to bed?"

Percival heard the female voice in the background.

"Hold on, PC," TJ said, covering the phone. "Babycakes, you see I'm on the phone. And, no, I'm not coming back to bed; I have to get home to my wife."

"Damn that. She don't—"

"Don't you start," he said, before slamming a door. TJ put the phone back to his ear. "Sorry about that, big dog. Now what's up?"

Percival took a deep breath and exhaled. "Okay. I got a call a few hours ago in the middle of the night. In so many words, I was told that if I attend the Million Family March, I won't be ordained."

"Who was it?" TJ asked.

As if they were standing in the same room, Percival shrugged.

"PC, you still there?"

"I have no idea. He never gave me his name, but, by the way he spoke, I really think he was the real deal."

"PC, trust me, you have nothing to worry about."

"How do you know that?"

"We built a twenty-million-dollar megachurch compound. We own three restaurants, two apartment buildings, and we're about to acquire eighty acres of prime real-estate for the mall thing."

"Me becoming a bishop has nothing to do with our land developing business."

"Now, that's where you're wrong. Did you forget the other golden rule?" TJ asked.

"What other golden rule?"

"He who has the gold makes the rules. We have the gold, and if we take our gold to another denomination, we'll strike a financial blow to the AME coalition."

He couldn't argue with that. TJ had a point, Percival surmised.

"The AME Bishop's council would be crazy to change their minds. And if for some insane reason they did, we'd just threaten to leave the AME faith and convert to Baptist. We wouldn't be the first to do it."

"Why would we do something like that?" Percival asked TJ.

"PC, think about it. Traditionally, the position of Bishop didn't and doesn't exist in the Baptist Church, but you still have self-appointed Baptist bishops springing up like weeds, right?"

"Right," PC said.

"So, by us converting the church, you can appoint yourself bishop just like others around the nation have done. The AME knows this.

"PC, we're going to this march and you will speak. This is our chance to take One World across the country and eventually to the Caribbean. Imagine the money, power, and influence we'll gain if you captivate one million black people."

*****

As usual, Percival had followed TJ's advice. They had gone to the march; he'd spoken; and now in 2004, TJ and PC had just gotten back from Philly where a congratulatory ceremony was held in honor of him receiving the Bishop of the Year award. It was the third time in five years that PC had been honored with the most coveted award of the AME clergy.

PC was driving back from the airport a little past midnight. TJ was sound asleep in the passenger's seat. PC waited at the downtown streetlight, behind the wheel of his Bentley, bopping his head. *"Some people got to have it. Some people really need it,"* he sang the song, *"Money, Money, Money,"* along with the O'Jays.

Like a ghost, out of nowhere, a crayon-black brotha of indeterminate age slowly walked across the well-lit downtown street, holding a large cardboard sign with big black bold letters facing the Bentley's front window.

**PREACHERMAN, THE HOPE FOR
TOMORROW IS LOST IN YESTERDAY, UNLESS
YOU TURN AROUND AND FIND YOUR WAY**

CHAPTER 4

"*T*J, wake up! TJ?"

"Stop shouting!" TJ put his hands over his face. "Home already?"

"Look, Man!" PC opened the door and jumped out of the car.

"Whachu doin'?" TJ asked while reorienting himself and opening the passenger's door.

The street was deserted.

"That man!" PC pointed down the street. "You didn't see him?"

"How could I? I was sleep."

It was past midnight on a Tuesday. They were on the outskirts of downtown, less than a block away from Capital Homes and the Grady Homes projects.

"Man, if you don't get back in this car and get me home," TJ said, now wide awake.

"You didn't see him?" PC asked again.

"PC, I haven't seen anything. But if you don't get back in this car, we'll probably be seeing the barrel of some carjacker's gun pretty soon. You do know that we're standing in the middle of the street in crackhead, carjacking central."

Still standing outside the Bentley, PC said, "I saw a man." PC wanted to say he saw the same man that he'd seen in the pool the night he almost drowned, but instead he said, "I saw a man carrying a sign made out of a cardboard box."

"PC, there's a lot of men and women carrying around cardboard signs in this area. And guess what?"

"I know that. But…"

"They all want one thing," TJ continued. "Money. The signs read: *Will work for food*, but what they really mean is give me some money to buy some crack."

Percival turned his head toward a vibrating sound somewhere not far off.

"Come on, Man, that ain't nothin' but some kid's bassed-up car stereo you hear in the distance. Come on now before their car pulls up on us," TJ said, looking in the rearview mirror at the approaching car's lights. "Gotta be some drug dealer playing his music loud enough to wake up Jesus."

Finally, PC got back inside the car.

TJ breathed a sigh of relief.

"This guy was different," PC continued as they drove toward the expressway. "I know you gon' think I'm crazy, but I just saw the man who saved my life all them years ago, back in that pool."

"Okay, PC," TJ said, wanting to pick back up on the erotic dream he was having before PC woke him.

"As sure as fat meat's greasy, I'm tellin' you I saw him."

TJ yawned. "I pulled you out that pool. It's late; you just think you saw—"

"The man was clean-shaven, had a bald head, and wore gray slacks and a white dress shirt. Looked the exact same as he had, way back when. The sign he carried had the words *Preacherman* in large bold letters across the top. It was like them words were speaking to me."

Ignoring Percival's tirade, TJ hit the massage button and reclined his seat. A few minutes later, as he was drifting off, PC became more and more incoherent and began to sound like the unseen "Mwa, Mwa, Mwa" teacher in a Charlie Brown cartoon.

"I can't believe you're falling asleep on me. I mean, you always expect me to listen when you have something to say." Percival shook his head. "Sometimes, I just don't know about you, Terrell Joseph."

"What did you just say?" TJ asked.

"Never mind," PC replied.

Now, heated, TJ sat up in his seat and glared at PC. "You always have something to say about what I do and how I carry myself. Did you forget, about how I took you under my wing when you were a lame backwoods hillbilly? If it weren't for me, you'd still be preaching at that church's chicken hole in the wall, New Bethel."

"If it weren't for you I wouldn't be going against God lying to your wife, a faithful member of my church."

"Your church? Ha! It was my idea to use the tithes and offerings to build a commercial and residential land developing empire. The money I've made us built the megachurch that we're in, the same one you so conveniently call *your* church. I lined the pockets of city councilmen, county CEO's, and mayors to get land zoned, permits, and building contracts, not you."

The gates opened as they slowly drove up the long driveway of the Money estate. PC put the car in park outside TJ's front door.

Turning to face TJ, PC began, "TJ, I respect what you've done. You're my best friend, the brother I never had. But, right now, I got somethin' to say and you gon' hear me out."

"Always about you, the great Bishop Percival Turner," TJ said, crossing his arms.

"No, but this time it is about me. Now I'm sorry if I take you for granted. I'll pray about it. But like I said, that man I saw downtown was the same man that pulled me to the top of that pool back when we were pledging Omega, back in college.

"PC, it was dark. I jumped in that pool. I was the only one besides you in that water. It was storming outside and midnight dark out; you probably imagined someone else—

"That's what I been trying to tell you for twenty years. It was dark, and that pool was even darker, but I saw that man clear as glass then, and I saw him clear as glass tonight."

"What do you want me to say, that I believe you, or I saw him too?"

Percival cupped his face with his hands and let out a long sigh. "TJ, it's late; we're both tired; and for the record, I appreciate you and everything you've done. It's not all about me; we're in this together. Without you, I wouldn't be me. Can't you see, Man? I look up to you. I care about what you think." PC grabbed TJ's hand and looked him in the eye. "Brotha, I love you, and don't you ever forget that. I just wanted you to see that man. I just wanted you to listen."

Percival's apology didn't fool TJ one bit. His mother had told him long ago to watch what people say, and listen to their actions. Percival's actions over the last ten years had been indicative of a person who cares about one thing: himself. "Man, you're right. It's late; we're both tired. We both said things we didn't mean. But, I just want to let you know this…" TJ took a second to get his thoughts together. "There's not a man on the planet that's more deserving of all the success you've reaped. I'm glad the AME yet again has recognized how much you mean to the church." TJ put his hand on PC's shoulder. "Congratulations, Mr. Bishop of the Year."

He nodded. "Thank you, Reverend. You just don't know how much that means to me."

TJ smiled, thinking that he needed hip boots for all the bull that came out of PC's mouth. "We still on for tomorrow night's game?" PC asked.

Lost in thought, TJ stared out the car's front window.

"Hey, Buddy!" PC, playfully backhanded TJ in the chest.

TJ jumped.

"Boy, you must be doing some heavy thinkin'," PC said.

"Nah, not really. Just tired."

"We still on for tomorrow night's game?" PC asked again as TJ got out of the car.

"Ah, PC, man, I completely forgot to tell you."

"Tell me what?"

"The brotha I was getting the tickets from got arrested the other day."

"Nooo. Really?"

"That's what I just said. You think I'm lying? You think I'd lie about tickets to a stupid basketball game?"

"No, no, of course not," PC said, shaking his head.

"Well, why'd you say *really*, like I was lying or something?"

"TJ, I apologize if I offended you. I didn't mean it like that."

"Well, tell me then, how did you mean it?"

"I just meant really, like, are you serious?"

TJ shook his head. "Man, I'm sorry. It's late. We been up practically twenty-four hours. Besides, we already know the outcome. Kobe and Shaq, 100. Hawks, 10."

"You and the wife should come over. We can watch the game together and you can let me know what you think about the sermon I plan to give Sunday," PC said.

"Sounds like a plan." TJ gave PC a pound before closing the door.

PC hit the button to the passenger's window. "Tomorrow evening, around seven?"

"Works for me," TJ replied. "Oh, yeah, when is the last time you spoke to Carmen?"

"Carmen? Man, I don't know. What? Seventeen, eighteen years I guess."

"More like nineteen, don't you think?" TJ smiled.

"Why you ask?"

"No reason. Just curious." He turned his back and walked away.

The purring sound of the Bentley's engine didn't fade as TJ walked up the cobblestone steps toward the door. He put the key in the lock and gently turned it before looking back and waving.

PC thought he was slick, sweating me, to see if I'd really go into the house. He wants to be all in my business; let's see what he thinks after I go snooping into his past tomorrow. "One, two, three," he said, gently opening the door and taking four quick steps to the alarm's control panel. He smiled, thinking he'd broken his old record of five chirps. He'd never sneaked into the house and disarmed the alarm in three chirps. He looked at his watch: 1:37. His girlfriend was still at the club. He could make it before she got off work, he figured.

"TJ, is that you, baby?" Barbara asked, sounding wide awake.

Damn! Damn! Damn! He sighed. "Yeah, Barbara, it's me."

"Come to bed, Honey. I haven't seen you in three days. I have an itch that needs to be scratched."

Scratch it yourself, he wanted to say, but instead he replied, "I'll do more than scratch your itch after I get back from Kroger. I need a beer to calm my nerves."

Barbara was at the top of the stairs leaning on the wrought iron railing surrounding the balcony, completely naked. *She's cute and in great shape, but she's still fifty.*

"I figured you'd want a beer, so I bought you a six-pack of Corona and two lemons." She started walking down the spiral staircase.

He wanted to scream. He couldn't believe this. If she were twenty five instead of fifty—

Interrupting his thoughts, she said, "Baby, I'll get you a beer. You just go upstairs and get in the Jacuzzi. I have the heater on so the water is hot, just like you like it."

Now it was his turn to smile, but he couldn't. His jaws locked up and his lips wouldn't crease. Finally, he managed a weak, "Okay, Babycakes."

One would've thought he was heading to the electric chair the way he trudged up those stairs.

He put his cell phone on silent before placing it on his closet shelf.

Thank God for Viagra, he thought as he swallowed one of the little blue pills before taking off his pants and climbing the Jacuzzi steps in the bedroom bathroom.

Thirty minutes later he lay on his back in their California king sleigh bed. Barbara on top. He just lay there wondering if Lexus was blowing up his cell phone.

Barbara twisted, turned, and pumped away.

*****

The phone rang.

TJ jumped. "What time is it?" he asked, turning and seeing Barbara's side of the bed was empty. He heard the answering machine pick up.

"You've reached the Money residence. I'm sorry no one is available to take your call. Please leave a name and number and me or Reverend Money will get back with you as soon as possible. Have a very blessed day."

He reached over and grabbed his watch off the nightstand.

"Mrs. Money, this is Dr. Wiley. Please call me as soon as possible. If I'm not in, leave a number where I can reach you," the voice said over the answering machine.

"I wonder what that was about," he said, looking at his watch.

"Sweet Jesus! One-sixteen!"

His legs gave out as soon as he tried to stand. He sat on the hardwood floor, next to the bed, cursing Barbara for trying to kill him last night and early this morning. All he wanted to do was sleep after he realized he wasn't going anywhere. But, no, Barbara wanted to have marathon sex.

Viagra, Corona, and a fifty-year-old horny aerobic-instructing workout fanatic do not mix, he thought while testing his ginger legs.

"Barbara? You home?" he pulled himself up and walked to his bedroom closet.

He picked his phone up from the granite closet shelf. Seventeen missed calls. He went to the last one and pressed *send*.

A second later, she picked up.

"Yeah? Whachu want?"

"Lexus, babycakes, I'm so sorry about last night. I was exhausted and my battery was—"

"You ain't gotta explain nothin' to me. I ain't yo' wife."

"Yeah, I know but—"

"But what, TJ? What do you want?"

"Babycakes, I want you. You should be my first lady when I take over my own super church."

"TJ, I'm real. You ain't gotta run game on me. I know the deal. You come over my place late at night or in the middle of the day before I go to work. We never go anywhere cuz you scared of being seen with a stripper. And that's cool. Really it is. I knew what it was before I first bent over and spread my legs."

"Ahh, come on, Babycakes, you know it ain't even like that."

"Psst. I can't tell."

"Soooo, what are the chances of me paying you to take the night off tonight?"

"Uhhhh, slim and none," she said sweetly. "Hold on. Someone's leaving." She paused. "It was Slim."

"Lexus? Lexus?" TJ looked at the words *CALL ENDED* on his cell phone. *No she did not just hang up on me. Lord, please tell me that, that., high-priced toilet did not just hang up on Dr. Terrell Joseph Money.*

After frantically pushing buttons and not getting the correct ten digits, he just went back to his dialed calls and brought her number up, took a deep breath, and pressed send.

"Babycakes, don't hang up. Hear me out. You're right. I'm not living right. I'm supposed to be a man of the cloth, a man of God, and treating a black queen like a sex slave is completely unacceptable. You deserve a provider, a nourisher, a man that can feed you spiritually and mentally, as well as physically; and if you forgive me and give me half, just half a chance, I want to show you that man." He paused. "You still there?"

"Uhm-hmm, I'm here."

"Babycakes, guess what I'm doin' right now."

"Racking your little mind, trying to come up with some more bullshit?"

Breathe, TJ, breathe. Tight-faced, speaking through clenched teeth, he said, "No, Babycakes. I'm heading to my car."

"I know you don't think you comin' over here," she said.

"No, I don't think, I know I'm coming over to my baby's apartment to give her five hundred dollars so she can go shopping. You already the finest woman on God's green earth; now I want you to be the best dressed tonight at the Hawks and Lakers game that we, me and you, are attending."

"TJ, are you for real? I mean, are you sure? What if your wife—"

"Barbara is only my wife on paper. How many times do I have to tell you that you're the only woman I have eyes for? You're the only babycakes in my life. I told you, I don't even share the same bedroom with Barbara anymore. Babycakes, you have to understand, the only reason I haven't divorced her is because I can't take the chance on the Board of Deacons denying me my own church. I already have one strike against me."

"I know; you told me. Your first wife, Phyliss, right?"

"Exactly. Heading up a megachurch is as political as it is spiritual, but after I have my own church it'll be just me and you."

"So, you mean to tell me you ain't still doin' her. I mean, she is your wife. She has urges."

"Would you do my wife?" TJ asked. "I mean, if you were me, and had a woman as fine and sexy as you." He paused a second. "That's what I thought."

"I didn't say anything."

"You didn't have to," he said, imagining all five feet eleven inches of Lexus standing in front of him naked with heels on. Sweat glistening and sliding down from the tip of where her long blond braids began, past the brown freckles on her face, between her perfect new D cups he'd paid for, and down to her shaven pubic area.

"Baby, you still there?" she cooed.

Now he was *baby* again. "Yeah, I'm here, wishing I was there. But, seriously, though. As much attention as I give you, I couldn't get it up with Barbara if I wanted to. Hell, my wife hasn't had sex in so long she probably has rotten cobwebs down there."

"TJ, that's nasty."

"I know, but so are the things I plan to do to you later tonight, my queen. Now, I can't stay. I'm just coming to drop off your money for this evening. I'll be there in a few." He ended the call.

35

He wore a deep smile as he walked out of his closet.
The smile was replaced by a look of shock when he peered
up.

Barbara was sitting on the bed with tears streaming
down her face.

*****

"Girl, you know how I am, but I just can't get it
together this morning."

"Carmen, you know I know. You're the most organized
person I've ever known. I bet the dust on your broom is
organized."

"If you saw me this morning, you wouldn't think that,"
Carmen said.

"Girl, it's that damn new medication you're on. You
said yourself that the doctor told you you'd be drowsy for
the first few days."

"I know. I know. Dealing with my HMO for the last
few months has really stressed me out."

"I can imagine. I still can't believe you can't do
anything about them just all of a sudden refusing to pay for
your medicine."

"Especially since I've been on the same meds for so
long, and I haven't been sick in years. And now all of a
sudden the medicine has been ruled experimental," Carmen
added.

Carmen grabbed her car keys off the dining room table.

"That boy is strong; he'll be fine if you miss one visit.
You know you don't need to be going up and down the
road this afternoon, feeling the way you do."

"I know you're right, Cheryl, but Samuel's my baby, and in three years, I haven't missed a visit," Carmen said into the phone while opening the apartment door to leave.

She dropped the phone and the gift bag she carried in her free hand.

He smiled.

"What the hell are you doing here?" she asked.

"And hello, to you too, Carmen," TJ said, walking past her into the apartment.

Suddenly, she felt dizzy.

TJ had his hands behind his back as he walked over to the mantle over the living room fireplace.

She closed her eyes. "Satan, I'm going to tell you one time. Get the hell out of my apartment, now," she said in a relaxed tone.

Ignoring her, he said, "A couple days ago, me and PC were in Philadelphia. Funny thing is I ran into an old friend of yours." He turned and looked around. Carmen was nowhere in sight. Just as he finished stuffing the framed photo down his pants, he turned again, and this time he found himself staring down the barrel of a large handgun.

Tears ran down her face. "I've wanted to do this for nineteen years, four months, and twenty-seven days," she said.

He slowly began taking steps backwards. "Carmen?" He held his arms out in surrender. "Please. Please, don't do this."

"Were those the words Tracy said, before you beat and raped her?"

"I, I don't know what you mean," he said.

The gun made a clicking sound as she pulled the hammer back.

CHAPTER 5

"*H*ello?" Barbara answered the phone.

"Hey, Beautiful. Can I speak to that husband of yours?"

There was a pause.

"Barbara?"

In the same drab, monotone voice she had used to answer the phone, she replied, "Yes."

"Maya and I are looking forward to seeing you two this evening," Percival said. "Of course, your little boyfriend, Percy Jr., is ecstatic."

"Uhmm, I…" She paused. "I won't be coming. I'm—"

"Barbara, I'm your friend and your pastor. I'm not going to pry, but I want you to know that I love you, and I'm here for you if you want to talk."

"TJ is not... I have to go," she said and hung up.

"Dad, what's wrong?" Little Percy asked after looking up from his new Madden Football 2004 Playstation game.

"I don't know." He frowned. "I just got off the phone with your aunt Barbara."

"Dad, she is not my aunt. She's Reverend Money's wife. I wish you'd stop talking to me like I'm twelve."

"But you're just thirteen," he joked.

"Fourteen. I'm fourteen, Dad," his son corrected. "She still coming over to watch the game?"

"I don't really know."

"Huh?" he asked with a blank look on his face. "Why don't you?" Little Percy asked, before putting the Playstation joystick down on the game table.

The elder Percival shrugged his shoulders.

"Is she sick, Dad?"

"Percy, what part of *I don't know* don't you understand?"

"Dad, you're her pastor. Don't you think you should find out?" He got up and started walking toward his father. "Come on, let's go over there."

At six two, with a mustache, and tipping the scale at two-hundred pounds, it was easy to forget that Percy was just barely a teenager.

"That's a good idea, but you're staying right here."

"Ahhhhhh, Dad. I've been in the house all week. Today is my last day in prison. Come on."

"Ahhhhh, Son," he mimicked. "I-ain't-gon'-be-able-ta-do-it. You should've thought about your actions before you hauled off and hit that boy at school."

"But, Dad, he called Mom the B word with the letters U-P on the end." He shook his head. "You and Mom just don't understand how hard it is being the son of a bishop. If I keep letting people talk about Mom or you, everybody'll think I'm soft."

"Number one, the boy doesn't know your mother; two, even a bishop's son has to follow rules; and three, you are soft. You should be thankful your mother gave that Playstation back."

Little Percival walked back to the couch and flopped down before crossing his arms.

Percival turned around and smiled. "I love you, too, Son."

*****

While driving to TJ's house, Percival got to thinking about how he'd been so much like Little Percy when he was his age. He knew he himself would've gone upside the boy's head, too, if he had called his mother Ms. Bitchup.

Percy was a freshman and the other kid was a senior and just as tall, even wider than Percy. Percival knew it was wrong, but he couldn't help but be proud upon learning that Percy had won the fight.

Thinking about his son made him lose track of time. Before he knew it, he was turning onto Reverend Money's horseshoe-shaped cobblestone driveway. "Doggonit." He popped himself upside the head, remembering that he was supposed to be following Maya back to the Mercedes dealership this afternoon.

He still couldn't believe she was making him return the SL 500 convertible. He'd spent eighty thousand on it, replacing her five-year-old Chevy Lumina.

You would think she'd be happy about the car he'd bought for her birthday. Turning forty was big. He'd surprised Maya with the sleek, silver convertible two days ago. And for two days she argued, calling Percival the shepherd in the castle. And he'd argued that it was his money, his castle, and he could rule his kingdom and provide for his queen the way he saw fit.

This morning, Percival had apologized and told Maya that they could take the car back. He didn't know particularly why, but this morning he decided to do something over the top to prove to Maya that he wasn't a shepherd living in a castle away from his flock.

Finally, after sitting in the driveway for a good ten minutes, thinking about Maya and what he could do to please her, he got out of his Mercedes truck and walked up TJ's cobblestone stairs. He rang the doorbell several times over the next five minutes. After getting no answer, he reached in his pocket and pulled out his phone. Seconds later, Maya's voicemail picked up.

"Baby, something came up. I'm over at TJ's. I'm running a little late." He lifted his arm. The sun beamed down on the platinum arms of his Presidential Rolex. "It's quarter til three. I'll meet you at the dealership at five instead of four," he said, talking to Maya's voicemail.

He knew she wouldn't answer. Maya never took her phone into the Northside Women's Day Shelter, where she taught Saturday morning GED classes to homeless women.

After hanging up, he dialed Reverend Money's house phone.

Still no answer.

He knew Barbara was home, because her Black Range Rover was parked by the front door. He contemplated calling TJ, but he thought that doing so would only make matters worse. Besides, TJ was probably the reason Barbara sounded the way she had.

A minute later, Percival stood on his toes, reaching over the top of the backyard privacy fence, unlatching the clasp. He walked around back, past the pool, to the edge of the waterfall, next to the fountain where he knew TJ kept a spare key.

By the time he walked up the deck stairs and over to the first set of French doors, sweat was dancing on his brow. Global warming had come to Georgia, he thought. July was always smoking hot, but today was hot enough to make Satan go find some A/C.

"Barbara, TJ, anybody home?!" he shouted from the kitchen. "Sister Barbara, it's Bishop Turner!" he yelled, walking around the first level. "Barbara, I know you're here, because you never leave the house without setting the alarm," he called out while waiting for the elevator.

The first set of French double doors leading to the master bedroom foyer was closed. "Sistah Barbara," he called out before opening them, "I'm coming in."

She was sitting at the foot of her and TJ's king-size bed, her back arched, fully dressed, her hands gripping the legs of her gray jogging pants. Her eyes were locked on the Plasma TV that hung from the bedroom ceiling. If it'd been turned on he wouldn't have been so confused.

Still staring at the screen, she flatly stated, "Bishop, I know you mean well, but please leave. I'm fine."

"No," he said, shaking his head, "you're not." He walked over to the bed and took a seat beside her. "Come here, Barbara." He reached out and took her small frame in his arms.

Immediately, her body went slack and she cried in his arms.

"Bishop, I cook; I clean; I read my Bible; I stay in shape. I'm always there whenever he wants me; I've never even considered stepping outside of our marriage. I think I'm a good woman."

"You are." He nodded. "You're a fine woman, Barbara Jean Money."

"No!" She shook her head. "I'm not. As TJ told some woman on the phone earlier, I'm just for show. The only reason he hasn't divorced me is because it would make it hard for him to become pastor of the new church."

"He said that?"

She nodded.

Unconsciously, he clenched his fists. "Who was he speaking to?"

She shook her head. "I don't know."

A box of rocks has more sense than TJ at times, he thought.

"This afternoon, I walked in while he was in the bathroom talking on his cell phone. I don't know which one of his women he was speaking to, but he told her that I meant nothing to him, that we slept in separate bedrooms." She looked up. "Bishop, what is wrong with me? What have I done to deserve this? I love Terrell with all my heart, but I can't take this anymore. I know this will only make the Cancer..."

"Cancer?" He grabbed her hand.

She dropped her head. "I have stomach cancer."

"Oh, my God. I am so sorry. Does TJ know?"

She shook her head. "He knew I went to see an oncologist a few weeks ago, but he never once asked me why, or what were the results of my biopsy."

"I am so sorry."

"Don't be. You haven't done anything," she said.

"When did you find out? How did it happen? What made you go see a doctor?" he asked in rapid succession.

"Around six months ago it became difficult for me to keep meals down. In hopes of reversing whatever was going on with my body, I started drinking Noni juice, wheat grass extract, Viviente juice, and other natural supplements. At times I could see some improvement, but ultimately my condition progressed."

"I noticed you've looked much thinner lately, but I thought that was due to all the exercise and aerobic classes you taught."

"I've actually slacked off on my workouts, and I've dropped half the classes I taught. Bishop, you know how healthy I eat."

He nodded.

"Well, I eat the way I do and work out so much because my grandmother and my oldest sister died from stomach cancer. I thought I could prevent it if I ate healthy and stayed in shape."

"But why haven't you told TJ?"

"I haven't told anyone. I don't know. I-I guess, I'm afraid."

"Afraid of what?"

"I don't know. Being alone, I guess." She dropped her head. "I mean, more alone than I am now."

"Sistah, although TJ and I have been friends and business partners for nearly twenty years, right is right and wrong is wrong. I love you and I will not let him hurt you any longer." He stood up. "Pack a bag. You're coming to stay with us for a few days. Percy and Maya will be overjoyed. And," he squeezed her hand, "I won't let anyone know about your condition until you're ready. Don't worry, I know TJ. When he sees that he's about to lose the best thing that ever happened to him, watch how fast he does an about-face."

She seemed ready to get off the bed before looking him in the eyes. "I don't want to die alone."

He sat back down and pulled her back into his arms so that she wouldn't see his tears. "Don't talk like that. No one is going to die until God is ready. You've fought too hard and too long to give up now. Jesus didn't give up on us." He pulled back from their embrace. He put his hand on her chin and turned her head to face him. "So don't you dare give up on Him."

"Thank you," she said. A hint of a smile creased her lips right before she stood up, took a step and collapsed onto the bedroom floor.

"Lord, please, no!" he said aloud while bending over her and trying to feel for a pulse. He couldn't find one, but he could feel shallow breathing on the side of his face.

Without another thought he scooped her up into his arms, hurried down the stairs, and out to his SUV.

Fifteen minutes later, he turned onto the street where Dekalb Medical Center was located. He slammed on the brakes just in time. He didn't see the old man. He started to exit the car when shock registered across his face. It was the man he'd seen in the pool, and again late that night last month. He was carrying another cardboard sign.

PREACHERMAN TURN AROUND BEFORE YOU SLIP AND FALL. TURN AROUND BEFORE YOU LOSE IT ALL

CHAPTER 6

"*P*astor, Pastor Money?" a voice called out.

Phillips Arena was packed as Lexus and TJ made their way through the crowd. TJ was surprised that so many people had shown up for a Hawks' game. He pushed through the crowd ahead of Lexus.

He turned. "Babycakes, did you hear someone call my name?"

"I ain't heard nothing but noise," she said, hands on her waist, looking like a ghetto, black Wonder Woman.

"Uhm! Uhm! Uhm! Lord, give me strength," he said to himself, watching Lexus walk in her glitter-gold heels. The way she moved the wind with her swaying wide hips had every man, and a few women, staring. And that glued-on purple, gold, and white Lakers mini-skirt left very little to the imagination. A man of little faith would think God was playing favorites when he created that woman.

"Pastor Money? It's me, Betty Mae, Betty Mae Jackson."

As PC would say, there was always something to take the joy out of life. And that something brought TJ out of his daze. Big-mouth Betty Mae-Tell-All is what many called her. There might as well have been a CNN news team with her.

"Don't look back," he said to Lexus as he hurried on. "Can you walk any slower?" TJ asked as he grabbed her by the arm.

He knew he'd taken a risk bringing her here, but what else could he do? He was about to lose the only woman he'd been with and he didn't need to use Viagra for. Besides, he had a private room on the club level in the arena. He hadn't given much thought to making it from the parking lot to the club level until now.

"I got three-inch heels on, Negro; whachu expect me to do, get in a runner's stance and come up sprintin' like a track star?"

"That would be better than running your mouth," he said, under his breath.

Lexus stopped right next to a crowded popcorn stand. She had a death grip on TJ's hand.
Her blonde micro braids followed her head movement. "Oh, no, you didn't," she said, waving a gold-glittered nail at him with her free hand. "You wasn't complaining about my mouth a few minutes ago in the parking garage, when it was on your—"

"Well, hello there, Sister Jackson," TJ said, drowning Lexus out, a nervous smile creasing his lips.

His heart was a beating drum at a heavy metal rock concert. He pulled away from Lexus and reached out and took Big-mouth Betty Mae-Tell-All's hand. "How are you this fine evening, Sister Jackson?"

She frowned and turned her nose up while giving Lexus the once-over. "Blessed and highly favored, praise God." Betty Mae turned to face TJ. "I don't see Sister Barbara."

He turned to glance at Lexus, who was standing wide-legged and smiling. She seemed to find the whole ordeal amusing.

"Oh, she's under the weather," TJ said. He extended his arm, while giving Lexus a

please-don't-embarrass-me look. "This is my niece, Lee-Lexora." *Why did I say that?*

"Lexora, what a unique name. I haven't seen you at church, young lady."

"Betty Mae, come on now, we missin' the game," a man that looked to be around Moses age said from behind Big-mouth Betty Mae.

"Frank Bivens, this is my pastor." Turning back toward TJ, she continued, "Pastor Money, and this is—"
"Nice ta meet y'all fine folks but I'm a Hawks' fan, been one since Bob Petit led the team to a champeenship back in '58. On any otha' circumstance I'd stay and chat but..." He grabbed Big-mouth Betty Mae by the shoulder. "Me and my sweetie gotta get ta our seats."

Thank you, Jesus, TJ said to himself as they hurried off.

Both hands jumped to her hips. "TJ Money, if you wasn't a preacher, I woulda told that bald-headed, silver-wig-wearing prune about her dried-up self. Who she think she is?"

TJ walked away quietly, leading the way as Lexus raged on.

"Lexora? You know my real name is Laticia," she fussed as they waited for the private elevator to take them to the club level, where they had a private room.

*****

Bringing her here had to be the absolute dumbest thing he'd ever done. His leg had vibrated the entire game. He dared not pull out his cell phone to see who was blowing him up. He'd more than enough drama dealing with Lexus. It was probably Barbara or PC, he thought.

Ninety minutes later, TJ and his colorful young date were walking out of the arena.

"TJ, I'm sorry for acting the way I did earlier," Lexus said as they rode the elevator in the parking garage.

The fourth quarter had just begun. TJ had been too shaken up by Betty Mae to enjoy the game. Lord knows what would happen if the church found out about him seeing a stripper. He might as well kiss his chance of pastoring the new church good-bye.

Lexus massaged his hand as they got off the elevator. "Baby," she cooed. "I know you risked a lot taking me to the game. You really do care about me."

He had his cell phone in hand. The suspense was killing him. He stole a peek at the screen.

Forty-three missed calls. Ridiculous. Barbara knows better than to be blowing up my phone. Just wait til I get home.

"TJ, are you listening to me?"

"Of course, Babycakes. I was just thinking about how good it is to be with the black Cinderella of Phillips Arena."

She smiled. "If you don't hurry and get me home before the stroke of," she looked at the Movado he'd bought her a week ago, "eleven, your Cinderella will turn into a naked sex goddess, and she'll be forced to enslave your manhood in ways only she can show you." She batted her long eyelashes and slowly licked her naturally swollen pink lips.

49

"If I wasn't a religious man, I'd respond in kind," he said, while dropping his cell phone back inside his front pocket.

*****

Last night had been better than he'd expected, and it would've been perfect if it weren't for Big-mouth Betty Mae and whoever had his cell phone number on perpetual redial. TJ couldn't remember a better fifteen minutes.

He rolled over, eyes closed, with a bright smile chiseled on his face. "Barbara."

"Barbara?" Lexus shouted from under the cover.

His eyelids sprang open.

"I ain't no damn Barbara. Negro, don't make me cut you. I don't care nothin' 'bout you bein' no pastor. Call me another bit—"

"Lexus," instantly alert and awake, he looked at her sternly, "there's no need for that type of language. I was asleep, Woman. I'm sorry."

"Sorry didn't have his face between my legs last night. Sorry didn't tell me he loved me last night."

He put his hand out. "Lexus, I don't have time for this." He got out of bed and looked around the room. "I don't see a clock. What time is it?"

"Time for you to realize that I ain't no damn Barbara."

He grabbed his watch. "Ten forty-seven!""Sweet Jesus," he said as he ran to the bathroom and washed up in the sink.

"Where's the toothpaste" he asked, rummaging through her cabinet. "Never mind; I found it," he said, taking off the top and squeezing some on his finger.

"Ten fifty-five. I can make the eleven-thirty service," he said, pulling his pants up before running out the door.

His heart raced as he put his cell phone on the hands-free cradle inside his Bentley. Right before dialing into his voice mailbox, he noticed that the forty-three missed calls he'd received last night had catapulted to ninety-one. "Good Lord," he said, thinking that Betty Mae had already gone to running her mouth. He took a deep breath before checking his messages.

"You have ten messages. Your voice-mailbox is full. You cannot receive any more messages at this time."

He pressed one.

"Terrell Joseph Money, it is 12:45 a.m. For the love of God will you answer your phone? This is Percival. Get to the emergency room at Dekalb Medical now. Your wife? Remember her?"

His heart raced. He looked down at his phone. He started to call Percival, but it was Sunday morning.

At 11:21, he pulled up to the curb and ran inside to the hospital information desk.

"Terrell Joseph Money!"

He turned around as Percival's wife took long, determined steps toward him.

When she was inches from his face, she stopped, rolled her eyes, and scowled. "Come with me," she said, turning and marching off.

"What happened? Is Barbara okay?" he asked, following behind her, oblivious to her cold tone.

Maya didn't look back or utter a word until she entered a women's restroom.

"Come in; no one's here," she said in a stern tone.

After he walked in and the door was completely closed, she lit into him. "Low-down, dirty, no-good, rat-snake dog." She pointed a finger. "I've stood by, played the quiet, subservient wife for far too long. I've watched while you brainwashed my husband, your ex-wife Phyliss, your current wife Barbara, and the entire One World congrega—

"Whoa, whoa, whoa. Hold on, Sister." He put his hands out in a defensive posture.

"Hold on, hell! That's been mine and everybody else's problem. We've been holding on while you've been steadily taking everybody down around you." She shook her head. "Unh-unh, not me. Not anymore. Years ago when the bishop lied for you about your whereabouts when that young girl, Tracy, was beaten and sexually assaulted, I suspected you were involved. And after I learned that your accuser was a member of your congregation, I went and talked with the poor girl's aunt, Mrs. Lewis."

TJ smiled.

I don't see what's so funny," she said, looking at the smile on his face.

"I was just thinking about something," he said.

"You need to think about this. You ruined that little girl. She was in a state mental institution and on medication for what you did to her."

"What I did?"

"There isn't an echo in here; you heard me. Mrs. Lewis told me that you had only one testicle."

Carmen and her big mouth.

"And when I asked why she didn't tell the police about the one testicle, she told me that her niece didn't mention it until long after PC lied for your child-molestin' behind. And since then, I've kept my eyes on your cheating behind. How do you think Phyliss got the VHS tape of you having sex with two women?"

Gritting his teeth, he said, "I don't know, but something tells me I'm about to find out."

"I hired a private detective. Phyliss was too good for you, and that's the only way I could think to break the spell you had over her."

"So you're the Judas that broke up my marriage."

"No, I'm the Maya Elizabeth Turner that exposed you for the rat that you are. Now Percival knows all about you. I told him everything while the doctors were seeing to Barbara. Until yesterday, he loved the ground you walked on. But now you've forced his hand. After I told all, you know what he said?"

TJ took a deep breath.

"Pulpit pimp. That's right." She crossed her arms. "He said you were nothing more than a pimp in the pulpit. He hates to admit it, but he finally realizes that he was wrong about you."

PC called me a pulpit pimp? After everything I've done for him. I made him.

With his voice breaking, he asked, "Where's my wife?"

Maya smiled, venom spewing from her mouth. "Sweat dripping from your forehead, fists balled up, your little beady eyes getting smaller than they already are. I know you wanna bust me dead in my mouth like you did that poor child you beat and raped. I pray to God that your wants overpower common sense." She looked up and put her hands together in front of her. "Lord, please let this fool hit me. I'll even close my eyes. Come on, Satan, do it. We can make Barbara a widow right damn now."

He wanted to explode, but instead he followed suit and closed his eyes, inhaled, and exhaled slowly. When he opened them, he was smiling. "Sister Turner," he shook his head, "the only hands I'm going to lay on you are healing hands. I just pray for yours and PC's soul."

"Don't worry about my soul, Negro. What you need to worry about is where you gon' live and what church you'll attempt to put under your spell. Because you will never, ever step your behind back up in One World or any of its affiliates. And you *will* leave town."

He put his hand out. "Hold on, Sister. I'm not goin' anywhere. As a matter of fact, I'm about to head up the new megachurch and PC will support me whether he likes it or not." He smiled. "And guess what, Sweetheart, you'll support me right along with your husband."

"I'm not your sweetheart." She uncrossed her arms and put her hands on her hips. "And since, obviously you haven't fully grasped the English language, I'll break it down so even you can understand." She paused. "I have enough evidence on you to not only ruin your already tarnished image, but I still have those tapes from the P.I. I hired years ago, and I have other evidence that will put you away for a very—and I emphasize the word *very*," she paused, her veins showing in her forehead, "long time. Now, if you don't believe me, just step one foot back up in One World."

She opened the door to leave the restroom.

He reached out in front of her and closed the restroom door.

"Maya, Maya, Maya. You can do all of what you've threatened."

"Promised!" she interrupted.

"And I can't stop you. And, yes, you'll ruin me, but," he pointed a finger in the air, "you'll also ruin your precious, creeping husband."

Her eyes widened.

"Ah-ha, got your attention now." He held a finger in the air.

"What?"

"Not what? The question should be how and who." He took a deep breath, "Maya, Maya, Maya—"

"Quit with the drama already," she said.

"I don't know how to tell you this but," TJ lowered his head and placed a hand over his chest, "it causes me deep," he paused, "emotional pain to inform you that… uhm," he nodded, "PC has an eighteen-year-old son…"

"That's a lie!" she shouted.

"A son that I have been taking care of for eighteen years. If memory serves me right, I believe you and PC have been married for, what, nineteen years now?"

"Lies!" she said.

"Oh, is it really a lie?" he asked, removing from his wallet the folded five by seven picture he'd been carrying around all week.

Maya's eyes became so wide TJ thought she was about to burst a blood vessel as he held the picture of PC's illegitimate son in front of her. There was no denying it. Carmen's son was the spitting image of PC.

"Congratulations on the new addition to your family. I could tell you about PC's other women, but I think this will be sufficient for now. And, oh, by the way, since we are being candid and frank, I think you should know that, on several occasions, cash-filled envelopes were exchanged with city officials to get things done, such as church zoning, building permits, and land development information. This cash, incidentally," he smiled even broader, "came from church members' tithes and offerings. Imagine the scandal it would cause if this information somehow found its way into the hands of the IRS, or worse, the local media."

She turned and ran out of the restroom in tears.

"Maya, wait. There's more. Oh, there is much more!" he shouted, as he pulled out his cell phone and called his old friend and college professor Drake Gardener. Time was a factor; everything had to be done before PC got back from Alabama tomorrow afternoon.

*****

"Mom, what's wrong?" Percy Jr. asked as they drove down I-285 on their way to pick up Percival from the airport. After church yesterday, Percival had rushed to the airport. A long time church member dying of AIDS was on her deathbed and she'd requested to pray with him.

"Nothing, just thinking," she replied.

"About what? Mom!" he screamed.

Maya looked at Percy sitting in the passenger's seat and then she turned her head the other way. "Jesus!" she shouted looking into the barrel of a scoped short-rifle.

A moment later, the driver asked, "Did you get the boy?"

"No. The contract was only for the woman." He paused. "Look." Drake pointed at the rearview mirror of the van they rode in.

"Shit!" the driver shouted.

"I guess it doesn't matter now," Drake said as he watched Maya's SUV jump lanes and run head on into an Atlanta city bus.

CHAPTER 7

*P*ercival sat back on the stained safari-print sofa that came with the apartment he'd rented the day after Maya and Little Percy's homegoing service. Was today Tuesday or Thursday? he wondered. If it was Thursday, then Maya and Percy Jr. would have been dead for three, almost four months.

Three months ago, the brown liquid had him gagging and throwing up. Now it just barely tickled his throat. He took a moment to look at the bright rainbow colors on the Dixie cup before balling it up and throwing it at some wastebasket that only he could see.

In front of him, on the coffee table, were a dozen, six-ounce Dixie cups left from the 24 pack he'd bought at the liquor store a few hours ago. To the left of the paper cups was a large bottle of Jack, and to the right was a smaller bottle of Johnnie Walker Black.

He blinked a couple times before pointing. "I beg to differ with you, Mr. Black. Neither you nor Mr. Daniels can make me believe that God is laughing at me." He reached out and pointed an accusing finger at the half empty bottle of Jack Daniels. "Don't look at me like that." Percival stumbled while trying to stand. "No, you're wrong!" He put his hands over his ears. "Stop screaming at me, both of you. It's me, not Him. I chose money over family." He pointed. "God tried to show me the signs; Maya tried to show me the signs, but I chose to ignore them. Terrell Joseph Money, the women, the money, the greed."

"Hey, Crazy!"

Percival jumped, then turned to the voice that startled him. He wiped his eyes and shook his head before blinking several times. "Maya?"

She stood in front of the apartment's single bedroom door, wearing nothing but a small white tank top.

"Sweetheart?"

"How many times I gotta tell yo' crazy drunk butt, my name ain't no Maya? It's Delicious."

He shut his eyes and squeezed them as tight as he could. "No. No. No." He shook his head.

"Yes, yes, and hell yes," the young lady said with her hands on her petite hips.

"What did you do with my wife?" She was just here. Where did she go? What have you done?"

"Fool, you got it bad. And I hate it for ya," Delicious said.

Even through the redness, the distant look Percival had was unmistakable. He seemed to be looking through the young woman who stood in front of him. He reached out. "I'm sorry, Baby. You were right. We didn't need it. I gave it all away. See, Baby?" he cried out.

"You is a real nutmeg," she said, pointing a small, burnt-looking glass tube at him. "First I thought you was gay, but now I see you done all the way lost it." She put the small tube in her mouth and lit it.

Who was this girl? And what was she doing with that thing in her mouth? He felt lightheaded. He tried to remember. How did she get there? He turned back around and pointed an accusing finger at the coffee table. "Which one of ya'll let this woman into my apartment?"

"Fool." She laughed, "I can't believe you been out here all this time talking to whiskey bottles." She pulled up her long tank top.

He turned back around and gasped. "You don't have on panties."

"No? For real?" she said, her voice dripping with sarcasm. "I offer you some of this sweet young snapper, and you out here gettin' nasty, stankin' drunk." She shook her head. "That's pitiful. Your friend was right. You done took a trip on Star Trek's USS Enterprise to Peter Pan's Never-Never land."

Turning back and focusing his stare on the whiskey bottles, he said, "Y'all told her that? I thought y'all was my friends. I see now that I ain't," he drew the letters out in the air, "A-I-N-capital T, got no F-R-ends. Friends fool you into thinking you doin' good when you doin' bad. Friends make you think you wading clear water in God's kingdom, when you swimmin' in a muddy Hell."

"Whatever." She waved a hand in the air before bending down. "I done did my part," she said, while sliding into a little red, white, and blue flag skirt. "I've already been paid. I got you out of your clothes. I can't make you stick it in. And if you want me to stay longer, you have to get me some more get-high, or ten dollars so I can get it my damn self."

"Get high?"

"Oh my God, you are lame." She held up the glass tube, shook her head, and walked toward the front door. "I'm outta here like last year." She turned her head back to Percival after wrapping her hand around the door knob. "If I would have known you was like this, I wouldn't have taken your buddy's money."

As soon as she opened the door to leave, a million sets of twins with guns drawn were standing before her.

Too much noise. He was falling, but where was the ground? Somebody done stole the ground, he thought, as he blacked out, crashing onto the gray, stained, carpeted apartment floor.

*****

"Preacherman! Preacherman!"

Percival heard a man's deep voice. The smell of urine and feces assaulted his nostrils before he opened his eyes. It had been the same nightmare, the one where he relived that fateful day—the day that ate his heart and swallowed his soul. The day his wife was shot in the head on the way to get him from the airport. The day his only seed was crushed by a MARTA bus on the freeway.

"Preacherman! Boy, I knows you hear me talkin' to you."

He slowly opened his eyes, but quickly closed them as the room's lighting streaked through his body and up to his head. He squeezed his eyes tight trying to nullify the pain. He felt as if two midget gangs were fighting inside his head.

"Preacherman?"

Another minute passed before he slowly lifted his head off the roll of toilet paper on which it had rested.

"'Bout time, Boy," the voice said.

With his eyes still closed, sitting up with his hands on his knees, groggy and disoriented, he asked, "Where am I?"

"You's in hell, Boy."

"Hell?" His eyes popped open.

"Nah, Boy, jail. I said you's in jail."

Percival massaged his temples.

"Let me get that there paper yo' head was layin' on," the man said.

He reached down, picked up the smashed roll of toilet paper off the dull gray concrete bench, and pitched it in front of him to the southern talking brother sitting on the toilet.

"Hey," Percival pointed, "you the man that walks around with cardboard signs."

"Am I?"

"I keep running into you. Who are you?" Percival asked.

"Boy, I thinks the question you should be askin' is, Who is you? I knows who I is. But you won't turn around to see who you is, and you s'pose to be a Turner."

"Say again?" Percival asked.

"Say what again?"

"Whachu just said."

"I said what you heard."

Maybe, just maybe he *was* in the pool. No. Percival shook his head. Remnants of the brown and white whiskey had his mind running wild. "Let's start over. My name is Percival Turner, and you are?"

"I know who you is. And that name don't have nothin' to do wit' who you is, Boy." The man smiled. "You is me and I is you."

Percival looked away to the other side of the cell, thinking the man in front of him needed professional help. It was then that he noticed the small Hispanic man curled up in a ball sleeping on the dirty concrete floor.

"Say, Youngin," the man called out, his bowling ball head shining like black gold. He had a broad nose and pinkish-brown thick lips that stretched across his entire face when they were creased like they were now.

"I've seen you a couple times, but other than that," Percival shook his head, "we've never met. You must be mistaken. I don't know you."

The man pointed a long dark finger in Percival's direction. "Now that's where you wrong, Youngin'. You knows me. You don't know you knows but you knows every human being that has ever lived on this here land. Some you knows better, some you knows worse. Like kin." The man shrugged. "You closer to some and some you ain't. But, Boy, you knows 'em all. You just don't know you knows 'em 'cause you won't turn around."

Yep. The man is certified crazy—crazier than a bedbug swimming in gin.

"I used to be jus' like you, Boy. Back in my hey day, fire and brimstone rained from my mouth as I let the Word go from my soul to the hearts of folk that came to hear the hope that spewed from my lips." He nodded, "Yeah, Boy, I was a preacha' man. Just like you is. And just like you done, I came down wit' the preacha' man blues."

Percival felt awkward listening to this man sitting on the toilet doing his business while speaking to him.

Finally he flushed the toilet, pulled his gray slacks up, took a couple steps, and sat down beside him.

"Since you won't turn around and recollect what I's sayin', I'm gon' help ya out. They calls me Poppalove," he said, extending his hand.

Percival looked down at the man's large, dark, ashy, calloused, and worse, unwashed hand. He couldn't ignore it. It was right in front of him. But still, there was no way he was going to shake it. He looked up into Poppalove's piercing big black eyes before crossing his arms. His crayon-dark facial features looked like they'd been chiseled out of a block of marble.

"Poppalove, huh?" was all he could think to say.

"That be me," he said, with a mile-wide smile. "Preacherman?"

Percival nodded.

"They gone. You can't change that. But you can change you, and you can change the world around you. A wise man once told a dying woman to not give up because she done fought too hard and too long. He went on ta' say that Jesus didn't give up on you, so don't give up on him."

I said that. I remember telling Barbara that the day before. But how did he... "Who are you? I mean, who are you really, and why are you here?" Percival asked.

"Like I's already said, I's Poppalove. But my Christian name is Nathaniel, Nathaniel Turner. See, I, like you, had visions as a child. From early on, like you, I knew I was sent to this here ground to lead the oppressed to the Promised Land. Only thing was, I didn't listen. I let pride, anger, and greed drive me into destroying men instead of building the ideals of men."

"Percival Cleotis Turner?" a jail attendant called out.

Percival's eyes stayed glued to the man's as he stood up and walked to the door. "Yes?"

The lock turned.

Finally, Percival gathered up the courage and exploded, "You were in that pool. You saved me, that night, all those years ago."

Ignoring the accusation, Poppalove said, "Preacha' man, I'm gon' tell ya one more 'gain. Now, you listen up good."

"You're free to go," a tall female sheriff's deputy said as the steel door opened.

"Before you can take a step forward, you have to turn around. Take two steps back."

Percival walked out of the cell while Poppalove was speaking.

"Tomorrow is hidin' behin' yesterday. Go back, Boy. Find it, and you'll find you."

He turned back to the processing desk before he walked through the second steel door. "What was I charged with anyway?" he asked the blonde, braid-wearing deputy.

"Are you serious?" a female officer behind the desk asked—smacking chewing gum.

"Yes, Ma'am." He nodded. "I'm embarrassed to say, but I was a little drunk when I was brought in last night."

She looked down at what looked to be some sort of file. "A little? You lucky you still breathin' as high as your B.A.L. was. Percival Turner, it says." She gasped, putting a hand over her mouth. "You're Bishop Turner." Immediately, she took the gum out of her mouth and sat up straight.

"Yes, that is…" he sighed, "*was* me."

"Bishop," the sadness in her voice was evident, "you've been charged with soliciting a prostitute and possession of less than one gram of crack cocaine."

"What? No, there must be some mistake."

"I wish there was. Lord knows I wish there was."

The look on the deputy's face tore at his soul. How many others would share her disappointed look? How many others would think he was the devil in disguise? Why, God? Why?

His eyes still closed, he tried to think. Slowly, he started remembering yesterday. He was sitting at Applebee's drinking coffee when a young girl invited herself to his table. And as for getting drunk, he really didn't remember having anything to drink other than coffee. He'd been sober a month. He'd finally started pulling himself together. One World needed him. And he needed the One World family. The deacons were excited when he told them he'd be returning in a couple of weeks.

So what happened yesterday after the young lady sat down? Is this what Poppalove meant by going back to yesterday to find tomorrow, or am I losing it? Or have I already lost it?

CHAPTER 8

*A*fter what had happened last night, TJ didn't think he'd have to worry about PC coming back to take over One World. What a year! At the beginning of 2004, his New Year's resolution was to be appointed pastor over the new church he and PC were building. Who would have thought that by October, TJ would be leading all of One World Faith AME?

Late last evening, after dropping the tape of PC being arrested off to Drake, he drove over to Janelle's. Every time he made a commitment to stay away from his old college psych professor, something came up where he had to enlist the man's help. Drake was well connected with the media, and the man was very discreet.

Running a church, a multi-faceted land development company, and making sure his position in the church was permanent, took more work than he'd ever imagined. And they say Tom Joyner is the hardest working man in America. If they only knew, he thought as he dried off. He'd just finished wrapping his hair in a scarf and was about to get into bed when Janelle rolled over.

"You might wanna check your phone." She pointed to the dresser. "It's been vibrating nonstop since you went to the bathroom."

He turned on the light and walked over to the dresser. *One new voicemail*, the phone read.

He pressed 1.

"TJ, I'm scared." Barbara said. "I'm having trouble bre-breathing. Please come."

It had been a little iffy since PC rushed her to the hospital three months ago, but for the most part, Barbara seemed to be doing well, TJ thought.

"Your wife?" Janelle asked.

He nodded. "I'm sorry. I have to go," he said as he buttoned his shirt.

"That's okay. I understand."

This was the very reason he had dropped the others and held onto Janelle.

*****

"Pastor Money?" the doctor called out.

His mind drifted back to last night. Janelle didn't ask questions. She just gave all of herself. She wasn't the best in bed, but what she lacked in skill she made up for in sheer determination. And she spoke in complete sentences. That was two steps up from the Black & Mild smokin', tattooed, ghetto diva Lexus.

"Pastor Money, sir?"

TJ had forgotten he was in the hospital with Barbara's doctor. "Uh, yes, I'm sorry, Doctor. You were saying?"

"I was saying that Barbara is in stage four. We opened her up and the cancer has spread to her liver, lungs, and kidneys. Her stomach is almost completely closed."

"Completely closed? I don't understand. How could you have let this happen? The doctor on duty last night said she was suffering from dehydration."

"She was."

"But you just said—"

"I know what I just said." Doctor Long had a don't-blame-me look on his face. "When Bishop Turner brought Mrs. Money in almost four months ago, I advised to the point of insisting that we go in and operate. But she refused."

"She what?" he asked with a dumbfounded look on his face.

"You didn't know?"

"Yes, of course I knew," he lied. "I just didn't know that it was this serious."

"Cancer, no matter what part of the body it affects, is serious," He spoke as if TJ were a child.

"I know that, Doctor Long, but..." TJ sat down on a beige leather recliner next to where his wife's bed would be once they brought her back from surgery. TJ continued, "She acted as if the cancer was under control. She told me back when she was first rushed to the hospital, that as long as she followed a strict diet, she'd be fine."

Off into his own world, ignoring whatever the doctor had just said, TJ interrupted, "Doctor Long, I don't care what or how much it costs, I want my wife to get the best treatment money can buy."

"Pastor Money, listen to me." Doctor Long put a hand on his shoulder. "There is nothing we can do. There is nothing anyone can do. Barbara will be lucky to live another month."

"Another month! Sweet Jesus!"

Doctor Long continued, "She can't keep any food down. So we're feeding her nutrients through a tube." Seeing the worry on his face, Doctor Long tried to reassure TJ. "Nothing I can say will nullify the pain you're going through, but I hope you can take solace in the fact that your wife isn't suffering. We have her on enough morphine and codeine to make her oblivious to any pain. We'll run an IV in her veins to keep her hydrated. We'll do everything we can to make her passing as peaceful as possible."

"Peaceful as possible! Morphine! So I'm supposed to sit back and hold her hand and smile while I watch her starve?"

TJ's last comment struck a nerve with Dr. Long. The compassion he had in his voice a minute ago was gone. Doctor Long asked, "When is the last time you looked at your wife, Pastor Money? She's five three and barely weighs eighty pounds. Did you not notice her size, the weight loss? She's been regurgitating the food and water that she's been swallowing for some time now. She's been starving for months."

TJ chin rested on his chest as he looked at the black dots on the floor. He shook his head. "Doc, I've been so busy these past few months. The only time I see Barbara is late at night when I get home, and even then, she's usually sleep."

Doctor Long shot him an are-you-for-real look. "You haven't spoken to her?"

No, I haven't, TJ wanted to say, but Doctor Long's wife was a prominent member of One World, and he didn't want anyone to think Barbara's and his relationship was anything other than perfect. Attempting to save face, he replied, "She's my wife; of course I've spoken to her."

He'd been busy because PC had lost his mind and given away all his money and assets. TJ hadn't asked him to sign over his interests in their collective businesses.

"Not long after she was diagnosed with cancer, I told Mrs. Money that if she didn't have surgery then, she wouldn't live another year," Dr. Long explained.

"And she didn't..." TJ began as a million thoughts went through his head.

Interrupting his thoughts, Doctor Long advised, "I suggest you have Mrs. Money moved to the Chateau Pontain Eddie McMichael Memorial Hospice in Buckhead. It's expensive but it's the most comfortable and, in my opinion, the best hospice in the state of Georgia."

"When should I—"

"As soon as possible," Doctor Long interrupted. "As a matter of fact, I can make the arrangements if you'd like."

Doctor Thomas Long had been practicing medicine for over twenty years, and in that time, he'd seen family members of terminally ill patients react in all type of ways once given the sad news. But he'd never seen anyone react with such scripted, false emotion. So, not trusting TJ to do the right thing, Doctor Long volunteered to make all the necessary arrangements so that Mrs. Money could die as comfortably as possible.

"Thank you. I really would appreciate that, Doctor Long."

An orderly and a nurse were wheeling Barbara into the room as they spoke. After the nurse took Barbara's vital signs and set the drip on the IV, TJ got up and reached under the covers, took her delicate thin hand in his, and said a silent prayer.

Her breathing was very deep, deeper than he'd ever heard. It was as if he was looking at a stranger. Her cheeks were deep bowls. Her forehead looked like a bunch of veins forming a road map to nowhere. Where was the vivacious, southern-talking fitness guru he'd married?

"I'll leave you to be alone with your wife." Doctor Long placed a hand on TJ's shoulder, as he stood over Barbara's bed, one hand braced against the rail, the other barely holding her hand.

He turned his head, and after he saw that he and Barbara were alone, threw up his arms and said, "Free at last. Free at last. Thank God almighty I'm free at last."

CHAPTER 9

●

$\mathcal{T}$he Dekalb County jail inmate receiving and processing area was full of family members and friends, either standing or sitting in beige plastic chairs, waiting for the release of, or a visit with their loved ones.

She had her back turned to him, but as he once had told her, if he lived to be God's age he'd never forget an inch of her body. And true to his word, he didn't. He knew exactly who she was.

The butterflies were raging in his stomach. For a moment, he was paralyzed, as the realization of how crazy he looked hit him. Percival was wearing a whiskey-and-Cheetos-stained wife beater tank top, two sizes too small. His hair wasn't so bad, only because short dreads were the latest craze among Atlanta men in 2004. Only thing was, if you got close enough, you'd see that his dreads were really uncombed naps. And the field of salt and pepper hair that grew wild on his face made him look like a middle-aged black wolfman.

How could I have let myself go like this? he thought while sucking in his stomach. He had so many questions for her, so many apologies. He smiled as he pulled down his shirt. As he approached her, blinding bright lights appeared and began to flash. Covering his eyes, he said, "Please get that camera out of my face."

A moment later, he opened his eyes and, instead of a camera, a microphone was thrust in his face. And then he smiled as Carmen Lewis turned around.

"Bishop Turner, how long have you been picking up teenage prostitutes?" a young reporter asked.

"What?" He shook his head. "No. She wasn't—"

"So, you did pay and engage in a sexual encounter with—"

"Get out of here before I arrest you. This is a jail, not a press conference," the female sheriff's deputy who had been sitting behind the glass a few minutes, ago said, as she grabbed the guy's arm and escorted him and his photographer out of the double glass doors.

"There are a lot more just like him outside," Carmen said, as she pointed to the double doors leading to freedom and public persecution.

Percival dropped his head. "How did you know? Why did you come?"

"No nice to see you, Carmen, how you doin'? Thanks for paying my bail. How've you been the last nineteen years?"

"Nineteen years? Wow. And you're still storybook-beautiful," he said with a starstruck look on his face.

She blushed.

"I'm sorry, Carmen, and thank you so much." He shook his head. "Right now, I'm, I'm really confused. Honestly, I don't know how this all happened. I mean, I don't have any idea who the young woman was, the one I was arrested with, nor do I know how she got into my apartment. And the media circus outside." He pointed to the door. "Why does everyone know more about what I did last night than I do?"

"You're Bishop Percival Cleotis Turner, only one of the most popular black clergymen in the country.

"Was."

"Was what?" she asked.

"I *was* a Bishop and I *was* popular, but," he held his arms out, "look at me now. I'm just an old drunk."

"Sweetheart." She smiled. "God made man. I've never read or heard anyone say that God made a drunk." She grabbed his hand. "God made you who you are. And try to deny it all you want, you're a bishop and you're still very popular. Your popularity had you on the news this morning and on all the black radio stations." She pointed outside. "And just look outside; they're here to get the dirt on the bishop, not some nobody-has-been drunk."

"But why, after all this time? Why did you?"

"Because you were there when I needed you most, and now I'm here when you need me most." She grabbed his shoulders. "Bishop, you're a leader. You brought me, and I'm sure so many others, to God. I couldn't let the police keep you in a cage." She shook her head. "And, no, I don't know what really happened last night, but I do know that you didn't do what the radio and TV are reporting."

He wondered how he could've allowed himself to sink so low. Could he have done something with an under-aged girl? *Lord, please help me remember.* "Thank you. Thank you for believing in me, Carmen."

"Bishop Turner," the female deputy called out. "I'm sorry about that ass... I mean, butthole. I wish there was another way out." She walked to Percival's side and in almost a whisper, she continued, "If it's any consolation, I agree with the lady." She looked over at Carmen. "My father had been on drugs, in and out of prison my whole life. And about eight years ago, I dragged him to One World and you preached a sermon about Lazarus rising from the grave. But you compared Lazarus to a modern day nig—I mean, black man. You said lazy, trifling, shiftless Leroy was Lazarus, and he needed to hear the voice of God working through man or woman."

For a brief moment, the deputy stood there, lost in her own thoughts. "I'll never forget the way my dad's eyes lit up when you said Leroy was among the breathing dead."

Percival remembered the sermon as if he had delivered it yesterday.

The woman continued, "My father's name is Leroy. And ever since that day, not only has he not missed one of your sermons, but he went back to school and got a degree in sociology. Now he counsels and helps ex-addicts and cons find jobs."

Instead of telling the deputy that he hadn't preached a sermon in over three months, he reached out and gave the young woman a hug. "Tell your father I said thank you." He looked at Carmen and then back at the deputy, realizing that he was Lazarus and Leroy.

He remembered. This stranger had taken him back to yesterday. This was what the man in the cell had told him to do. Remember. Go back to yesterday and you'll find tomorrow.

A minute ago it was a wrap. Percival was done, dead, and ready to be buried; and now he was a determined warrior. He didn't know exactly what he had to do, but he did know where to start.

He turned back to Carmen and held his hand out to her, "My queen, shall we?"

Without a word, she smiled and took his hand. This was the Percival Cleotis Turner that she'd loved for nearly twenty years.

With his head held high, Carmen in tow, he marched through those doors like a proud soldier going off to war.

"Bishop Turner, are you going to seek treatment for your drug addiction?" one reporter asked as soon as they walked out of the jail.

Percival just smiled, waved, and kept walking.

"Bishop Turner, was she worth it?"

He stopped for a moment to get a look at the man who had asked such an idiotic question. *What did he mean, 'Was she worth it?' I went to jail. Is anyone worth losing their freedom over.*

Carmen was glad he stopped. She could have tapped him on the shoulder, but he looked entirely too determined to break stride and follow her. But his stop gave her just enough time to walk in front. He didn't know where she was parked. There was no telling where they'd end up if he continued leading the way.

"Bishop Turner, now that you've lost everything you've worked for—your home, your family, your money, and now quite possibly your freedom—how do you feel?"

Were all reporters dumber than a bag of bricks, or was today Ask-a-Dumb-Question Day? Percival wondered.

Reporters and cameramen filled the sidewalk and street as they continued following Percival and Carmen another two blocks.

Percival had one foot in Carmen's Green Ford Expedition before he responded to the last idiotic question he had paid attention to. Relaxed and confident he said, "I feel... I feel God and that makes me feel good. Yes, as you so clearly stated," he singled out the reporter with the checkerboard fedora on his head, "I've lost the world, but I haven't lost my soul." He stepped out of the vehicle. "You see, it took losing everything, and the wisdom of a strange, homeless man, a sheriff's deputy, and this woman next to me, to realize that all the money in the world don't mean jack-diddly-squat if the good Lord ain't at the head of every decision you make."

Percival pointed a finger in the direction of the journalist. "The Lord said it is easier for a camel to get through the eye of a needle than it is for a rich man to enter the kingdom of heaven. And, hey, I have to answer for enough as it is; I don't want to be the one pushing the camel through a needle when God calls me home."

The small crowd broke out in laughter.

*****

Carmen had been on the highway for about five minutes before the silence was broken. "I would ask if you're hungry but I'm afraid you'll say yes, and, God, you smell like a cool breeze off a donkey's butt. So, I'm taking you to my place where you can either take a bath or I can hose you down out on the patio."

For the first time in he didn't know how long, he laughed. "What about my clothes?"

She held a finger in the air. "Okay, we're going to burn those before birds start dropping from the sky." This time Carmen joined in on the laughter.

Bonding with Carmen had always seemed so easy, so natural.

"I live up the street from Marshall's. While you're getting cleaned up, I'll go out and get you a shirt and some pants."

"I know what you said earlier, but I still don't get it. I mean, your niece, Reverend Money, you, me, us. I guess," he paused, "what I'm asking is why?"

They were pulling into a parking space at a small apartment complex. There were only three buildings on the newly paved street. By the looks of them, the apartments were at least twenty years old, but they were very well-maintained and they looked to have been painted recently.

As they walked to her front door, she said, "Bishop, when I was a little girl, my mother told me and my sister that the two times in a real man's life that he truly needed a woman was when he was in prison or in the hospital."

CHAPTER 10

*E*ighty-seven close friends and family of the Moneys were gathered in Reverend Money's solarium to view the body. Soft Gospel music wafted throughout the stop-sign-shaped room. Barbara Money looked at peace lying in her blond oak casket. Reverend Money had spent over a hundred thousand dollars adding this room to the already seven-thousand-plus-square-foot mansion in Stone Mountain, Georgia. For hours at a time Barbara would come in here to meditate, stretch, read, or just kick back and stare at the sky through the tinted solarium glass ceiling, almost like she was doing now. The only thing was that her stare, now, was eternal and behind closed eyelids.

TJ had finally gotten away to call the attorney handling the New West End Mall development project he and Percival had worked on the past few years.

"You've reached the law offices of Gant, Bernstein and Brownlow. Our hours are from nine a.m. to six p.m. Monday through Friday. If you know your party's—"

He cut the message short by pressing 221.

"Gerald Bernstein," the attorney answered on the first ring.

"Gerald, Reverend Money here. I hope you have good news for me."

"I wish I did, Reverend, but—"

"Come on, Man, don't give me no buts, not after all the palms I've greased, babies I've kissed, and, I don't even want to talk about the two hundred thousand I've given your law firm since we started this project three years ago."

"Reverend, we've done everything we could. We even offered Ms. Harris two hundred thousand for that matchbook she calls a home. She just won't sell."

"Won't sell? Hell, I know that, that's what I've been paying your firm to handle. For five years we've pushed the homeowners into selling; the few that refused, we waited them out—waited for the city to increase their taxes and when they became delinquent, we bought their property in tax sales. Now, five years and 1.8 million dollars later, you mean to tell me you can't find one, just one legal loophole to put that old woman out on her behind?"

"There is no loophole to find," Gerald said.

"There's always a loophole, and if you can't find one, you create one," TJ said.

"Reverend, you know we can't."

"No, I don't know what *we* can't do. I do know that *we* can't let me lose all the money that *we* put in the pockets of the city commissioner, fire marshal, and whoever else. Sweet Jesus, man, all the zoning requirements and building permits have been paid for. I have commitments from Parisians, Neiman Marcus, Rich's/Macy's and Magic Johnson Theatres." He paused a second before speaking much slower. "Do you not understand the severity of the situation? This is a $200 million dollar acquisition. I'll be the first African-American to build and own a major shopping mall in this country. I have one year. One year, or I lose everything that I've invested. And If I lose," he paused for emphasis, "then Gant, Bernstein, and Brownlow lose."

"You wouldn't."

"Do you really wanna take that chance and find out?" TJ asked, thinking how fast he'd get on the phone to some FBI agents he knew. Once they learned of the bribery, it would be all over for the prestigious Georgia law firm.

"Reverend? Reverend Money, are you alright in there?" Deacon Jones asked after knocking on the master bedroom's double French doors.

TJ removed his cell phone from his face. In a broken tone he replied, "I ju-just nee-need a minute."

"Can I get you anything?!" Deacon Jones shouted from behind the huge doors.

"No-no, I-I'll be-be down in a few. I just need a minute. I can't bear to see my Barbara lying in a wooden box," TJ said, while wishing this old man would go back downstairs and leave him alone.

"I understand, Reverend. I can't imagine what you must be goin' through. Sister Money was a good woman. But at least her sufferin' is over and she's home now."

I wish you would join her, TJ wanted to say. Instead, he just went back into his bedroom restroom to resume his conversation.

"Gerald, you still there?"

"I'm here. I'm so, so sorry about your wife. I didn't realize you were at her wake. I'll be here until around midnight. You can call me back..."

"No-no-no. Don't hang up. The wake is being held in the solarium on the first floor. I'm in my upstairs bedroom. Besides, it ain't like Barbara's going anywhere. She's dead, just like this deal if *we* don't find a way to get that old woman to sell."

Gerald continued, "No one knows that you're behind the mall project."

"Everyone will when I announce the name," TJ said.

"The banks, the city—everyone thinks Legacy Investments is a large but privately owned White corporation," Gerald said.

"And what does any of that have to do with getting the old woman to sell?"

"Everything." The smile Gerald had on his face was evident by the tone of his voice. "To Ms. Harris, Legacy Investments represents the greatest of evils."

"Tell me something I don't know. Stevie Wonder could see she hates us."

Gerald continued, "It's not about what Ms. Harris hates; it's about what she loves. She's a Christian woman with Christian values. She only leaves the house for four things: the bowling alley, the grocery store, her daughter's house, and church."

"Enough said. I see where you're going. Call you back in a coupla' days," TJ said. Shortly after hanging up, TJ took the elevator to the main floor where the solarium and a room full of well-wishers were.

"Reverend Money?" a voice called out as he entered the solarium.

TJ turned, and in front of him stood a stunningly beautiful young woman in black chiffon.

"I'm so sorry to hear about your loss. I didn't know Mrs. Money very long but the little time I did, she made a lasting impression on me and my aunt," the young woman said.

She stood almost close enough to feel TJ's racing heartbeat.

Although he was speechless, his thoughts weren't. *Okay, Lexus had the best body out of all the women I've had. And as far as faces are concerned, it's a toss up between Janelle, and my new lady friend, Kim.*

Reaching out and taking his hand, she continued, "I've heard so much about you, Reverend Money. I'm very honored to meet you."

He smiled. "The honor is all mine, Sista..."

"Shemika. Shemika Brown," she said as he held her hand.

He was looking at Eva Langoria from *Desperate Housewives*, but with deep, dark, smooth, coffee skin, Angelina Jolie's lips, and J-Lo's behind.

"I don't know how you got past security at the front gate, but I'm glad you did," the Reverend said with a smile plastered across his face. "So, Mrs. Brown?"

"Ms.," she corrected. "Ms. Shemika Brown."

"So, Ms. Shemika Brown, do you have a church home?"

"No, Reverend Money, I don't go to church like I should. But I am saved."

Still holding those soft hands of hers, he asked, "So, Ms. Shemika Brown, what type of work do you do?"

"I'm a sex therapist."

He coughed.

"You okay, Reverend?"

He waved an arm, signaling for her to give him a second. "I'm fine. And by all means," he smiled even wider, "call me TJ or Rev."

"Okay, TJ. And you can call me Shemika."

He smiled.

"Are you hungry, Rev?"

"No. Why do you ask?"

"Because you're looking at me like I'm dinner," she said.

They laughed.

Sister Parker materialized out of nowhere. "I'm so sorry about your loss," Deacon Jones's girlfriend said as she stepped between TJ and Shemika.

So caught up in the moment was he that TJ hadn't even seen her coming.

"If anyone knows, I know what you're going through," Sister Parker said. "Pastor, you know it's been two years since my Orlando was called home." Maggie switched her stare to Shemika. "And before he was even in the ground good, I had a line of men knocking down my door."

"Yes, Ma'am," TJ said.

"Reverend, I just stopped by to pay my respects. If I can do anything, anything at all, please give me a call," Shemika said as she handed him her card.

Sister Parker reached out and tried to snatch the card from Shemika's hand, but TJ was too fast.

"That won't be necessary. We at One World take good care of our pastor," Sister Parker said as she grabbed TJ's hand from Shemika.

Turning to face the Reverend, little five-foot-two-inch Maggie Parker looked up and continued, "As I was saying, Reverend, a single, successful, prominent widower like yourself might not see them coming, but mark my words," she pointed in the air and switched her gaze back to Shemika, "the vultures and dark-skinned buzzards will be circling, if they aren't already."

Taking his hand back from Sister Parker, Shemika said, "Again, Reverend, I want to express my deepest sympathies to you and your family. I'm sorry I can't stay longer, but I have other business to attend to." Shemika made eye contact with Sister Parker before continuing, "That is, after I buzz around and circle the room one good time."

As she turned and walked away, TJ let out a sigh of relief as he watched Shemika's black chiffon dress wiggle in all the right places.

CHAPTER 11

*C*armen's apartment was small but cozy. The furniture was stylishly contemporary, making the two-bedroom apartment look like a model.

There were no photos of friends, or family, on the round, glass end-tables nor were there any on the mantel over the marble fireplace.

"Here you are," Carmen said, returning to the front room. Percival was standing in front of her fireplace, admiring the detail in a colorful painting that depicted a young, sultry Billie Holiday wearing a red dress, performing in a crowded nightclub.

After handing him a towel and face cloth, Carmen said, "Make yourself comfortable. The bathroom is down the hall to the left. I'll be back shortly."

At thirty-nine, Carmen still looked and had the body of the twenty-year-old woman he'd met years back.

After taking a hot shower, he walked around the apartment with a green and blue beach towel wrapped around his waist.

He walked into what must have been a guest bedroom. It consisted of a full-size dark wood sleigh bed, matching armoire, chest of drawers, and a night table with an alarm clock and lamp on top. He thought it strange that this was the only room not decorated in different shades of green.

For the first time since Maya's and Percy's accident, Percival felt warm inside without the help of alcohol. The warmness is what had him feeling guilty. He felt like he was somehow betraying Maya—being unfaithful to her memory. It was way too early to feel warm—way too early to feel good. If he had had something to wear, he would've put it on, left, and caught the bus home. This wasn't right.

He left the room and, a few steps later, was standing outside Carmen's closed bedroom door wondering what secrets were behind it.

As soon as he turned the bedroom doorknob, he heard noise coming from the front of the apartment. Just as he got back to the living room, the front door swung open.

"I forgot to ask you what size you wore," Carmen dropped a large plastic Marshall's bag on the hardwood foyer floor, "so I bought you this sweat suit," Carmen said, reaching in the bag and removing a money-green FUBU velour top and bottom. After handing him the clothes, she put a hand over her mouth. "I didn't know."

"You didn't know what?" he asked.

She pointed to his mid-section. "That you were so far along. When is the baby due?"

He looked down at his round stomach and burst out laughing. A minute later he replied, "Don't be so quick to laugh," He pointed to her nicely proportioned chest. "All that up there is going to change places with," he pointed to her mid-section, "all that down there."

"All what, down where?" she asked, pulling her pink Baby Phat tee up over her stomach.

"Yeah," he pointed to her stomach, "the road is flat now. But in a few years, that same road is going to be a hilly highway, with several streets of stretch marks."

"Uhh, that would be not. Open your eyes, Bishop. Look at me." She slowly did a three-sixty with her shirt still up around her bra line. "Are you looking?"

Starting to feel self-conscious about wearing nothing but a towel around his waist, he said, "Let me put on those clothes and I'll get back to you."

"What, you too holy to recognize African art?"

He turned and headed for the restroom down the hall. "I'm a holy man, not a dead man."

A few minutes later, he came out of the bathroom and walked into the kitchen looking like a forty-four-year-old rapper.

"I can make a mean Texas omelet," Carmen said as she started taking things out of the fridge.

Percival put a hand on her butter-colored shoulder. "Carmen, before you get started, can we sit down a minute?"

She came over to the kitchen table.

He took her hand as he pulled out a kitchen chair. "You have no idea how much I appreciate everything you've done."

She blew him off with a wave of her free hand. "It's nothing."

"No, it's everything. And I don't deserve your kindness after the way I..."

"Percival."

"No, let me finish. Carmen," he paused, "the least I can do is give you an explanation."

"You don't owe me anything, Percival. Whatever went on in that apartment yesterday is between you, that woman, and God."

"I wasn't talking about yesterday. I don't even know what happened with that myself. I'm talking about us, my abrupt departure, and never calling." Percival took a deep breath and collected his thoughts. He hoped Carmen would say something like *'let's leave the past in the past'*. But that was just wishful thinking. Her face was ice as she waited on him to begin.

"Carmen, TJ did some terrible things. He was an unfaithful husband. But when you heard the passion and vigor with which he spoke, when he preached the Word or talked about the Lord, his eyes would sparkle and you just knew he was hand chosen by God to spread His glory."

"Percival, in one of your sermons you spoke of false prophets, how Satan knew the Word better than anyone, how Satan would come at you from the front, back, left, and right. Do you remember?"

"Yes, I've spoken on that so many times, but TJ is a man, and no man is free of sin. Look at me. Hell, me and you, my drunkenness, and then there's the money." He paused. "Carmen, Maya would always ask why we had to live so far above ordinary people—why did I have to own a car that cost more than most of the congregation's homes. And you know what I'd say?"

Carmen shook her head, no.

"I'd tell her that the house, the clothes, the cars, and the jewelry was a status thing. Black people wanted *more* and I had the *more* they wanted; the *more* is what drew them to the church. I was a symbol of success—the American pie every black, white, red, brown, and yellow man strove for."

"But what does that have to do with TJ?" she asked.

"Give me a minute. You'll see," he said. "Carmen, I went as far as quoting from the book of Psalms and Proverbs, telling the story of Solomon and how God blessed him with riches. I told her the story of Job, and how in the end God blessed him with so much more than he initially had." He paused.

"And..." Carmen said.

In a lower tone, he continued, "Maya would always say the same thing. We had too much. She told me that one day I would choose money over her and Little Percy. She'd remind me that gluttony is a sin, and the love of money is the root of all evil. When I would say that I love God, family, and my fellow man, she would counter with, 'and don't forget money. If you weren't in love with money, then you'd give it all up and live a humble Jesus lifestyle. You'd use the excess to set up learning institutions, shelters for the homeless, battered women, and drug abusers."

"You set those programs up," Carmen interrupted.

"I know. I would tell her that, and she would ask me if there was one illiterate adult walking the streets, if there was one homeless person, cold and dying on the Atlanta streets, if there was one scarred and battered woman without counseling or shelter? That's about the time I'd blow up and say something like, I'm doing my part, or, I can't save the world, and she'd say, 'Jesus did.' And then I'd really get mad, feeling that I got no credit from my own family for what I'd done. I'd say something like, I'm not God. And she'd come hug me and whisper in my ear, 'You're His shepherd, his messenger, and through Him all things are possible, even saving the world."

The doorbell rang.

"You expecting company?" Percival asked, relieved for the break the door gave him.

"No," she replied with a perplexed look on her face. "I'll be just a minute," she said, getting up and walking to the door.

She looked through the peephole. She turned her head toward Percival. "I have no idea who they are," she whispered.

Percival walked up behind her.

"Yes, can I help you?" she asked through the door.

"Ms. Lewis? Ms. Carmen Lewis?"

"I know that voice," Percival whispered.

"This is she."

"My name is Jebediah Jones."

Percival smiled. "Deacon Jones is a good friend of mine from One World," he said as she turned the lock and opened the door.

Carmen ushered Deacon Jones and Deacon Wiley inside. "Can I get you something to drink, gentlemen?" she asked.

"No, thank you. We won't be long."

"Deacon Jones, how are you?" Percival extended his hand toward his friend.

Ignoring Percival's hand, Deacon Jones said, "I've seen better days."

"How'd you know I was here?"

"The television," Deacon Wiley answered. "Everyone saw you leaving jail with her." The word *'her'* came out of his mouth like bile.

"I see you don't waste much time," Deacon Jones said, shaking his head in disapproval.

Waste much time. What did he mean by that? This doesn't sound like the same man who came to me in tears a few years ago. The man whom I took into my home the same day he lost his job and walked in on his fifty-year-old wife in bed with his nineteen-year-old son—her stepson.

Deacon Jones continued, "Percival, I've known you for about twelve years now. You know how strong I am in my faith."

So strong you tried to commit suicide after you caught your wife on all fours with nineteen- year-old Jonah behind her?

"You know that Jesus is the front, rear, and center of my existence."

"As He should be," Percival said, wanting so bad to say what was really on his mind.

"This morning, Reverend Money called the board together for an emergency session. The reason was to discuss your behavior over the past few months."

TJ. That's how they found out about Carmen so fast. He must've seen her with me on television. But how did he pull the deacons together so quickly?

"As a man of God, and at one time your friend, I asked Reverend Money and the board that I be the one to come and tell you what we've decided."

"What do you mean, what you've decided?" Percival asked.

Deacon Jones pointed his index finger at Percival. "What you did—what you've done is an abomination. You were a bishop. But you've taken to the devil's poison. You've let Satan come into your life and take control. Not only are you a drunk, a child molester, a drug addict, and a criminal, but you're an embarrassment to the church."

"I lost my wife and my son, and I am not—"

"Ah-ah-ah," Deacon Wiley interrupted, waving a finger in front of Percival's face. "Job lost everything, but he didn't turn to the world. He didn't forsake God. Jesus lost his life, but he did so you could be here today." Deacon Wiley looked down on Percival. "You call yourself a Christian, a Bishop, a man of God; and look how you honor our Lord and Savior."

Deacon Jones broke in, "You're not fit to lead anyone. And if you continue to forsake God, you will be doomed to eternal damnation."

Carmen exploded, "That's enough!" She stood directly in front of Deacon Wiley. "I cannot believe what I am hearing. Bishop Turner built One World. He changed the lives of so many. If it wasn't for him, where do you think you two would be today?" Not giving them a chance to respond, she continued, "You cowards are no better than the U.S. justice system. No, you're worse. You've convicted a man without even listening to his side. If anyone will suffer in hell, it'll be you two."

"Satan, I rebuke you!" Deacon Wiley said as he pushed Carmen on her forehead with an open palm.

Stumbling and finally losing her balance, she fell to the carpet.

Without hesitation, Percival went into action, throwing a wild haymaker.

"My nose." Deacon Wiley attempted to stop the blood from pouring by cupping his hands around it. "I think you broke it!"

Ignoring the fat little man, Percival turned and extended a hand to Carmen. "Are you okay?" he asked, helping Carmen to her feet.

"I'm fine, but I don't think he is." Carmen pointed at one of the two men who were now scurrying from the apartment.

Carmen and Percival stood at the apartment building's entrance.

"Not only has the Board expelled you from the church, but the Bishop's Council is in the process of revoking your appointment!" Deacon Jones shouted.

"You can't do that without Reverend Money's approval," Percival said as the deacons were getting into the X5 BMW SUV that he had given to Sister Parker the month after Maya and little Percy had passed.

"Reverend Money's approval?" Deacon Jones laughed. "It was his idea to excommunicate you and revoke your appointment in the first place."

CHAPTER 12

"**S**ome say the good die young. And others say the good never die. The good that Barbara Money did lives through the countless women and children at the One World Faith shelters she and Maya Turner spearheaded." TJ scanned the church looking for Shemika Brown. "A person's life is not measured by time, but by their deeds. And as you all well know, Shemika Brown lived her life for the Lord."

The church fell completely silent. TJ realized two things: He'd just called his wife Shemika Brown, and he had just spotted PC and Carmen a few rows back from the front.

Is PC smiling at me? I can't believe he has the audacity to step foot inside my church.

TJ went on as if he'd never brought Shemika's name up.

*****

After the services and the burial, instead of going into the church banquet room, where the funeral procession was gathering to eat dinner, TJ walked across the street to the church administration building.

He stood over the Louis the XV office desk, admiring the reflection that stared back at him through its shiny green granite-speckled top. He smiled because all this used to be PC's—the floor-to-ceiling book shelves, the art work that decorated the apartment-sized office, the expensive eclectic furniture—everything. If nothing else, PC had exquisite taste, TJ thought as he sat down in the saddle-brown calf-skin leather massage chair behind the desk.

Neither the dreary off-and-on rainy day nor his wife's funeral dampened his upbeat spirit. The rhythm to which Shemika Brown's body danced, as she had walked away from him at Barbara's wake, had consumed his thoughts all day. TJ knew it wasn't right for him to be thinking about the woman in such a way while delivering his wife's eulogy, but he couldn't help it.

Not another thought crossed his mind before he picked the headset up off the desk and dialed the woman's number.

"Hello. Shemika?"

"Yes? And this is?"

"Bishop Money, I mean, Reverend Money. Did I catch you at a bad time?"

"No, I have a couple of minutes before I go into a group counseling session."

"What type of counseling? I may need some myself."

"I hope not," she said.

"You never know," he replied.

"On Thursdays, I counsel a group of women on the art of pleasing a man in bed."

Sweet Jesus, I have to have this woman. "You're right. That type of counseling I don't need."

"I thought so."

"Look here, Beautiful, I want to see you right now but I can wait until this evening."

"You don't waste any time, do you?"

"Time's not promised. I live for today, 'cause God ain't never promised another tomorrow."

"I thought you were burying your wife today."

He put his feet on top of the desk. "I am. I mean, I did."

"How about tomorrow?" she asked. "I've had a long day, and I still have a long way to go before it's over. When I leave the office, all I'll want to do is go home, light some candles, put in a Kenny Lattimore CD, and take a nice, long, warm bath."

The way she dragged out the words *long* and *warm* had TJ hotter than a harlot in hell. He had to come up with something extravagant to get rid of his country-ghetto in-laws before his rendezvous with Shemika, so he called a travel agency as soon as he got off the phone with her.

Ten minutes later, TJ entered the banquet room just in time to bless the food. He dropped his head and lowered his voice, "I want to thank everyone for the flowers, cards, money—everything. Without the support," he extended a hand toward the table where Barbara's family was seated, "of my in-laws, and you all," he turned and reached out to the hundreds of friends and church members in attendance, "my One World Faith family, I don't think I would..." he paused to take out a handkerchief to wipe his eyes.

"Take your time, Reverend," a voice called out.

"We love you, Pastor Money!" a female voice shouted from the back of the room.

"I love you, too," he said, making a wide arc with his arms. "I love you all." His chin dropped to his chest. "Please forgive me, family. I—I just need some alone time to talk to God," he said, leaving the red carpeted banquet room.

If he hadn't lifted his head when he did, he would've walked right into the life-sized ice statue of Barbara that stood next to the rock fountain near the banquet hall entrance.

"That poor, poor man. All he's gone through this year. I'm surprised he's still standing," TJ heard someone say.

He felt bad being deceptive, but he couldn't figure out any other way to get out of listening to the don't-you-remember and remember-the-time stories. Besides, Shemika had him so hot and bothered, he couldn't wait to get over to Janelle's.

*****

Late that evening, with Janelle's scent all over his body, and Shemika on his mind, TJ drove home listening to some vintage George Benson.

"Turn your love around. Don't you turn me down," he sang.

As soon as he turned the corner onto his street, loud rap music drowned out George Benson's greatest hits CD.

What in God's name? He sped through the security gates outside of his estate. Every single light appeared to be on.

He pulled around to the front door and jumped out of the Bentley.

"Sweet Jesus! What in God's name is going on?!" TJ shouted as he entered the den.

"Bruh law, Bruh law, let a nigga pour you a drink," Barbara's alcoholic brother, Red, said from behind TJ's wet bar in the den.

"Negro, have you lost your ever lovin' mind?" He pointed to his drunken brother-in-law. "You wearin' my clothes. And you sittin' behind my bar, drinking my imported *Chateau Elan* out of the bottle.

"Ah, Bruh law, stop trippin'. Half dis here," he held up the bottle, "is my sister's. Half. She own half, and she won't be drinkin' it, so I'm drinkin' her half."

"Half? Negro, only half you get is half my foot up your behind," TJ said, snatching the bottle out of his hand and hitting the remote, shutting off the music on the main level.

TJ put the bottle down on the bar's glass countertop and grabbed his brother-in-law's small arm.

"How you gon' handle me like dis'? You know I got a pro'lem." He grabbed the open bottle. "But for real, though, guess what, bruh law. As long as I got dis' here," he held up the bottle, "I ain't got no pro'lem." He laughed.

"Come on, Man," TJ said, pulling Red toward the elevator.

"Everybody, look!" Barbara's mother pointed in TJ and Red's direction as they entered the basement gaming room. "Big-money Money is in this motha sucka'," Barbara's mother sang. "Ho', you try to steal my books if you want, while I'm talkin' to Money man, and see if I don't slap yo' ass into next week," Barbara's mother said to her daughter while looking at TJ.

Every light and electronic device in the basement was on. The women were playing spades and drinking the reverend's liquor like it was Kool-aid. Barbara's stepfather and her other brother, Blue, were hitting each other in the chest while the music blasted.

"Big-money Money, I bet you can still drop it like it's hot." Barbara's mother tapped her Bruce-Bruce-looking daughter on the shoulder. "Karen-Sue, go over there and show yo' Bruh law how to drop it like it's hot."

"The word is brother-in-law!" TJ shouted.

Before TJ knew it, this five-foot, three-hundred-plus-pound woman was dancing and bending over in front of him.

"Touch your toes, Babygirl. Shake it like a salt shaker!" Red shouted.

"Go, Babygirl; go, Babygirl, go!" the others shouted.

Stunned, TJ didn't move. He didn't even breathe until the biggest butt he'd ever seen was wiggling and jiggling closer and closer to his mid section. And worse, she had a thong on under her table cloth-sized, see-through sarong.

"Pop it! Pop it! Pop that thang like yo' momma taught you, Girl. Don't make me get up out this chair and show you how to pop it on a Negro, cause you know I will." Barbara's seventy-something-year-old mother began to rise.

Oh, double-hell nah. With the remote in hand, TJ pressed the power button, but they kept shouting and dancing as if the music were still playing.

TJ put his hands in the air. "Everyone, quiet!" he shouted at the top his lungs. At that moment, he'd never been happier to have fifteen thousand dollars to spend at one time on other people. "Barbara always wanted to go to Disney World. So, as a tribute to her memory, I booked and paid for an all-inclusive trip for everyone," TJ announced.

They all looked at each other.

"What dat all come wit'? Cuz right about now a nigga' broker than a ugly, one-legged hooker," Red said.

"Yeah, me too," Blue said."

"Both ya'll just shut up. Just shut the hell up. Ya'll just ig'nant for no damn reason. Da' man done damn said all-inclusified. Dat' means he done paid for everything, fool," Barbara's mother explained.

"Ah hell, in that case, I thinks we needs a drink to cele'bate," Red said, before turning up the bottle.

One would've never imagined that Barbara had come from such a dysfunctional, backwoods family. TJ looked around at the four drunken supersized women and the three French-fry-looking men that either had no teeth at all or had a mouth full of gold. Half of them had never been out of Coldwater, Mississippi. Mickey Mouse thought Be-Be's kids were bad. Imagine what he'd think when Be-Be's grandparents showed up.

*****

The black version of the Beverly Hillbillies were packed and gone before ten the next morning and TJ was pulling his shiny red Hummer into Ms. Harris's one-car driveway at 10:30 a.m.

It was mid-November and the woman had two green box fans in the windows. As old as the house looked, TJ wouldn't have been surprised if Ms. Harris had a wood-burning stove in the living room.

Every house on the street looked like a mini prison with bars on the doors and windows. And still, the crack heads and prostitutes had found a way to get past all that steel. Several of the houses TJ had purchased on the street had been broken into. No doubt to get high or turn tricks in.

I don't know what's more disgusting, roaches or crack heads. Yes, I do. Crack heads. At least roaches scatter when the lights come on, TJ thought.

The sun was shining on this cool November day. The crack heads, dealers, and prostitutes were out doing their business as if they had received permission from Bush himself.

Why would anyone want to live like this? TJ wondered as he knocked on the white burglar-barred door.

"Yes, can I help you, young man?" a heavyset older woman with gray hair tied up in a bun stood at the door wearing black and white Air Force One high-top Nike tennis shoes, baggy jeans, and a black and red Atlanta Falcons Jersey.

"I'm looking for Ms. Harris, Ms. Gertrude Harris."

"I'm Girty. What can I do ya for, Son?"

Do you for? Girty? Next thing you know she'll be pushing her rap demo on me. He took off his hat. "Ma'am, my name is Reverend TJ Money. I'm the pastor over at—"

"One World Faith," she interrupted. "My daughter and son-in-law are members."

"Ms. Harris, can I come in, please? I have a dilemma. We have a dilemma that I think together we can solve."

She turned the key in the deadbolt. "Sure, come on in, Baby."

The house was much bigger than it looked from the outside, but it was still only slightly bigger than TJ's bedroom.

He was about to sit down on the gold sofa wrapped in plastic but thought better of it. There was no telling whose behind had been there.

"Ms. Harr... Uh, I mean, Girty, as you know," he cleared his throat, "Legacy Investment Management Enterprises, or as they like to be called, LIME, has used underhanded tactics and they have literally taken these poor people's homes. We at One World are doing everything we can to reach out to the families who've fallen victim to their underhanded practices."

"Only three lost their homes; the other fourteen sold out to the Man. Not me, though. No, Sir." She shook her head. "They'll have to get past a twelve gauge, a Mac-11, and my favorite," she smiled, "my late husband's, nickel-plated Smith and Wesson .357."

As crazy as it sounded, TJ had no doubt that she was serious.

"Ms. Harris, uhm, I mean, Girty, I don't think you'll have to shoot anyone. Unfortunately, LIME has petitioned the courts to exercise a law called eminent domain."

"Eminent do-who?"

He sat down beside her and took her liver-spotted hand.

"Girty, eminent domain is when these large corporations come into an impoverished neighborhood and get the government to force everyone to sell their homes at market value so they can put up a Wal-mart, a shopping mall, or some other business that the government deems better for the community."

"Ah, hell, that ain't right." She shook her head. "That's just plain wrong," she said.

"I agree."

"Can they really make me sell my home?" she asked.

He took a deep breath and exhaled before nodding. "I'm afraid so. It usually takes a couple of years, but in your particular case, because LIME has bought up all the houses and land in the area, and yours is the last one they need, the courts will expedite the process and—"

"Cut to the chase, Reverend. How long do I have?"

"Sixty…" He shrugged. "Maybe ninety days?"

"Sixty days! Reverend, I was born seventy-one years ago in this here house." She pointed to the white and beige checkerboard linoleum kitchen floor. "Dr. Martin Luther King Jr. stood right in that kitchen and drank R/C with my brother Grip when they were students at Morehouse. Presidents have come and gone. Black leaders, movements, hell, even Jim Crow has come and gone. Tornadoes, storms, floods—everything—they've all come and gone." She pointed toward the large front window. "Those streets have poured with generations of black blood. But you know what, Reverend? The Harris home is still standing."

TJ sat there listening with little concern for what she was saying.

She turned and looked TJ in the eye. "You know why black folks ain't ever gon' overcome, Reverend?"

He shook his head. "No."

She grabbed his hand. "Because we don't hold nothin' sacred. We buy and sell everything. If we can make a dollar, we'll sell it. And when Whitey get rich off what we done sold him, we wanna complain. When he take our boys off to fight a war against folks we don't even know, folks that ain't ever called us Nigga, or lynched or raped our men and women folk, what we do, Reverend?"

"Uh, I don't know."

"Yes, you do, Reverend. You know good and damn well what we do. We get on that idiot box," she pointed to the floor-model TV against the far wall, "or we be up in church singing 'Lift every Voice and Sing' when we should be liftin' every fist and swingin' at them same folks that trick us into selling our land, our people, and our souls."

Switching gears, she continued, "I know what you saying is right, Reverend. The city done already tripled my taxes. In forty-two years I ain't never paid over eight hundred a year, and last year my taxes shot up to twenty-four hundred dollars. So I shoulda' knowed they was gon' pass some law and find a way to take my hist'ry away from me. But I got a trick for dey ass." She nodded. "Uhm-hmm, yes the hell I do. Just let 'em come try and rob me of my hist'ry. I'm gon' buy me some mo' guns, and I'm gon' take as many of them wit' me; you just watch. So, Reverend, you tell them pencil-pushin mother-suckers to bring it."

TJ squeezed her hand. "Girty, we don't have to resort to that. There's a way we can beat them, legally."

Her face lit up. "There's a way I can keep my home?"

"Not exactly, but we can make sure LIME doesn't get it. We can kill their mall development plans, and," he pointed a finger in the air, "in a couple of years you can move back into your home."

"How?" she asked.

"You'll have to sell your home to me, I mean, the church. I'll have to make this home an extension of One World. Unfortunately, because it will technically be a church, the city won't allow anyone to live in it. I'll have my attorneys draw up the necessary paperwork and I'll give you a check for, say, $75,000 and I'll turn the house back over to you in a coupla' years. How does that sound?"

"Sounds good." She looked up to the ceiling and put her hands in the air. "Thank you, Jesus." Looking back at him she continued, "Thank you, Reverend. You truly an angel, but I can't take your money."

"Excuse me."

She shook her head. "I can't take your money. Now, I'll sign over the house. But, no, I can't take your money. You doin' me a favor."

"No, Girty, I insist. The church insists. For the next couple of years you need somewhere to live. The seventy-five thousand will be for you to find a place. Do some traveling. Enjoy your golden years. Besides, we have to make everything look legitimate. We don't want the government to say you gave the church this house just to stop the development."

She agreed and they finally wrapped up the reverend's visit.

A few minutes later, TJ was walking to his car.

Ms. Harris shouted, "Reverend, ain't it a shame what happened to that poor bishop that used to be over at your church?"

"Yes, Ma'am. Yes, it is," he said.

"At least the girl came forward and told the police the truth. They say the police are lookin' for the man that gave the girl the date rape drug that she was paid to slip into that poor Bishop Turner's drink."

CHAPTER 13

"*P*impin', let a Nigga holla at ya!" the young man across the street shouted as Carmen let Percival out at the curb in front of his apartment building.

Percival turned his head.

"Yeah, you, Pimpin', I'm talkin' ta you." The young brother pointed at Percival.

Two others, no older than sixteen or seventeen, sat on the hood of an old rusty Camaro across the street, watching their friend struggle with his penguin strut. The boys were all dressed alike, wearing beige, prison-issue-looking work pants right above the knees, and nightgown-like white T-shirts.

"Look here, Pimpin', a Nigga be scopin' you out and, uh, I been checkin' your game," the boy said while fidgeting. "I know you be likin' that bottle and thangs, but," he opened his closed fist, "I got that fire-ass dirty white for ya, Dog."

"Boy!" Carmen shouted, while getting out of her truck.

Percival jumped at the sound of her voice.

"If you don't get outta here, I'm gon' take yo narrow behind to jail myself," Carmen said. "You wanna go to jail, young man?"

He reached down and pulled up his pants. The swagger he had all but disappeared. He shook his head before replying, "No, Ma'am."

"And all you all," she pointed across the street, "don't be on this block tomorrow when I come by. You need to be in somebody's school instead of on these corners selling that crack."

Just like that, the three young drug dealers were gone.

"Woman, are you crazy?" Percival asked with a perplexed look on his face. "They could have shot you, shot both of us."

"And how do you think they would get away from the police? Just look at their pants." She laughed.

"Carmen, this is not a joke. These young kids today kill people for no more than looking at them cross-eyed."

"They're killing people every day selling that crap. What?" she put her hands on her hips, "I'm supposed to stand by and do nothing while they sell death to our people?" She shook her head. "I'm not scared of what they could do or what they could've done to me. I'm scared of what would happen to them, to us, to their children that haven't even been born yet if I don't stand up and say something. Percival," she grabbed his hand and spoke in a softer tone, "I've seen so many young men over the years just like them, and for many years I stood by and said nothing."

Carmen's words caused him to take a good look at the sadness and despair that blanketed the hood where he lived. So caught up in his own misery, he'd forgotten why he woke up every morning before his wife and son had died.

His own self-destructive behavior had only added to Satan's joy.

"You wanna go somewhere, have a cup of coffee, and talk about what you've been through?" Percival asked.

A tear rolled down her face. She shook her head. "No, not right now. I have to go. I just need to be alone a while." She squeezed his hand. "I'll be alright. I promise." She smiled and walked to her SUV.

Percival stood there and watched her get in and drive away before walking on the colorful autumn leaves that covered the stairs leading to his basement apartment.

What a day! What a week, he thought while unlocking the burglar-barred door of his small, one-bedroom apartment. *Barbara's funeral, my arrest, Carmen. Should I have invited her in?*

He walked inside.

"No way. She'd think I was a pig, and she would've been right. But as you are my witness, Lord, I promise I will never, under any circumstance, let you down again," he prayed. "My youngest son is with you, Father God, but I have millions, billions more that I can and will save if you will give me the chance and the strength. My wife is with you, Father God, and she knew you, but there are so many more mothers, wives, daughters, that need to meet you, and if you'll allow me, I'll shepherd as many as you see fit into your kingdom. In your name I pray. Amen."

He closed the front door.

For the first time since moving into the apartment, he was sober. He couldn't believe he'd lived like this for four months.

*****

I must've been drunk when I leased this rat hole, he thought as he lay across the couch, sore, sweaty, and exhausted.

He'd spent so much time on his hands and knees, the roaches eventually gave up running away when he'd scrubbed one of their gathering spots. They simply moved to an area were he hadn't scrubbed, until there was not one dirty spot in the entire apartment.

It had taken all evening and night, and every towel and rag he had, but when Percival had finished, the apartment was sparkling.

It was 6:18 in the morning. He'd been lying across the couch for several minutes, waiting for feeling to return to his knees and back. The pain he felt after the first couple hours of cleaning turned to soreness, and now he was just numb, too numb to move. The only thing that seemed to be going full speed was his mind.

Every time he tried thinking about something pleasant, his mind kept drifting back to TJ.

Even after TJ had spearheaded the movement to remove Percival as bishop and pastor of One World, he still didn't think the man was an inherently evil person. He should know; he'd known the man for over twenty years.

The pounding on the door brought Percival out of his daze. Who the heck was beating on the door this time of morning? It was barely light outside. He dragged himself off the couch and limped to the door. He was so tired that he didn't even ask who it was. And where he lived, that wasn't very smart.

His eyes suddenly came alive as he recognized the woman in front of him.

"Don't!" she shouted, extending her arms towards him.

He slammed the door so hard the walls shook.

"Preacherman, I didn't know you was no bishop!" she shouted. "When dude gave me five hundred that night, I didn't know who you was!" she shouted from behind the door. "Before I got out the county this morning, I told the police everything. Now, don't get it twisted, Preacherman. I ain't no snitch, but I got played too. That's the only reason I talked."

He freed the chain and both deadbolts before opening the door.

A bad nightmare stood in front of him. She looked completely different than she had that night. Instead of wearing a little more than a red, white, and blue head scarf around her waist and a tight little half shirt, she now had on loose fitting jeans, a multi-colored sweater, and a matching blue jean jacket.

She's just a child.

"On the real, Mr. Preacherman, I'm sorry," she said, while looking down at the leaves that covered the cracked concrete walkway in front of his door. "I just came by to apologize. I told five-O, I mean the police, that some guy gave me five hundred dollars to slip a liquid Tylenol-like capsule into yo' drink."

He had a mind to let her in, but thoughts of that night made him think twice.

"What kind of capsule?"

She shrugged. "The man just told me that it would make you relax and make it easier for me to convince you to let me come home with you."

"I never left the table," he said. "So, how did you slip something into my tea?"

"Remember when I dropped my purse?"

"No." He shook his head. "Outside of the TV football game I was watching before you came up, I don't remember much of that night at all."

"Well, I did, and when you looked down, I slipped the Mickey in your glass. The man that gave me the money told me he would be watching and following. He said he'd give me another G, if I got you back to your apartment and had sex with you in your bedroom."

"Why would you do something like that? That man could have put arsenic or some other type of poison in that capsule. I could have keeled over right there in Applebee's. Why?"

"Money." She shrugged. "What else? I mean, look at me, Preacherman." She stepped back and held her arms out. "You see what I am."

"Yeah, I see," he said studying the young lady who had drugged him.

"And?"

He knew what she was, but he thought back to yesterday when Carmen stood up to the manchild that had lost his way. "I see one of God's angel queens."

She laughed. "One of God's angels? Man, you seein' way too much." She shook her head. "Preacherman, I'm a seventeen-year-old crack ho'. Been one since I was fourteen; be one when I'm forty."

"You must need glasses because I know I have 20/20 vision, and I see a seventeen-year-old black angel queen who cares about people."

"Preacherman, you seriously got me twisted. I don't care nuttin' 'bout you." She looked him up and down. "And ain't nuttin' but two people I care about—the dope man and my next trick."

"If you don't care, why'd you tell the police the truth? Why're you standing on my doorstep at," he looked at his Timex, "6:27 in the morning, apologizing?"

"Me getting locked up wasn't part of the deal. And furthermore, if there is a God, I ain't trynna' speed up my trip to hell by messing over a Preacherman," she explained.

"Did the police ask who paid you to drug me?"

"Yeah, they asked me who dude was and I told them I didn't know, that I ain't never seen him before that night."

"If I show you a picture, do you think you might recognize him?"

"I guess, maybe." She shrugged her shoulders. "I don't know. It was dark."

He turned the dead bolt on the steel black screen door. "Follow me," he said, turning and walking toward the kitchen.

He didn't wanna believe it was TJ, but who else could it have been?

After removing a yellow rubber magnet from the refrigerator, he showed her a picture and pointed to Reverend Money. "Is this him?"

"Nah, but that's him right there." She pointed the deacon out in a picture taken at last year's *'Bring the New Year in with a Full Stomach'* homeless and hungry dinner.

"Are you sure?" he asked.

"Yep. You can't forget the face of a man that looks like a black Abraham Lincoln."

Percival grabbed his hat and jacket off the coat rack by the door. "You're welcome to stay if you like."

"How you know I won't rob you?"

"Whachu gon' steal? Besides, I have a gut feelin' about you." He put an arm on her shoulder. "Somethin' tells me that you're a very special queen."

She jerked away. "You don't know me."

"I know your soul."

"There you go, talkin' out the side of your neck again. What you think, your whiskey bottles gon' beat me down if I try to steal somethin'?"

He smiled. "Nope, they aren't talking to me any more. I have a new friend."

"Oh boy, here comes the God spiel."

"I'm not talking about God. He's an old friend. I'm talkin' 'bout you, my new friend," he put his arm around her, "Delicious, Tasty, or whatever your name is."

"Deidre', Deidre' Denise Davis," she said to his back as he hurried out the door.

CHAPTER 14

"*J* shoulda known! I shoulda known!" TJ growled while banging on the steering wheel. He was angry, upset, confused, and relieved all at the same time. Angry because Jones had not sent someone else to meet Delicious like he'd told him. Upset because getting rid of PC was occupying too much of his time and energy. Confused because he didn't know his next move. And relieved because Jones was the only one who could prove he had anything to do with drugging and setting PC up.

He'd just turned off Ms. Harris's street. TJ was heading for the expressway. *Think, TJ, think. You have to come up with a plan.*

He merged onto the I-20 freeway with no destination in mind. He drove three hours to Montgomery, Alabama, and then back to Atlanta, still with no clue as to what to do about Deacon Jones. The closer he got to downtown, the heavier traffic got. The November sun was fading back into the clouds when he exited the freeway near downtown. He decided not to deal with the five-thirty rush-hour interstate traffic.

He wasn't having a lot of luck sorting things out in his mind, so he pulled into a dirt lot across the street from a Triple A parking garage.

"Dear God, grant me wisdom and strength in my time of confusion. Show me the path which I should take. In Jesus' name I pray. Amen."

He closed his eyes and thought back to when he had first met Lexus's cousin, Delicious. Her boyfriend/pimp had just beaten her and she was staying with Lexus until she could get on her feet—so she had said. TJ had only met the young girl once at Lexus's apartment about a year ago. The desperation in her eyes had said what she didn't have to say: Money was her God and she'd do anything for it.

At the time, TJ didn't know the young girl was hooked on crack. But watching her, listening to the way she spoke of the man who sold her up to six times a day, TJ knew she couldn't survive without someone guiding her steps.

He knew that one day he'd need her; he just hoped that the number she had given him would still be valid when he did, and it had been.

But what he couldn't figure out was why she came clean with the cops. She was as liable as anyone for drugging PC.

All of a sudden, a bright light caught his attention. It was the neon Triple A sign across the street. At the same time it lit up like a red sun, the solution to a potentially disastrous situation popped into his head.

He pulled the Hummer out of the dirt lot and into the parking garage across the street. Minutes later, he walked out of the garage and looked at his cell phone—6:13 p.m. He opened the phone and was about to dial Jones's number but changed his mind.

*****

Nearly an hour later, TJ got out of the taxi, buttoned his black London Fog knee-length jacket up to the collar, ducked his head, and started walking.

Deacon Jones lived in a quiet neighborhood of older, modest, ranch-style brick homes. He had no idea if Jones was home. And if he wasn't, that was fine. The deacon kept a spare key under the flowerpot on the front porch.

TJ was tempted to look from left to right to see if anyone was watching. But if they were, they couldn't see his face. So, he just kept his head down and moved with a determined stride until he walked up to the garage. There, he cupped his gloved hands to the tinted window, and looked inside. The shiny bronze 1969 Deville was parked inside. He breathed a sigh of relief, thankful that Sister Parker's BMW truck wasn't inside. He hadn't thought about what he'd do if she was there. Another sign from God, he thought.

The door was opened just as he bent down next to the flower pot.

"Reverend, what brings you to my neck of the woods?" Jones asked.

"I was on my way to surprise you with the news, but my car broke down around the corner."

"What news?" Jones asked while backpedaling and turning around. "Come on in. I'll just be a second. I have to get my keys," he said, while walking toward the back of the house.

"It's sort of a surprise. Something Sister Parker and I cooked up," TJ said.

"Surprise? I just got off the phone with Maggie. She didn't tell me nothin' 'bout no surprise!" Jones hollered from somewhere in the back of the house.

"It wouldn't be a surprise if she said anything, now would it?"

"Guess not. That woman is something else, you hear me? It's pitch dark outside, and that woman is out speed walking to South Dekalb Mall."

"I thought she lived on Clifton Church Drive," TJ said.

"She does."

"That's at least a five-mile walk," TJ said.

"I know what you thinkin', Reverend. But she don't listen to me. She say she been walking since she marched in Selma with Martin Luther King, back in the sixties. I'm just glad she carrying the little .22 derringer I gave her." Jones was putting his arm in a green ski jacket while walking into the living room.

"I had to find some batt'ries for my flashlight." He waved an orange, block-like light in the air. "Pray to God we get you running so we can get on with my surprise," he joked.

TJ stood up.

"You ready?" Jones asked.

"Not yet. I need to use your computer a minute."

"Sure. You know where my office is," he said as he sat down in a blue and white recliner. "Take your time, Reverend. The computer's already on."

"*Jeopardy* fan, huh?" TJ said, pointing to the 27-inch television before turning and heading toward the deacon's office.

"My favorite."

After sitting down in the folding metal chair behind the brown particleboard desk, TJ turned on the lamp that sat next to the monitor.

After he double clicked the Microsoft Outlook icon, the e-mail screen popped-up.

After pressing NEW he pressed the letter M and scrolled down until he spotted her address. PARKER_MAGGIE1@yahoo.com.

He typed the message and was out of the office in under three minutes.

After sending the e-mail, he quietly got up, went into the deacon's bedroom, over to the old army chest at the foot of the bed.

Jones was a Vietnam Vet and an ex-Atlanta police officer. He'd been retired for going on twenty years and had been a gun collector ever since.

CHAPTER 15

*P*ercival parked his small blue pickup two blocks away from Deacon Jones's house. Not by choice— it was the closest he could get.

What in God's name? he wondered as he walked up and weaved through the small crowd of onlookers standing behind a large block of yellow crime scene tape. Police, paramedics, Sister Parker, and Reverend Money stood outside the deacon's house.

"Sir, you have to stay behind the yellow tape," a white officer said with a lisp.

"Let him through. That's Percival Turner," a detective said, waving for the officer to let Percival pass.

The officer brushed up against Percival as he ducked under the tape.

"Hey," Percival said, looking back at the officer.

The man just winked and smiled.

What was that all about? Percival wondered.

"Turner?" The detective who had cleared him held a finger in the air. "Give me a minute. I need to ask you a few questions," he said before walking into the house and dismissing the two officers he was speaking with.

They, too, looked at Percival sort of funny, like there was some inside joke everyone was privy to—everyone but him.

The crowd was quickly growing on the other side of the yellow tape barricade.

Feeling self-conscious, Percival walked over to Sister Parker. "What happened?" he asked.

TJ put his arm around Sister Parker's shoulder. For a minute, it looked as if she cringed when TJ put his hands on her.

"I didn't log on to my computer until this morning. I had to feed the dogs when I got back from my walk. I had just spoken to Jebediah before I went for my walk," Sister Parker cried.

"Shhh. Shhh. It's okay. He's with the good Lord now. There's nothing you could have done," TJ said, as he held her and looked at Percival with an emotionless glare. "Jones, uhm, Deacon Jones committed suicide. He sent Sister Parker an E-mail..."

"First my Orlando, and now Jebediah," she cried.

"What did the E-mail say?" Percival asked.

"I'll answer that," the detective from a minute ago interrupted as he approached.

They were all standing in the grass next to the porch. The November wind made it seem like it was 33 degrees outside instead of 53.

"Come with me, please, Mr. Turner."

He nodded and followed the detective around to the back of the house.

They were standing on a small, wooden, platform deck when the wind started to pick up. Percival put his hands in his pockets, wishing he could go inside.

Void of any emotion, the detective said, "Mr. Turner, Jebediah Jones shot himself in the head last night."

"Noooo!" Percival closed his eyes and shook his head.

"When did you last see or speak to him?" the detective asked.

He shrugged. "I don't know. It's been a while."

"What's a while? Yesterday, last week, last month?"

"I honestly can't tell you. Oh, yes, I can. I spoke to him about a month ago. Right after I—"

"Right after you got out of jail," he said, looking down at a small notepad.

"Yes."

"What did you to talk about?"

"He was with—"

"Charles Wiley," the detective interrupted.

"If you know everything, why are you asking me all these questions?"

"I can't share the actual details, but I want to show you this." The detective handed Percival a piece of paper. "This is a copy of the E-mail that he sent to Maggie Parker last evening. She only saw it this morning after logging into her account.

My Dearest Maggie,

I've been living a lie for some time now. I can't live like this any more. I love you, Maggie Parker, but I am in Love with PC Turner. Have been for some time now.

PC and I fell in love while I was going through a hard time after I left my wife. He took me into his home with his wife and son. That's when our affair began.

After his wife passed, he broke it off with me. He wouldn't take my calls. He completely shunned me. I couldn't tell anyone. I wouldn't tell anyone. I couldn't sleep, I couldn't eat. I didn't know what to do. So I started following him.

Each woman was a dagger to my heart. Each woman he picked up off the street and took back to his apartment killed a small piece of me. Eventually, my hurt turned to anger. I was and am a God-loving, and God-fearing man, and when I found out he was coming back to One World, I couldn't let that happen. So, I hired a prostitute to lure him back to his apartment. Afterwards, I called the police and waited with a video camera. When they arrested him and the teenage prostitute, I got it on tape and sent it to FOX news. Maggie, I am so very sorry.

Good Bye
Jebediah Joseph Jones

"Bullshit!"

"Excuse me?" the detective said.

Sweat broke out on Percival's forehead, and his hands were trembling. *TJ is the only person who calls me PC.* "That E-mail!. Jebediah Jones did not write it," Percival said.

"What do you mean?" the detective asked.

He couldn't tell the detective what he was thinking. He had no proof. Besides, his credibility was less than zero right about now. "It just doesn't make sense." Percival shook his head. "I've never had an affair with Jebediah, or any other man," he said before walking off.

"Lord, please make me weak. Take the strength and the desire to kill from my heart," Percival prayed aloud while taking long, determined steps around to the front of the house.

He couldn't stop clenching and unclenching his fists. Beads of sweat were forming on his forehead. He bit his tongue to keep from screaming.

And there he was. Satan. Directly in his line of sight on the other side of the driveway, with his three piece black and white pinstripe suit on—his white collar identifying him as a man of the cloth.

No longer did PC asked the question why; he just wanted to know *if.* If he could strangle the evil life force out of the man before the police could pull his hands from around TJ's neck.

His mind was cloudy; he couldn't think about anything but killing the evil that was causing him so much pain.

TJ had no idea how close he was to hell. He had his back turned while speaking to some people on the other side of the crime tape. Percival was only three steps away from catching a murder case before something and someone caught his eye.

Poppalove had on the same clothes. As usual, he held a cardboard sign over his head.

PREACHERMAN RUN AWAY FROM THE HATE BEFORE IT'S TOO LATE. RUN AWAY. FIGHT ANOTHER WAY. FIGHT ANOTHER DAY

CHAPTER 16

*L*ast month, the suicide e-mail had done what Delicious and Jones couldn't do—ruin PC. Now, two days before Christmas, the deacons' council was in its last session until after New Year's. They'd been in session for over an hour. Most of that time, TJ sat in his chair counting the water spots on the glass top that covered the sixteen-foot round table, while nineteen of the most boring men on the planet discussed the Jones/PC allegations.

"Does anyone have anything else to add before the votes are cast?" Deacon Wiley asked.

Oh no, why did he have to ask that? Everyone knows good and well Deacon Harris 'Pig' Higganbottom always had to have the last word, and his last word usually meant a State of the Union address.

"Deacon, you have the floor," Deacon Wiley said to Pig.

It took a moment for the deacon to get his wide girth out of the black leather seat. The sun's glare from the window behind Pig was blinding until he stood up and became a human eclipse.

In his nasal voice he began, "Acts one, twentieth verse." He pointed a stubby finger in the air. *"'For,' said Peter, 'it is written in the book of Psalms. May his place be deserted; let there be no one to dwell in it. May another take his place of leadership.'"* Pig scanned the room until he locked his eyes on TJ. "What does this verse mean?" He banged his fist on the glass. "It means the Church has been deserted of its leadership. Now that a shepherd of men has come from the bosom of our fallen and disgraced leader, we must not hesitate in making soon-to-be Bishop Money's appointment permanent. Although a cloud of doubt looms as to our former leader's sexuality, that cloud of doubt rests only over Mr. Turner's head."

The deacon raised his arm and pointed to the large window in back of him. "For there," he paused, "is God's light shining through to us. We must move swiftly. We must move now, and—"

TJ stood up and applauded. "Thank you, Deacon, for your words of encouragement and enlightenment."

*****

Two hours later, TJ was leaning back in his office, shoes off, feet on his desk, the phone headset in his ear. He and Shemika had been together every night for about six weeks. In that time, he hadn't even thought about being with Janelle, Pam, or anyone else.

"Yeah, Babycakes, I tell you I didn't ask for it. I didn't want it. I was happy just serving God as PC's loyal servant. Being elected senior pastor was the furthest thing from my mind. "No," he paused. "Not at all. I had no idea. He'd never given me any reason to think he was gay," he said as the French double doors swung open.

TJ didn't realize that his mouth was wide open upon seeing PC enter the office. He hung up the phone and put the headset on the desk. "PC, how've you been?" he asked. "What brings you to One World Faith?"

"You brought me here," PC said as he approached the desk.

TJ quickly removed his feet from the desk and stood up. The office was still the same as PC had left it back in July.

So much had changed in such a short time, yet so much remained the same, PC thought looking around the large room that was once his second home.

Two elephant ear plants and a rubber tree plant were in front of the wall of stained glass windows at the end of the room. A dark, wooden bookshelf filled with everything, from the Bible to books on the restructuring of post war East Germany, took up two walls in the octagon-shaped office. Besides the large desk TJ sat behind, a black ergonomic leather sofa and two matching chairs made up the décor in the office.

PC's face was filled with emotion as he spoke. "I loved you more than I loved myself, for longer than I can remember. I lied and protected you from the police when even I had my doubts about your innocence. I lied and protected you while you disrespected and cheated on both Barbara and Phyllis. I sided with you against my wife. I did all of this because I believed—not you," he shook his head, "not the man—I believed in you. I believed in what I thought I saw in your heart. I trusted you. There was a time when I would have died for you without even blinking. I thought you were a good man, a man anointed by God, until..." he put his head down, "until the day I read that e-mail." He raised his head and pointed a finger at TJ. "The e-mail you sent to Sister Parker."

"I sent?" TJ put a hand to his chest.

"That's when all that love, trust, and faith turned to anger. And by the time I was only a few feet away from you, Satan had entered my heart and that anger manifested into a burning ball of hate that I never want to feel again. If it weren't for a man carrying a cardboard sign standing off in the crowd of onlookers, you woulda been a memory."

TJ put his hands in his pockets. He didn't want PC to see them trembling. "Have you been drinking?"

"No, I haven't had a drink since the night you gave Deacon Jones the drugs that had me hallucinating."

"You talking crazy, PC. I think you better leave," TJ mustered up the courage to say.

PC took a step closer to the desk. TJ took a step back. Now his back was literally against the wall.

"Leave? No." He shook his head. Very calmly he said, "I won't go anywhere until I tell you how I know that you killed Deacon Jones."

TJ's voice went up an octave. "He shot himself."

"I don't think so. In the e-mail you sent, you identified me as PC. No one calls me PC but you. Everyone calls me Percival, Bishop, Pastor, or Reverend. You're the only one who's ever called me PC."

"But—"

"Deacon Jones had a phobia of being shot. There's no way he would've or could've shot himself. And last but not least, you and I both know that I am not gay. Not only did you kill a man of God, but you tarnished his good name. For that, God will judge you."

"Are you God now? Or are you His only begotten son who has come back to save mankind? You must think so, because you've been passing judgment on me since college. PC, if it wasn't for me, there wouldn't be a One World. You wouldn't have the cars, the money, nothin'."

"If it weren't for you, who knows, Maya and little Percy would probably still be here. Deacon Jones would be alive and a little girl's life wouldn't be ruined."

"Little girl? You must've been talking to Carmen," TJ said.

"Carmen's helped me open my eyes to a lot of things the last couple of months. And let me tell you something else, Reverend, Bishop or whatever else you call yourself: One of these days I'll bring you to your knees and then," he balled up his fist, "I'll crush you like the piss-ant devil you are."

Loud and shrill, TJ countered, "Devil?" He patted his chest with an open palm, "Devil?" He walked around the desk and stood in front of PC. "Look in the mirror, PC; that's where you'll find the devil. That's where you'll see the man who profited from all my work whether it was unsavory or not. The mirror is where you'll find the man who had an affair with a married woman less than six months after he himself got married. That's where you'll find the man who fathered a child with that same married woman and passed the child off as the son of the woman's then husband."

"What are you talking about?"

In a much calmer tone, TJ said, "Come on, PC, don't play stupid."

"Stupid?"

Taunting him, TJ waved a finger in front of him and sang, "What tangled webs we weave when we practice—"

"Untangle this web," PC said, gritting his teeth and grabbing TJ by the neck.

TJ couldn't breathe. In no time, he was on the hardwood office floor clawing at PC's arm. The more he struggled, the tighter PC's grip became. TJ saw the murder in PC's eyes as the life began to drain from his body. "I can't breathe." TJ barely squeezed the words out of his mouth.

CHAPTER 17

"That's the point," Percival said as he let go of TJ's neck.

TJ wheezed and coughed uncontrollably for a couple minutes while Percival stood over him glaring—looking at the man responsible for so much pain, so much misery.

"You-you—" TJ whispered while trying to catch his breath, still coughing.

"All we've been through. All I've had to put up with because I believed in you. Twenty-four years..." Percival shook his head.

TJ made it to one knee. Pointing a finger at Percival, he said, "You-you should've..." He coughed.

Percival interrupted, "This is your church, your building now, but the people will never be yours. And someway, somehow, someday, I'll find a way to get them to see the truth. The good Lord speaks of false prophets, and He also speaks of those who expose and destroy them," Percival said as he walked out of the office.

"When I finish with you, you're gonna wish you killed me," TJ whispered after Percival was gone.

*****

While driving home, all types of thoughts bounced around in Percival's mind.

The first thing he noticed upon turning onto his street was the same young men Carmen had run off a month ago. Time line is off here. This was at the time of the suicide. They'd moved two blocks down to another corner and were posted up on another beat-up car.

It had been a month a some change since Deidre' had shown up on Percival's doorstep filled with heartfelt apologies. Deidre' liked Carmen, but Carmen seemed indifferent or a little scared of Deidre'.

Carmen was a middle-aged woman who lived a sheltered life. Aside from going to the gym, work, and to the movies, she didn't do much else. She was a loner, an introvert.

On the other hand, Deidre' was an extrovert. She'd been on the streets since she was fourteen. She'd done whatever it took to survive. She'd seen hell, danced with the devil, and smoked from his pipe.

When Percival had first met her, at Applebee's, two months ago, you would have sworn she was in her early thirties. However, over the past few weeks her face had begun to fill out, and her dull, hard-looking skin had started to shine like the African sun. And smart, the girl was a whip.

Percival breathed in the winter air and looked around at the strings of colorful lights that decorated yards and trees as he got out of his truck. Funny how no matter how poor they were, people always managed to light up the streets around Christmas, he thought.

He walked through the dirt and leaves down the stairs to what was once his dull gray and beige drunk tank. Now, thanks to Deidre' and Carmen, the apartment was a colorful small piece of paradise in the ghetto.

After turning the key and opening the door, his eyes widened. He couldn't believe what he was seeing, right in front of him, only a couple of feet from the door.

"You like?" Deidre' asked with a shy, little-girl look on her face, which was weird. It was hard to believe she'd ever been a little girl, and anyone who came in contact with her knew that she was anything but shy.

"Like? This is unbelievable."

Deidre' stood next to a painting with her hands behind her back. That shy look was instantly replaced with the most brilliant smile.

The last six weeks had been difficult for both of them. She was in and out, sometimes gone for one or two days at a time. Percival knew what she was doing, but instead of trying to convince her to stay off the streets, off drugs, and out of the flea-bag hotels and alleyways where she turned tricks, he encouraged her to do what she loved most, and that was painting.

Three days after she had more or less moved in, Percival surprised her with a twenty-four by thirty-six inch stretched canvas, an assortment of paints, and an easel.

If it weren't for the paint supplies, Percival believed, she wouldn't have returned from her many street journeys. He knew he should've been talking to her about AIDS, drug awareness, or a number of things, but he didn't. What could he tell her that she hadn't already heard or seen? Instead, he had encouraged her to love herself.

They had had conversations about God. He'd used the messages that were in the Bible to illustrate right and wrong.

Every time he woke up or came home and she was gone, he'd have an overwhelming urge to go look for her, but he knew he couldn't find her. Only God could.

"I'm standing here witnessing the hand of God working through you, Deidre' Denise Davis." He reached out and she stepped forward and into his arms. "Thank you," he whispered.

"You really think it's that good?" she asked.

"Better than good; it's genius." He pulled away from her to admire the picture in front of him.

"Just look," he pointed, "the detail is impeccable."

"You think?"

"I know."

He was glad she'd made him promise not to take a look at it until she was finished. He had no idea what she had been painting. For hours at a time she'd be engrossed, sitting on the stool in the far corner of the front room, her back against the wall, listening to her CD's on little Percy's boom box.

Over the past few weeks, since she'd begun, Percival had become a Jada Kiss, Common, Mos Def, Kanye West, Talib Kwale, and Nas hip-hop fan. They were Deidre's favorite artists, and these were the only CD's she would listen to.

These six young men were what Percival called God's prophets of hip-hop. He had had no idea that there was so much positivity in rap music.

She pointed to the picture and began to explain, "The dove-winged black men and women in purple robes flying over the department store escalator are angels."

135

He nodded.

"The long department store escalator represents the stairway to heaven," she explained. "The hand that your wife and son are standing on as they ride up the escalator is the hand of God."

Tears formed in Percival's eyes.

"The blue sky in the background represents freedom."

The apartment was getting cold. Percvial wanted to step back and close the door, but he was so overwhelmed with emotion he couldn't move.

"The cloud-colored gates at the top of the escalator are sort of self-explanatory," she said.

He nodded. In a barely audible low tone he said, "I understand the Heaven's gate concept, but what does that mean?" He pointed.

"I painted 1372 Promised Land Avenue in the middle of the gate to represent what people seemed to have been trying to find since the days of Moses. When you told me the story of Moses, and used today's black woman and man as the oppressed and lost people trying to find the Promised Land through alcohol, crack, or the dollar bill, it gave me the idea for Promised Land Avenue."

"Wow." He shook his head, tears free-falling down his face. All choked up, unable to speak, he pointed to the numbers 1372.

She smiled. "Oh, that's this address, Silly." Deidre' used her arm to make an arc around the room. "This is my promised land. You've shown me that if I look deep enough inside myself, I can find the solutions to all of my problems. "Not one time did you try to stop me from using drugs or turnin' tricks. You never judged me; you just showed me mad love. By doing that, you made me want to listen to you, and by listening, I learned a lot about life and about myself. I ain't gon' lie. I been out there turnin' tricks and getting' high the month and some change I been here. But I can't live like that any more." She began to cry. "I won't live like that ever again."

Percival tried to pull it together, be strong while he listened.

"Every time I looked at a trick, I saw you. Every time I lit the pipe, I saw you. Because of you, I've been clean for seven days. I know that ain't long, but it's a lifetime to an addict." She grabbed his hand. "Trust me."

He wiped his eyes with the sleeve of his coat.

"I ain't got no desire to get high or let anyone use me like a toilet ever again. You made me realize that God's greatest gift to me is my life, and if I am of God then my body doesn't belong to me." She paused. "It belongs to God. And by poisoning my body with drugs and different men, I'm poisoning God."

"I guess God got it goin' on," Percival said as he noticed something else in the painting. "Deidre'?"

"Yes?"

He pointed. "You painted that picture inside my face."

She smiled. "Sort of. It's an abstract outline of—"

"My face," he interrupted.

"No, it's your likeness. It represents the face of God. I used your face as a depiction of what I would like to think God looks like. That's really who I saw before I turned a trick or lit a pipe. If they can paint Jesus, Moses, Abraham, and the others White, and in the likeness that they can identify with, why can't I paint God the way I want to see Him?"

Percival stood there freezing, his mouth agape. "Deidre', this is your calling. You have to share your gift with the world."

137

A voice from behind them interrupted, "I don't give a rat's ass who the ho' shares her gift with, as long as they got paper."

Deidre's eyes became frisbees. "Big Rod!" Terrified, she took a step back and fell to the ground bringing the easel and paints down with her.

Percival turned and stood face to face with a man close to his height, but that's where the comparison ended. Percival had picked up maybe ten pounds since college, but he was still built like a basketball player. The man in front of him was built like a building.

"So, this where you been hidin'. You done found you an old, hard-up, has-been preacher trick."

"No, Big Rod. It-it ain't like that, Baby." She scurried backwards. "It ain't like that at—"

"Shut your mouth and open your legs," he said as he hit the palm of his fist with a small baseball bat.

Deidre' was shaking her head no while she scooted back on the floor. "No, Rod. Not here, Baby. Not now. I'll go with you. I'll do anything. But please, please, not here."

CHAPTER 18

*T*J got up and went to the phone on the other side of the desk. Next, he went back to where PC had choked him. Before lying on the hardwood floor beside the desk, he dialed Shemika's number.

"Yeah, what up, folk?" a hard-sounding female voice answered.

"Good afternoon, may I speak with Ms. Brown?" he asked, wondering who the ghetto boo was who had answered Shemika's phone. There was no response. And rude, he thought. It sounded like the woman had dropped the phone.

"Hello?"

"Hey, Babycakes. I catch you at a bad time?"

"No, Sweetie. I always have time for my boo."

He smiled. "I just had a little altercation, but I'm okay. By the way, who answered your phone?"

"Oh, that was my cousin, Joanne. She was on my other line, but she's off now."

"No, I ain't!" TJ heard the gruff-sounding woman in the background.

"I can call you back—"

"No, no. I can talk. What happened?"

"PC, Percival Turner, the ex-bishop happened. Would you believe he came into my office and attacked me while I was taking a power nap?"

"You lyin'!"

"Babycakes, I'm serious as a heart attack. I woke up with the Negro's hand around my neck.

"Are you okay, Sweetie? Where is he? Did you call the police?"

"Calm down, Babycakes. I'm fine. It's him you should be worried about."

"What happened?"

"Like I said, he snuck up on me and hit me with something hard and heavy."

"He hit you? I thought you said you woke up with his hands around your neck?"

"Uh, they were. I did. If you would've let me finish, I would've told you that the man choked me after he hit me with something."

"I'm sorry, Sweetie. It's just that I love... I mean, you have me worried. I won't interrupt again; tell me everything."

"Well, after he hit me and started choking me, we scuffled. Next thing I know, I'm on the ground with his hands around my neck. I couldn't breathe. I was about to pass out when God breathed life into me and gave me the strength of Samson. I reached out and locked onto his wrist and said, 'Satan, loose me.' Like magic, I removed the death grip he had on me with ease. And with my other hand, I reached around and... wham! One punch and there was blood gushing from his nose. I got up and looked him in the eye while he held his nose. 'Leave this House of

God. Now!' I said, pointing toward the doors. Babycakes, Satan is real. I know, because after I told PC to leave I saw hell in his marble, black eyes."

"You must've been terrified?"

As she was speaking, TJ had an idea. He jumped up, reached in his back pocket, removed all the money from his wallet, and hid it inside the office sofa. "Terrified?" he said, "if anything, I was mystified. Babycakes, I'm a man of God. I fear nothing and no one but the Almighty."

He placed the phone on mute. In one sweep, he pushed everything off the desk, scattering papers and folders all over the marble floor.

"My sweetie, Reverend TJ Mike Tyson Money."

He jogged to the front door of the administration building and dropped his wallet by the door. He pressed the unmute button. Breathing heavily he said, "Babycakes, I abhor violence." He took a minute to catch his breath. "Lord knows I do. I tried to be diplomatic and diffuse the situation Martin Luther King-like, but, regretfully, I had to go Malcolm X on his black behind."

"Baby, I'm worried. You sound so out of breath. You want me to come over to the church while you deal with the police?" she asked.

While she spoke, he jogged back into the office and laid down in a pile of papers in front of the desk. "No, no, that won't be necessary. The only reason I called them was because PC somehow stole my wallet."

Damn, Sweetie, I—"

Interrupting her, he said, "Police are here; gotta go."

After hanging up, TJ pushed the phone back under the desk.

"Ohh! Uhhhhhhh!" TJ moaned as he heard footsteps on the marble office floor.

"Sir. Sir." An officer knelt by his side.

"Ohhhhhhhhh! Uhhhhhhhhhhhhhhhhhh!" he moaned.

"Can you hear me?"

"Wa-water," TJ mumbled, bringing two fingers up and putting them to his lips."

"Water, you want water?"

TJ nodded.

"Joe, call the paramedics while I get this man some water."

A moment later, the other officer knelt beside his partner. "Sir, here you go," he said, holding the paper cup to TJ's lips.

"Are you okay, Sir?" the cup-holding officer asked.

I'm on the ground moaning like I'm dying and this guy asks me, if I'm okay.

"Can you tell me your name?" the other officer slowly shouted.

I was nearly choked to death, not stricken deaf and dumb, TJ wanted to say, but instead he replied, "Bishop, I mean, I'm Reverend Terrell," he coughed, "Joseph Money."

"Over here," one of the officers said and pointed as the paramedics came into the office.

After checking his vitals, his blood pressure, and doing some other minor routine tests, the blonde-haired, sparkling-green-eyed paramedic asked him if he could stand. After being helped to his feet, she said, "I suggest you let us take you to Crawford Long."

"No." He shook his head. "I have about five hundred HIV-stricken children in Somalia that are depending on me for medicine. I have to make some phone calls and make sure the medicine I bought in London will arrive by the first of next week. The kids," he coughed, "are much more important than I am."

"Are you sure?" the petite, creamy-skinned paramedic asked.

He nodded. "Very sure, Ma'am." He smiled as he squeezed her hand.

"Okay, then." She jerked her hand from his grasp. "Well, I guess we're done here," she said as she and her partner made their way out.

Her nametag read: K. Martin. She wasn't wearing a ring, and TJ saw how impressed she was when he spoke about the children. He made a mental note to send her a dozen long stemmed roses along with a thank you card with his phone number on it.

One of the officers walked back over. "Sir, would you like to give us a statement?"

"Yes, I'll give you a statement, and afterward I want Percival Cleotis Turner arrested."

The officer righted one of the two chairs that was usually left in front of the desk. "Have a seat, Sir," he said as he walked over by the window and pushed the other chair across the floor to where TJ was now sitting.

After sitting down and turning to a fresh page on his notepad, he said, "Go ahead; start from the beginning."

"Since I've taken over this church as its pastor, the former pastor, Percival Cleotis Turner— that's P-E-R-C-"

He put a hand up. "I got it. Give me a second here." He took a minute to radio in the name and some other relevant information. He looked at the victim again. "Continue, Sir."

"Okay, well, PC, as I call him, has been harassing me. I haven't told anyone because he just lost his wife and son back in July."

"What do you mean, 'harassing you'?" the officer asked in a dull monotone while keeping his eyes focused on the pad.

"He's called me several times and has threatened to kill me and burn the church to the ground. But this is the first time he actually put his hands on me. I was sitting at my desk talking on the phone, trying to arrange for some medicine to be transported from London to Ethiopia, when—"

The officer looked up. "You told the medic Somalia."

"Yeah, that's what I said."

"No, sir, you said Ethiopia."

TJ's hands shot in the air. "Whatever. Anyway—"

"So what was it?" the officer interrupted, "Somalia or Ethiopia?"

"Somalia, Man. Look, I'm traumatized. An hour ago I was on the floor struggling to breathe. Why are you giving me a hard time?"

"I'm sorry, Sir, but I have to have the facts. Please take your time and continue."

TJ took a deep breath. "Anyway, PC came into my office and started mumbling some mumbo jumbo about him being Satan in the flesh, before attacking me."

Without looking up from his notepad, the officer asked, "How did you end up on the floor on the other side of the desk?"

"The man is much larger than me. He was choking me." TJ reached out toward the officer and cupped his hand in a choking gesture. "I struggled to stay conscious. I guess he dragged me. I don't know. I just blacked out. And when I woke up, the office was ransacked and completely vandalized."

"By the looks of this room, I'd say he was looking for something," the officer said. "Do you have any idea what the perpetrator may have been looking for?"

"Huh? What? No! He was looking for me. The man is not stable, I'm telling you. He tried to kill me."

"Sir, is this your wallet?" The other officer walked back into the room carrying a Ziploc bag with a wallet in it.

He felt his back pocket. "Yes, it's mine. I didn't know it was gone."

He pulled the bag back. "I'm sorry, we have to dust it for prints. You have to come down to the station to pick it up."

"Sweet Jesus! Why you need fingerprints? I just told you who the killer was."

"Killer? No one was killed," the officer taking the report retorted.

"I was almost killed, and if it weren't for some divine intervention by God, I would've been dead." He pointed to his wallet. "I need my wallet. I have a thousand dollars in it. A thousand dollars that I have to take downtown to the North Avenue Harriet Tubman Battered Woman's Shelter."

"Sir, there is nothing in this wallet but your ID, some credit cards, and a Blockbuster Video card," the other officer said.

"What? Oh no," TJ said. "He stole the church's money, too? I want him arrested for murder, attempted murder, armed robbery, and vandalism."

"You didn't say anything about a weapon in your report."

TJ closed his eyes and took a deep breath. "Trust me, he had a gun. I saw an imprint of it while he was choking me."

"But you didn't actually see a gun, did you?"

"I—" TJ placed his hands over his eyes. "Lord, give me strength." Slowly, he removed his hands. And slowly TJ said, "I was robbed, vandalized, attacked, and left for dead, and you guys are sitting here asking me questions like I'm the crim—"

The office holding the Ziploc bag interrupted, "Sir, please relax. We're just doing our jobs."

"Your jobs? That armed and dangerous psycho could be assaulting and shaking down some other man of God. And you're standing around like—"

"Sir, a unit has already been dispatched to a residence we have on file as the perpetrator's last known address."

CHAPTER 19

$\mathcal{T}$he brick house standing in front of Percival had to be somewhere in his late twenties, early thirties, but he dressed like one of the young kids selling drugs on Percival's block. The black 50 Cent T-shirt he wore came to his knees. He had to walk wide-legged to keep his black jeans from falling down to his ankles.

His mouth sparkled with platinum and diamonds. "Now you want my mercy? After you done disrespected me and ran off with my paper. I run a ho'-fa'-hire bi'ness not a people-finding agency," he said. "After you done disappeared for a week, I gotta track yo' trick ass down. And you want me to show you some mu'fuckin' mercy?"

Deidre' braced her back against the wall and stood up while Big Rod continued hitting the palm of his hand with the baby baseball bat.

She nodded. "You right. You right, Big Rod. I'm sorry. I'll make it up to you, Baby. I'll stay out all night for a week. I'll—"

Big Rod interrupted, "I'll hell. I'll tell you what you gon' do. You'll lay yo' ass down right there and spread yo'

funky-ass legs is what you gon' do, and I mean right now."
He looked at Percival, whose mouth was wide open.
"Preacherman, I'm gon' show you how you gotta treat
these ho's when they try to play you."

Percival took a step in Big Rod's direction. "I must be
out of my mind letting you talk to one of God's queens this
way." He pointed to the door. "You see the door. I suggest
you use it."

"You see the door. I suggest you use it," Big Rod
mimicked in a singsong, child-like voice. After looking
Percival up and down, he said, "Nigga, is you out your
rabid-ass mind?"

"No, please, no," Deidre' cried as Rod pushed past
Percival and stepped on her leg with one of his beige boots.

Percival ran over and grabbed the lapel of Big Rod's
Atlanta Falcons starter jacket. "I said... leave!" Percival
slung the big manchild aside. Big Rod Stumbled before
losing his balance and falling into the small kitchen table.

Before Percival could do any more damage, Big Rod
was on his knees in the middle of broken glass and what
was left of the table.

"Get back, Nigga," he said, rising to his feet, gun in
hand. "You think I won't put one in you 'cause you a
Preacherman?"

Standing between him and Deidre' was Percival, whom
Big Rod frowned upon as he sized the smaller man up.
"Nigga, you ain't no better than me. You just like me. Only
difference is I'm using dope, guns, and hope to keep my
ho's in line. And you usin' a book, written by a Nigga ain't
nobody ever seen, to keep yo' ho's in line. Psst. Ya'll
preachers got that trick bag on lock, and ya'll makin' long
paper doing it." He waved the gun. "You got your game,

I'ma' give ya' that." Big Rod patted his chest with his free hand. "I got mine."

"God ain't a game, Son. He's real, and He loves you even though you hate yourself."

"Hate myself? Nigga, please. Psst!" He waved off Percival's comment. "Now get the hell out my way 'fore I blast yo' people pimpin' ass."

"No!"

"No? No? Nigga, you wanna repeat that?" Big Rod asked as he took a step forward, turning the gun sideways with the barrel lined up with the middle of Percival's forehead.

Unmoved, Percival said, "There's only one Nigga in this room, and it's the man that let's a gun talk for him."

Big Rod took another step.

"Do what you have to do, 'cause I'm not moving." *Father God, I ask you to take me in place of her. Spare this child's life.*

With the gun's barrel now on Percival's forehead, Big Rod said, "Pimp', it ain't that serious."

Percival silently thanked God as Big Rod's arms went down to his side.

"You wanna put claims on a crack ho', go ahead. Tramp ain't even worth a bullet."

Percival opened his eyes just long enough to see Big Rod pull his pants up and walk to the front door.

He closed his eyes and continued praying. *Father God, come into her heart and take away her sorrows her sins, and her pain.*

Deidre' didn't say a word. Percival flinched when he heard the door open, but still he kept praying.

"Hells naw, I can't go out like no sucka'," Big Rod said before pulling the steel sleeve back on the black death he held in his hands.

Deidre' screamed.

Percival's eyes popped open just in time to see the gun again aimed at his head. A world of fear jumped into his body and spread to the core of his soul. Not the type of fear that causes a man to beg for his life, but the type of fear that a father has for his endangered children.

Holla back from heaven; tell a Nigga what it's like and I might decide to change my nigga ways, Preacherman," he said, walking forward.

Out of nowhere, two officers barged through the burglar-barred screen door.

"Police, drop your weapon!"

Big Rod's gun was maybe two feet away from the middle of Percival's forehead.

"Drop your weapon, now!"

With his eyes, Percival pleaded with Big Rod to do as the officer had commanded.

"Can't let her play me," Big Rod mouthed before pointing the black gun down at her.

"Nooooo!" Percival shouted as he lunged forward.

A single gunshot was fired.

Deidre' screamed.

Big Rod and Percival collapsed to the floor.

The young man was dead before he hit the ground.

Less than three baby steps away, Deidre' sat against the corner, balled up, holding her knees. "No. No. No," she repeated over and over until Percival and the police rolled Big Rod's heavy body off of him.

"No!" Percival shouted at the officer who was reaching down to comfort the little girl who was in a grown-up body.

150

Percival crawled to her. "Shhhhh. Shhhhh. It's over," he said, holding her in his arms. He'll never hurt you again." He rubbed her back.

Minutes later, the apartment was flooded with police.

"Ma'am, Sir, uhm, I have to ask you to wait outside," a detective kneeled down and said.

On their way out of the apartment, Percival stopped next to Big Rod. Deidre' kept her face buried in his chest as he looked at the black manchild that had fallen victim to his own ignorance. Percival shook his head before praying for Big Rod's soul.

"Are either of you injured?" an officer asked.

"No, Sir," Percival replied.

By the time they made it outside, there was an audience.

"It's freezing out here," Deidre' said as she held onto Percival for dear life.

You would have thought that the six Atlanta police cars that pulled up were there to disperse the block party forming in the street in front of the four-unit apartment building.

It didn't matter how late or how cold it was, when there was any kind of drama in the hood, black folk came out in droves to see what was happening.

Hours later, they were still waiting to get back inside the apartment. The night wind was howling. It was 7:12 p.m. and Deidre' sat in the back of a police cruiser while Percival stood outside. The county coroner had taken Big Rod's body away an hour ago. The crime scene had been secured, and their statements had been taken. So what was the hold up, Percival wondered.

It didn't look like they were going to get back inside the apartment anytime soon, so Percival walked up to the lead detective.

"Detective Regal, we're exhausted. Is it ok if we—"

He waved. "Hold on," the detective mouthed as he spoke into an earpiece.

"Yeah, okay. Copy that. Ten-four," the detective said before calling for a blue suit.

He pointed. "Percival Cleotis Turner, right?"

"Yes?"

A uniformed officer walked up. "Sir, put your hands behind your back, please," the officer said.

"Why?"

"Percival Cleotis Turner, you are under arrest for attempted murder."

CHAPTER 20

*a*nd the Lord said, Vengeance is Mine. This verse came to mind as TJ stood on the stage behind the electronic soundboard podium. He stomped his feet and clapped his hands while the Angels of Faith Concert Choir sang.

After spending Christmas and New Year's behind bars, I bet PC wished he had killed me now.

And now, in February, Percival was still a resident at the Fulton County Jail. And by the looks of things, he would be there for some time.

Over the last four months, TJ had lost a hundred thousand dollars, and PC had lost his freedom. But despite TJ's loss, he was determined to make 2005 a great year.

In November, he'd paid a hundred grand for the title that he would never hold in the AME. He'd been scammed, and even at the threat of going public, the AME still wouldn't appoint him bishop.

It took some quick thinking and masterful convincing, but TJ had done it in record time. He warned the Bishop's Council, that if they didn't make him bishop, he would convince One World to convert from African Methodist to Baptist. And since the title of bishop wasn't traditionally held in the Baptist church, TJ could and would anoint and appoint himself.

And now, just a few months later, One World Faith AME was One World Faith Missionary Baptist.

"Come on, family." He pumped his arms in the air. "Give a big hand to our own Angels of Faith Concert Choir."

As the electronic choir platform descended, Bishop Money pressed the button on the podium and caused the church lights to flash different colors and shoot lasers throughout the packed megachurch auditorium.

A minute or two passed before he stole a glance at his watch. Shortly afterwards, he double- clicked the main light's foot dimmer under the podium. The lowering of his arms matched the pace in which the church lights dimmed. By the time the lights were barely on, the church was dead quiet.

Bishop Money turned to the purple-and-gold robed Angels of Faith Concert Choir to his left rear, and then he turned to his right rear where the One World Faith Orchestra sat. Satisfied, he clicked the podium's foot pedal again, returning the church lights to their normal brightness.

After turning back to the congregation and bracing his arms on the sound board podium, he began, "Please be patient with me; God is not through with me yet. Wow! What a song. So prophetic. So true."

He backed away from the podium and took a couple steps to his left. "I ask you, family. I ask you as your Bishop, your friend, your brother in Christ. Please be patient with me. Because," he stuck a finger in the air,

"God is not through with me yet. No, he's not. Before I'm a bishop, before I am a leader, I am a man." He dropped his head and took a step down from the six-stair church stage. "A man that is not free from sin. A man that errs, a man that is not afraid to err, and I am a man that knows that I don't have all the answers." He paused. "That's why I turn to you, family."

"We still love you, though!" someone shouted.

Sporadic laughter followed the outburst. "I love you, too," TJ said. A fake smile spread across his face. "But seriously, family, lately I've been second guessing some of my decisions and I need your help. You've heard what some people are saying."

"No, what are they saying, Bishop?!" someone shouted.

"Just last week, in the *Crossroads Gazette*, a journalist wrote an article entitled 'Big Business and the Church'. In this article, the journalist alluded to the church being more of a social club and a business than it was a place of worship. He said in his article that ATM machines in the church are just another way that I've found to milk my followers."

"No, he didn't!" someone shouted.

TJ nodded. "I'm afraid he did. And ever since I've read the article, the journalist's words have weighed heavily on my mind, as does the rising number of our women who are getting raped, mugged, and killed after leaving ATM machines. Family, this is the reason why I had the four ATM's installed in and around the church vestibule.

"You single mothers know how it is being mother, father, doctor, cook, teacher, and so on. John-John has the chicken pox and baby Jane's teething. You can't bring them to the church daycare, and you sure can't come to service with no sick babies. But you want to serve Him and give God his portion. What do you do? You ran out of stamps a week ago, and you don't wanna carry the kids in the post office to mail your tithes. What do you do?"

Bishop Money stuck a finger in the air, "I'll tell you what you do. You go through the well-lit, twenty-four-hour drive-through ATM and tithing booth I'm having built on the church grounds." He paused.

"Am I wrong for wanting to protect my church family? Am I wrong for caring so much about the health and welfare of my beautiful sistas and brothas? Am I wrong for building a twenty-four-hour drive-through ATM and tithing booth so you can give to God at any time, so you can continue to receive His glory all the time?"

A ripple of nos resounded all the way from the upstairs balcony to the front row.

Again, Bishop Money looked at his watch while gathering his next thought. "The journalist was correct in his assessment of a couple of things." He held a finger in the air. "One, church is big business. The biggest. God is the most important and biggest business there is."

"Amen to that!" someone shouted.

"Preach on, Man! Preach on!" another shouted.

"Can I get another amen?" the bishop asked.

He got several.

"The journalist was also correct in his assessment of the church being a social club. I don't know about any of you, but I'm proud to say I come to church to socialize with Jesus's people. I'm proud to say that I'm a member and I hang out at God's club." Again, he glanced at his watch. He began wrapping up the service.

He'd cut the service thirty minutes short and still didn't get off the grounds until two-thirty. But when he did merge onto the I-20 interstate ramp, he tried to break the sound barrier, speeding downtown to the apartment where he'd just moved Shemika into.

They'd been seeing each other since the day after Barbara's funeral. As much as Shemika tried to play the role of a refined, intelligent woman with class, she was nothing more than a hood rat in drag. If she weren't so good in bed, he would've discarded her long ago. Granted, she had a body better than most women in rap videos, but it was the way she used it that kept him coming back.

He almost called in sick after reading the text message she'd sent while he was driving to church this morning. And he would have, if he hadn't had to justify the ATM machines.

Thirty minutes later, TJ pulled into the underground parking garage of the penthouse apartment he sub-let to Shemika.

A threesome, her text message promised. He couldn't wait.

He hadn't had two women at the same time since the little coupe' de' grace with Lexus and her dopefiend cousin, Delightful, Delicious, or whatever she called herself. And since then, he hadn't stopped fantasizing about having another.

Shemika thought she was clever the way she rationed out her sex, but he was smarter. The next time she tried to hold out, TJ decided he would just conveniently remind her that he owned the penthouse apartment she was leasing.

Once he got off the elevator and walked down the red carpeted hallway, her apartment double doors swung open.

"Sweet Jesus," he said, trying not to drool.

"You like?" she asked.

His eyes were about to fall out of his head. In front of him stood a goddess, body oiled down, her copper complexion shining.

Shemika stood in the doorway, legs spread, hands on her hips, wearing three-inch stilettos and nothing else.

"I love."

"Love is a hard word," she said as she tilted her head and continued rhythmically and sensually massaging her oily, copper-bronzed body.

"I have something even harder," he said as he entered the apartment and closed the double doors.

You couldn't tell the sun was shining by looking around the large apartment. The curtains were drawn. The only light needed came from the fireplace and the trail of candles that surrounded the den. The sounds of the S.O.S Band wafted from the wall speakers that were in every room.

She grabbed his hand. "Let Momma Meow make you growl," she purred as she backed up to a cleared area in the middle of the den.

"No one's gonna love you, the way I do," the S.O.S. Band sang.

There was no rescue in sight as TJ found himself drowning in her aura, mesmerized by the quiet rhythm, which her swollen red lips and wet tongue danced to as sensual words of ecstasy rolled off her tongue.

"Oh-my-God," he said as she did a stripper move, spreading her legs and arching her back before dropping into a squatting position eye-level with his crotch. As she slowly undid his belt with her mouth, he asked, "Ba-ba-babycakes, where is your friend?"

"I'm her," Shemika said.

"Excuse me?"

"I'm gonna show you how I can be every woman you'll ever want or need," she cooed.

I rushed church service, popped a Viagra, and almost killed myself speeding to get here and there isn't gon' be a threesome?

"No need for that." She pulled the condom out of his back pocket. "I got everything covered."

He was turned on like never before, but there was no way he was going to do anything without a condom, so she better have everything covered including his manhood, he thought. His flesh inside hers was a sin, fornication. As long as he used a divider, something that didn't cause their juices to mix, he was fine.

The doorbell rang.

"You expecting someone?" the bishop asked with a sly grin on his face.

"No."

A second ring.

It was a secured building. No one could get in unless they were buzzed up, unless it was someone who already lived there. Shemika had just moved in; she didn't know anyone. Besides, the type of people that lived in the building wouldn't associate with the likes of her. So, she had obviously let a friend up earlier, and that friend probably went upstairs to the bar on the roof. That friend had to be the other one-third of the threesome that was promised.

"Aren't you going to open it?" the bishop asked while standing on one leg as she removed the second leg of his pants.

"No. I'm busy pleasing my man," she said.

"What are you doing, TJ?" Shemika asked.

"What does it look like I'm doing?" he said, walking to the door. "You think you slick," he said, with his head turned to the side. "I think your friend is gonna like Mr. Wiggles," he said, looking down at his rock-hard manhood.

"Come in; join the party," the bishop blurted out as he opened the double doors.

"Terrell Joseph Money?"

Shock registered on his face. "Carmen?"

CHAPTER 21

" *B*ishop, come on, Man. Let's go. It's yard call. Time to give us sinners some of that good God game," one of the young brothers doing time in the county jail said after jumping off his bunk and heading toward the dorm's steel door.

Percival was lying across his top bunk reading *Last Man Standing, the Geronimo Pratt story*.

In many ways he felt like the man he was reading about. The former minister of defense for the Black Panthers had spent twenty-six years in prison before his conviction was overturned. Twenty-six years for a murder he couldn't have committed. Geronimo Pratt had been set up, just as Percival had been, nearly five months ago.

Percival climbed down from his bunk, having no idea what he was going to discuss out on the yard. He really didn't feel like moving. He would've been content staying inside the concrete walls of the Fulton County Jail, but he couldn't. He'd been ministering to the brothers on the rec yard everyday since arriving, and he couldn't stop now. They were hungry for the mind food he cooked up from the recipes of knowledge he'd received and was receiving from the ancestors he read about every day.

"Yo, B, hurry up, 'fore they close the doors," another inmate called out.

He'd been in the county lockup for 121 days. When Carmen comes, it has climbed to 121 and it appears to be the same day. Last week, the attorney that had been appointed, urged him to accept a deal he'd been offered three months ago, back in January.

If he had plead to petty theft, terroristic threats, and simple battery, the hundred-thousand-dollar bond would've been reduced and he'd be released until the sentencing hearing, looking at only two years probation and a hundred hours of community service.

"Yo, Bish, what's on your mental?" a young brother named Hassan asked.

Two men from two different generations, two different religions, faced with the same problem, walked side by side out to the concrete, fenced-in rec yard.

"I was just thinking about the offer my attorney presented me with."

"Don't let yo' public pretender get in yo' head. How many times I done tol' you. They ain't got nothin' on you, Bish. It's yo' word against Bishop Cashmoney's. You need to file pro se and represent yo' damn self."

"That'd be suicide. I don't know anything about law."

He shook his head. "Yo' public pretender don't, either. Come on, Bish, you think he care about what happens to you? Don't matter if he Black or White, what he care about is green, and you ain't the one breakin' him off. The system that got you in here is feedin' him."

Hassan had a point. In the very beginning, when they had initially met, Percival told his attorney, Mr. Jarvis, that he wanted a jury trial. He made it very clear to the man that he wasn't interested in pleading to crimes he didn't commit. And yet, several months later, Cornell Jarvis was still trying to convince him to take the deal.

Hassan continued, "Atlanta may have a black mayor, police chief, and city government, but they all just Master's overseers. The Law is color blind; it don't care nothin' about what you done and who you was." He paused. "Excuse my French, Bish, but as far as the Law is concerned, you ain't nothin' but a Nigga, a slave on the world's biggest plantation, the U.S. Ask Michael Jackson, or OJ."

A crowd of maybe fifteen to twenty-five inmates had gathered around Hassan and Percival as they stood over by the fence next to a broken basketball goal.

Percival leaned against the thirty-foot cage while addressing Hassan. "No, little brother, that's what *the powers that be* want us to think. As long as we think we're Niggas and slaves, we'll act the part. In today's age, they no longer need to use whips to make us pick cotton. Now, they just lock our minds up," he pointed to the side of his head, "and threaten to take away whatever rights they dangle in front of us. They don't have to lend our men out to different plantations for breeding purposes. Now, we do it without their prodding, at least their physical prodding."

Percival had had no idea that he was as lost as he was before picking up the first book outside of his normal realm of Christian reading. There was nothing else to read except romance novels and Donald Goines' street books. So, it was by default and not by choice that he had picked up Tony Browder's book, *The Browder Files*, almost four months ago. Little did he know *The Browder Files* would be the beginning of his journey into the soul of Blackness.

In the past, if it weren't the Word or Christian-related material, Percival didn't read it. But now, thanks to Carmen, a whole new world had been introduced to him through the cultural awareness books she had been sending.

He looked around at the crowd that had gathered. "You see, ABC, all about Caucasians; NBC, nothing but Caucasians; CBS, the Caucasian broadcasting system; newspapers, schools, and even our churches are responsible for our mental programming. And the way we are programmed precipitates our actions, hence, causing us to be deaf, dumb, and blind."

"Programmed? Bishop, you make us sound like we robots," an older brotha said.

Percival smiled. "Oh, but we are, Mr. Freeman. We don't think. We've forgotten how. We let others who never meant for us to be free put whatever in our heads they want us to believe. The biggest misconception, and our biggest problem as a people, is that we think—and I place an asterisk on that word *think*—that the Emancipation Proclamation gave us our freedom, when in fact, as Hassan said, we are still slaves. Even the church feeds and fuels the misconception of freedom."

"The church?" a young brother asked.

Percival continued, "Show me where Jesus called himself a Christian. Show me where Jesus said He was a Muslim. Show me where He proclaimed to be a Jew." Percival paused to look in the faces of the inmates who had gathered around him.

"But, like a political party, or a street gang, we blindly follow either tradition or our spiritual leaders, instead of researching and reading for ourselves. And if we just did a little historical reading, we would see that the plantation is not the U.S. The plantation is our mindset, and two-thirds of the slavery we endure is self-imposed. That's why, if you ask me now, I'll tell you I'm a man of God and not a man of man conforming to any one of the big three—Christianity, Islam, or Judaism."

The crowd as usual was captivated by the words he spoke.

The one hour a day he spent on the rec yard was the only time he didn't think about Deidre' or Carmen.

This day was different, though. He couldn't get Carmen off his mind. For a little over six topsy-turvy months, Carmen had been his inspiration, while Deidre' was his motivation. And the thirty-four biographies, autobiographies, and cultural awareness books he'd read in the past few months were his spiritual-freedom education.

Carmen had gotten him to see that he was a good person who had done bad things, like almost every man who had ever lived. He smiled as he thought of the conversations he and Carmen had had while they sat up, sometimes all night, waiting for Deidre' to come home. And then there were other times when they'd just go to the park and walk and talk for hours. There were also those times when they sat outside, on her apartment patio, holding hands and just enjoying the silence.

"Bishop, you goin' or what?" an inmate asked, interrupting his thoughts.

"Going where?" he asked, forgetting that he was still out on the rec yard.

"Visitation. They called you a few minutes ago," the young brother said.

CHAPTER 22

*C*armen boldly strode past him into the huge, candle-lit apartment.

"What are you doing here?"

"I should ask you the same, Bishop Terrell Joseph Money," she said, turning to face him.

With the palms of his hands, he made a feeble attempt to cover his shame. "Babyca-uhm, Shemika, throw my pants over here, please."

"I can't get near you at the church, and your house is a gated fortress. This is the only place I can hope to be able to appeal to you," Carmen said as she removed her cell phone from her pants' pocket.

He looked Carmen up and down. She wasn't half bad. He put a hand to his chin.

With her body glistening in the candle light, and wearing nothing but a pair of black stilettos, Shemika seductively sauntered up to Carmen. After dropping TJ's pants in front of his feet, she extended her arm. "Hello, my name is Shemika Brown, and you are?"

"Carmen Lewis."

Do these two women resemble each other, or am I just seeing what I want to see?

Carmen took Shemika's hand. "I'm a friend of Percival's." She turned back toward TJ. "Speaking of which—"

Still holding Carmen's hand, Shemika interrupted, "Percival Turner, TJ's friend?"

Carmen continued looking at him, "Former friend. Friends don't destroy the lives of their friends with lies, and deceit."

"I agree." He smiled. "And friends don't assault, rob, and vandalize their friends, either," he replied.

Shemika let go of Carmen's hand and ran a red painted fingernail down her arm. "Carmen? Can I call you Carmen?"

That's my girl. All TJ could do was smile.

Carmen turned her head. "Yeah, whatever," she said as she swatted Shemika's hand away. "You have to drop the charges. Percival won't take the deal, and rightfully so. Please, Terrell, please," Carmen pleaded.

"Carmen, your hair is so soft." Shemika ran a finger through Carmen's shoulder-length hair. "I love the way it hangs off your shoulders. It makes you look like a mini-me red-bone, Naomi Campbell." Suddenly, Shemika looked to her left. "What the hell was that? I think I saw a big-ass mosquito or something."

"You're seeing things," TJ said.

Carmen turned to Shemika and grabbed her arm. Looking the younger woman in the eye she said, "I am not into women."

"Hmmmm." TJ put a hand under his chin. "Maybe if you were into women, I could be persuaded to drop the charges."

"What? You have got to be joking," Carmen said, a look of horror on her face.

"Am I smiling?"

"Come on, Terrell. I'll make sure Percival is out of your life for good. Don't do this to him. Don't do this to me. Hasn't he suffered enough? Haven't *we* suffered enough?"

"I don't know." He shrugged. "You tell me."

"You're serious," she said.

"As a heart attack," he replied. "Now, if he goes to trial you know he's looking at a minimum of ten years."

"That's if he's—"

"Ah-ah-ah." TJ waved a finger in the air. "Not *if* but *when* he's convicted. But if you—"

Shaking her head, Carmen said, "No! No! No! I can't."

"You love him, don't you?" He laughed. "Oh, the irony of it all. The hand maiden falls in love with the master. She bore his first child. The master's wife doesn't know. A few years later, the wife, too, bore the master's child. The story doesn't go quite that way, but your situation reminds me of the story of Abraham. I bet PC doesn't even know he has a son that's in prison for murder."

The shock on Carmen's face spoke volumes. "How did you—"

"I know everything." He smiled. "It would be a shame if somehow PC found out some of your innermost secrets."

Carmen's tears only encouraged him. She dropped her head. "You'll have all the charges against Percival dropped?" Her voice was soft, full of pain and defeat.

"As soon as I can meet with my attorney and get down to the D.A.'s office."

"What about the things that you think you know about me and my son?"

"I've already forgotten," he said, unfastening his pants.

She turned and pointed a finger at Shemika, who was now sitting cross-legged on the arm of the beige leather sofa in the den. "She can't touch me. I'll do whatever you want. I don't care if she watches, but she can't touch me. And I just wanna let you know I've been recording and taking pictures with my camera phone, so if you go back on your word..."

What Carmen didn't know was that TJ knew what she had been doing with her phone. It was so obvious. He wished she hadn't said anything. Now, it would possibly be more difficult to steal her phone and destroy it after he finished with her.

And where PC was concerned, Carmen didn't have to worry about TJ going back on his word. PC was ruined. There wasn't much more TJ could do to him that hadn't been done already. Besides, TJ didn't want the negative publicity that a trial would bring. There was no telling what would come out.

When Cornell Jarvis, PC's attorney, had called the other day and informed TJ that PC wouldn't take the deal, TJ had decided then to drop the charges. Although he was paying PC's public defender to keep him abreast of the case, TJ still wasn't going to inform the attorney of his plans.

Minutes later, Carmen came out of the bathroom wearing cream-colored panties and a matching bra.

"Sweet Jesus, PC is a lucky man," TJ said, watching the woman walk toward him. The loose-fitting blue pants, white blouse, and matching jacket she'd worn hadn't done justice to her flawless body.

"I haven't been with PC, at least not since...you know."

He clasped his hands around her neck, like PC had done to him. He wanted her to feel as helpless as he had.

"Terrell, stop. You're hurting me," she cried as she dropped to her knees.

"Babycakes, come here," he called out to Shemika. "I want you to share this moment with me." He smiled at Carmen.

"Ouch!" He let go of her neck and grabbed his lower back. "What the? Woman, did you just stick me with something?"

"What?" Carmen said with a confused look on her face.

He turned. "Shemika, did she just stick me with something?"

"Had to be the mosquito. Now do you think I'm seeing things?" Shemika said.

He looked down. The Viagra was wearing off. This was not happening. He couldn't let a mosquito ruin his threesome.

CHAPTER 23

*F*rom behind the plexiglass window, Carmen waved, as Percival walked into the room. In the 121 days he'd been in the Fulton County Jail, he'd never seen the visitation area so empty. This was the first time he didn't have to wait for another inmate's thirty minutes to be up before he could sit down in the open, phone booth-like visitation station.

Of the twenty-four cubicles that snaked the length of the room, only six chairs were occupied. The thin, stainless-steel partitions that separated each visitation booth hardly provided any privacy.

After sitting down, Percival picked up the black phone receiver on the wall.

"Hey, you." She smiled. "How are you?" She put a hand over her mouth. "Forgive me. That was a dumb question."

"No such thing," he said, shaking his head. "But for real, I'm good. Real good. I know I don't look it, but I am."

"This is a first. I've never heard of a happy black man in jail."

"Now, I didn't say all that." He smiled. "I'm not happy that I'm in this place. I'm happy that I'm at," he tapped a finger to the side of his head, "this place. Seeing so many misguided men, young and old, come through these revolving doors has made me realize that my calling is to introduce, or shall I say re-introduce them to Jesus."

"I thought you wanted to get your church back?"

"I do, sort of, but after seeing and hearing some of the trials and tribulations that these men have endured, compiled with what I've heard and gone through with Deidre', I feel that I can do more good coming into prisons than I can pastoring a large church."

"Can't you do both?" she asked.

"Yeah, but I can't give 120 percent to both. And these young folk today definitely need all of my attention." By the look on her face, he could tell she wasn't quite convinced.

He continued, "I think I can really get through to wayward young men and women. I think I can show them the Jesus that they've never seen. I think that, after seeing Him, they'll be able to see themselves for the kings and queens that they really are."

"Do you really think they'll listen?"

"If I didn't, I wouldn't be so adamant about doing it. You sound like you're not convinced."

"I don't know. It's just that..." She shook her head.

"Carmen, what's wrong?" he asked, a worried look shrouding his face. "You're crying."

"I've done something."

"What? To who? Deidre'? Is Deidre' okay?"

Deidre' was in good hands. Carmen had taken Deidre' into her home on Christmas Eve, the morning after Percival was arrested, but that still didn't stop him from worrying about the gifted young woman. It had been two months since she'd written or come to see him. Valentine's Day was the last time he'd seen her crooked-tooth smile.

"Deidre's fine." Carmen opened her purse. "She's still working nights at Food Depot."
She wiped her eyes with some tissue. "I've never seen anyone more determined. All she does is work, sleep, go to GED class, and study."

"Good. I'm proud of her."

Carmen blurted out, "I lied to you. I'm sorry. I'm so sorry, Percival," she cried.

"Carmen Lewis, look at me," he said, looking deep in her watery, hazel eyes. "You may have lied with your mouth, but your heart doesn't lie. And, Woman, you have a good heart. You've saved me from myself. You've saved me from my own ignorance. So, there is nothing, and I mean nothing, that you can tell me," he paused, "that will change the way I see you. You'll always be my Assata, my Winnie, my Harriett, my—"

"I was married the day we met outside of the police station."

"Say, say what?"

"Turner, keep it down," Officer Godfrey, the visiting room guard, said from across the room.

Her eyes pleaded for understanding.

"Did you just say that you're married?"

"Yes, no." She shook her head. "I *was* married."

Not only am I an adulterer, but I've slept with another man's wife. God, forgive me.

Her chest slowly rose and fell before she removed her hand from the window.

"It was 1983. I was fifteen and Ray was twenty-five, but he didn't look a day over eighteen. Half the girls in high school had a crush on the big city teacher, basketball coach and former pro basketball player from New York City. Even the guys at school thought he was the epitome of cool with his Shaft fade-afro and his thick, long sideburns. Anyway, a few months after we started seeing each other, my father followed me to his apartment."

Percival tried to mask the pain and hurt that stung his heart. He tried to listen, but it was hard. "How did your father know?" he asked.

"He didn't, but Thomasville, Georgia, was a small town. Everyone knew everyone, and someone must've seen us together."

He nodded.

She saw the pain in his face. She couldn't look at him. She had never meant to hurt him. She'd stayed up all night, praying that Percival would understand. He needed to know. And he needed to know now.

"Well," she put her head down, "Ray and I were on the couch in the living room. I was fully dressed but Ray was on top of me wearing nothing but his boxers when my father kicked in the door. Before Ray got to his feet, my father hit him in the head with a shotgun. I shouted for him to stop. I told him that Ray hadn't touched me, but he didn't listen. Next thing I know, Daddy jammed the double barrel of his shotgun into Ray's mouth, knocking teeth out. Blood splattered everywhere. Everything happened so fast. Ray didn't have a chance to cover up or defend himself. All I could do was stand behind the couch and scream. With the gun in Ray's mouth, my father calmly told him that he was either going to marry me, or he'd arrest him for statutory rape."

"Your father was a police officer?"

"He was the sheriff in Thomasville."

"So, you married Ray?"

"Yeah. A month later, at city hall. My father thought it best for Ray to resign from Thomasville High, take me, and move up to Atlanta with my sister Sharon and her two daughters."

"Why didn't you ever tell me this?"

Her head still down she asked, "Why would I tell you? When I met you, all I wanted was for you to recant the story you told the police. And after I fell for you, I knew you wouldn't hold me or touch me if you knew I was married. And at the time, after what I'd gone through with Ray, and what I'd seen my nieces go through, I needed to believe in men. I needed so bad to be touched and held by a good man."

"Carmen, look at me, Queen."

She looked into his watery eyes.

"I understand. I really do. And if I was the man that I am today, I would've gone back inside that police station. I know sorry is not going to change anything; I've said it a million times to you, to God, and to that poor child's soul."

Carmen momentarily turned away from him, knowing he had no idea what had happened to Tracy once TJ had molested her. The years of therapy... of pain, and then, and then...

"Carmen?"

"I'm sorry, I just... I just... I don't know." She cried, thinking about her oldest niece, her big sister, and what had happened to both of them as a result of what TJ had done.

"I'm so, so sorry, Carmen."

"I know. I know you are," she said, putting her hand back up to the window.

They shared a moment of silence. Neither of them wanting to speak, but both knowing that they had to bring closure to it all so that they could find peace within.

She sighed. "I was sixteen when Ray and I got married and moved to Atlanta. Ray took a teaching job in the suburbs, and I enrolled at Washington High. For some time, I suspected Ray had other women, but I was in love. It wasn't until our second year of marriage—my father had just passed away and I was in my senior year of high school when Ray threw all discretion out the window. He stayed gone for days at a time." She paused to wipe the tears away. "Over the next year and a half, I had to be treated for two different types of venereal diseases.

Percival just shook his head.

"Both times Ray begged, apologized, and swore it would never happen again. The only reason I didn't leave him after the second time was because I became pregnant."

"You had a son, right?"

"I lost—" She sucked her bottom lip in and put a hand over her mouth.

"Carmen?"

She shook her head.

"Carmen?"

"I'm..." She waved a hand at him. "Give me a second." She took her hand and used the back of it to wipe the tears. "I lost my baby. For the third time Ray gave me a disease, and this time, because of the infection, I miscarried."

"I am so, so sorry." Percival wanted more than anything at that moment to be able to hold her, take away her pain, her grief.

"Leaving Ray was the hardest thing that I'd ever had to do." She closed her eyes. "Even harder than burying my father. But I did. I left the man that had become my world. The man I'd loved so hard that I thought I'd die without him. I wanted a family more than anything, Percival, but I knew it was never going to happen. I thought I'd never trust or want another man. That is, until…" she paused, "until I met you."

He smiled.

"My plan to seduce you backfired when I fell in love. You were so passionate, sincere, and naïve back then. No matter how bad or evil they were, you always saw the good in people. I think that's what hooked me. But when you cried and asked the Lord to forgive you after we made love, I felt terrible. I knew then that I'd made a mistake. You didn't know it, but I also prayed. It was the first time since my father passed away, but I prayed for the Lord to forgive you and punish me for seducing you. And since that day, I haven't stopped praying.

"I didn't think I'd ever speak to you again. And I completely understood. I was just glad that you came into my life and restored my faith in men. And I was most grateful that you brought me back to Jesus. Because of you, Percival, I even forgave Ray."

So engrossed was Percival in Carmen's story, he didn't want to turn around and look at the clock.

"I called Ray a couple months after you and I… you know…"

He nodded.

"He was unemployed at the time and had lost a lot of weight in the year that we had been apart. Ray told me that the weight fell off because, most of the time, he was in too much pain to eat."

"What was wrong with him?"

"He was under a doctor's care for a degenerative disc in his back. It had something to do with the knee injury he sustained when he played pro ball."

"Tell me you didn't take him back."

"I loved him, Percival. I was convinced that if I could bring him to Jesus, he would repent."

"Did he?"

The expression on her face said it all. "Three months after Ray and I got back together, I came home from work early because I was having severe labor pains."

"You were pregnant again?" he asked.

"Wrap it up, Turner," Officer Godfrey said, tapping him on the shoulder.

He turned around. "A few more minutes, please," he pleaded.

He held out his palm. "Five minutes, Turner. No more."

Percival turned back to Carmen.

"Where was I?"

"You were pregnant and you came—"

"Oh, yeah. When I opened the door to my apartment, I saw a naked woman wearing my cooking apron, standing in my kitchen, frying my chicken on my stove. I won't go into detail as to what happened next, but let's just say they left in a hurry, and I never talked to or saw him again, until his funeral two years later. But, to answer your original question, yes, I was pregnant. I gave birth to your son, Samuel Percival Lewis."

CHAPTER 24

"*I*'m pregnant."

He sat up in the bed, let out a long, loud yawn, and stretched his arms. For the last couple of mornings he'd awoken feeling like he was king of the world. He seriously doubted that it would be possible, but he had to at least attempt to get the three of them together again. But how? Carmen had left the apartment in tears eight nights ago.

"TJ, did you hear what I just said?" Shemika asked.

He turned and looked up at her.

She stood next to the bed with her arms crossed.

"Good morning, my love. How are you this lovely spring morning?" He pulled the satin sheets back.

"I said I'm pregnant." Her robe fell open as she put her hands on her hips. "Well?"

He put his arms in the back of his head and smiled, thinking about his upcoming trip overseas.

"Aren't you going to say anything?"

"What do you want me to say?"

"I just told you that I was pregnant."

"And?"

"And you could say something?"

"Okay. Do I know the father?"

She looked him up and down. "Look in the mirror."

He looked at her and smiled.

"Why you smiling? Did I say somethin' funny?"

"Yes, you did. Shemika, you are hilarious." He laughed, extending an arm in her direction. "Look at you. You should see yourself, going off on a tangent. I should be the one ranting and raving. You had unprotected sex, got pregnant, and now you're making a feeble attempt to mask your shame by accusing me of fathering your mistake."

"What? Negro, are you serious? You think I'm a…" she pointed a finger toward herself. "I can't believe you think I've been sleeping around. So, now I'm a ho'?"

"Your words, not mine."

"Fuck you, TJ!"

Stay calm, TJ. Anger will get you nowhere.

"Negro, you need to open your eyes and unball your fists."

He did as she asked, slowly creasing his lips. "Shemika, if you're pregnant, I believe you. But me being the father is impossible. Let me explain, so even you can understand." He spoke as if she were a child. "Number one," he counted on his fingers, "I always use protection. Two, I have a low sperm count. And three, if you're indeed pregnant and you haven't been with anyone else, you'd better get used to being called Mary, and you'd better drop the Terrell from my name."

She crossed her arms. "One," she counted on her fingers, "you're the only man I've slept with since I met you. Two, you have a low sperm count, not a no sperm count. And three, seventy percent of condoms have microscopic holes in them. And four, I will not name our son Jesus, because there is nothing miraculous about this baby I'm carrying, Daddy."

He'd known it would eventually come to an end, but he didn't expect it so soon. He had just moved her in, and now he had to move her out.

"Where do you think you're going?" she asked as he started dressing.

"To Africa. That is, after I go home, shower, and wait on the limo that will take me to the airport."

He was dressed and on his way to the door when Shemika decided to block the way.

So, you just gon' leave?"

He smiled.

She stepped aside and waved an arm in the air. "You know what, TJ, I don't even care."

He had his hand on the door knob.

"I wonder what your precious One World congregation will say when they find out that I'm having the great Bishop TJ Money's bastard baby, less than a year after your wife died."

"Hold on. Don't go spreading any stories. Wait until I get back and I'll pay for the abortion."

"Ain't gon' be no abortion," she said as he opened one of the double doors.

Turning back to her, he said, "I doubt it, but if in fact you are pregnant, and by some miracle it is mine, you will get rid of it; end of story."

CHAPTER 25

*T*here were ten dormitories in the eight-story Fulton County Jail.

In the dorm where Percival was housed, there were 40 two-man cells that circled the second tier, and forty on the bottom. The jail was so overcrowded, sometimes fifty inmates were forced to sleep on cardboard-thin cots, scattered near the far wall, under and around the stairwell.

Today, there were only twenty-eight inmates sleeping on the floor, but later on, there would be more arriving.

The electronic cell doors automatically opened at six every morning. That's when the best meal of the day was carted to the first-floor common area. Percival never imagined the day would come when he would salivate at the thought of powdered eggs, a slice of orange cheese, hard grits, and a small carton of white or chocolate milk.

The next two meals of the day were much worse. For lunch, the county jail inmates would get a brown paper bag containing a peanut butter sandwich, a discolored bologna sandwich, a small bag of plain, half-stale potato chips, a soft apple, and a carton of milk. The only identifiable supper meat was the dried-out baked or greasy fried chicken that was served on Saturdays.

Percival never missed breakfast. Sometimes he ate lunch, but besides chicken day, he'd never eaten supper. He had something against eating what he couldn't identify. And it wasn't unheard of for something to be crawling or wiggling around in the dinner salad.

He ate just enough to give him the energy to get through the day. His daily regimen of push-ups and sit-ups only took up an hour. With the exception of the hour he spent out on the yard, the rest of his day was dedicated to reading and studying.

Listening and seeing the unity and discipline that Hassan and other Muslim inmates exuded, inspired him to pick up their holy book, the Quran.

Like most people, he didn't know much about Muslims, other than what he'd learned on television or heard from someone else. Before he'd started reading the many books Carmen had sent and continued sending him, he'd always thought that Muslims didn't believe in Jesus, hated white people, didn't eat pork, and worshipped a pagan god whom they called Allah.

Needless to say, he was shocked and angered when he finished reading and cross-referencing the Quran with the Bible a month after he had picked it up. He was angry because his entire Christian upbringing had been a farce. Angry because of the lies he'd been told about Islam. Angry because the media had good Christians thinking that Islam was a hate and pagan religion, when in fact it was a religion of love—another path to pull sinners out of the wilderness and put them on the yellow brick road leading to God.

Percival had no intention of converting, or anything like that. He had simply set out to understand why so many men had come to prison professing Christianity, but left as Muslims.

"Open Dorm 4," a loud voice boomed over the dorm's loudspeakers, interrupting Percival's meditation time as he sat cross-legged on the floor near the dorm's sliding steel double doors.

He stood as three young men carrying blankets, sheets, and toiletries walked into the dorm wearing orange jumpsuits and blue, slip-on sneakers. Three floor cots were sure to follow. Percival sat back down paying little attention to the new fish.

His eyes were closed and his back was up against a wall when Hassan called out, "Yo, Bish?"

Percival blinked several times. Same size, height, a little lighter; same signature pig pug nose, and then the eyes. The man in front of him had the same penetrating dark eyes—Percival's penetrating dark eyes.

"If my man here," Hassan looked at the young brother next to him, "was a shade darker, and you had three less wrinkles, you wouldn't be able to tell you two apart. Yo, Bish, I'm gon' let you two break bread." He gave the young brother a pound. "If you need anything, Black, just holla. I'm in Cell 24," Hassan said before walking off.

Percival got up and extended his hand as the young man looked him up and down.

Percival's hand was left hanging. With his arms crossed in defiance, the young man said, "So, you the ex-big balla', Bishop Turner?"

Percival thought carefully, going over in his mind what he was about to say.

"You'd think, that after eighteen years, you'd have something to say."

Percival didn't quite know what to say, but he did know that the words running through his mind were insufficient.

"Man, you look like one of Jerry's kids with your head tilted and your mouth hanging open," Samuel said.

"I'm sorry," Percival said as a lone tear ran down his face.

"Come on, Dog." Samuel shook his head. "We in jail. You can't be doin' all that."

"I didn't know," Percival said.

"I know you ain't know. I don't fault you for shit. Momma played us both. Man, she didn't have no right—"

"Your mother did it for me."

"And that makes it right? Come on, Man. Don't even try and play me like that."

For three days Percival had awaited Samuel's arrival. He couldn't have been more skeptical, but, then again, why would Carmen lie? For three days, Percival had pondered that very question. And over the phone, for the past three days, Carmen had explained that she'd put all of Samuel's pictures up in a closet with everything else. She'd presumed that if Percival had seen a picture of Samuel, he would know.

"Can we go into my cell and talk?" Percival asked Samuel.

"Yeah, whatever. Just don't try and take up for her. I don't care how you slice it, she was dead-ass wrong."

As he and Percival walked into the small, claustrophobic cell, Samuel said, "People told me for years that I looked like you. I even saw the resemblance on TV, but I didn't pay no 'tention." He shrugged. "I had no reason to. Momma gave me pictures and told me all about this cat named Ray who she was married to before I was even born. She had me thinking that he was my pops."

Percival used his cell toilet for a seat and offered Samuel the bottom bunk. "I understand you don't too much care for me," Percival said as Samuel sat down on the bunk.

"I ain't gon' front. Unlike my mom, I keep it real. Yeah, you right. I didn't and I still don't like you. And just 'cause you my old man, that don't change a thing."

Percival nodded. "I can respect that."

"Don't you wanna know why I gotta problem with you?"

Percival leaned forward. "Yes, I do." He shrugged. "But I figure if you wanna tell me, you will."

"Like I said, I'm real." He patted his chest. "I ain't gotta problem lettin' you know the deal."

He could see that the young man he hoped to call *Son* was hurt. But there was nothing he could do about yesterday.

"It's one thang to get your hustle on, but, Man, you was playin' on religion to get rich. I ain't no hater, and I ain't no angel, either; but I can't get down with no holy roller runnin' game on the *Don't knows*, like Momma"

Percival nodded.

"Man, every single Sunday," he paused, "for I don't know," he took a second to think, "eight, nine years since you started comin' on TV, Momma made me watch your eleven-thirty service. What you said sounded real good, but it wasn't no secret how you was livin'. You and your man. What's his name, Dollar?"

"Money. Terrell Joseph Money," Percival corrected him.

"Yeah, that dude. You and dude was big ballin' like rap superstars. The big daddy Benz and Bentleys, the Yo' MTV cribs. And don't let a local celebrity die or get killed; you be the first one on V-104 announcing that you was paying for they services. They were celebrities; they had life insurance and money. They folks could pay for they funerals easy, but let a homeless John Doe die on the streets of downtown, one who ain't got no family or moneyand what was done for him?"

"I agree with you one hundred percent. I cared and yet I didn't care. I was so bent on building my congregation—"

"Hold on. I ain't finished," Samuel said, waving his arms. "You gave mad money away for scholarships. You even gave some of the houses away that ya'll built, but that's all game. Don't let someone say something negative about the good Bishop Turner or, now, Bishop Mo' Money to a One Worlder; they liable to pull a pistol on ya."

Percival got up, took two steps, and sat down beside the angry young man.

"Man, people is stupid. They be up in church blessin' people to death when you can't tell the preacha from a pimp," Samuel said.

"Everything you said is somewhat true. I abused my power. I took advantage of people, but I truly believed that what I was doing was right. I didn't realize my wrongs until my family passed away. My wife had repeatedly told me that we weren't living like God wanted us to. In my arrogance, I would show her scripture that seemed to facilitate the lifestyle I was leading. I can show you all through the Bible, Samuel, where God speaks of endowing his loyal servants with an abundance of wealth.

"I felt like I was doing a lot of good and bringing people to God. I just wanted to expand my efforts by opening more churches and investing in more real-estate ventures. That way, I could bring even more people to Jesus and at the same time serve as an example to people of color that we, too, could share in the American dream of being wealthy."

"If that was the case, why did you give it all up?" Samuel asked.

"I realized that I had been wrong. As you said in the beginning, I had used the Word to get rich off the backs of hardworking people. I was playing poker with my people and using God as my royal flush. I fell in love with money and power, and once I realized what I'd done, I wanted to repent. So, I gave it all away. Once I lost my family, I no longer cared anything about myself. I didn't care about this life; I only cared about finding favor with the Lord so that he might forgive me and accept me into his kingdom." He smiled. "And when I was at the lowest point in my life, He sent an angel to rescue me from my own misery."

"Come on, Man, you doin' too much," Samuel said.

"Nah, that's the problem; I'm not doing enough. And that angel is your mother."

"I hear what you saying, and it sounds real good. But so did all those hundred million sermons I was forced to listen to. Luckily, I prepared myself for this. "Yeah, Momma rushed down to Jackson State Penitentiary last month when I told her that I was being brought back to the Fulton County jail to go back to court for a new trial. She figured I would see you and the truth would come out, so she told me about you. Once I realized that she was serious, I got up and left the visitation room. I haven't talked to her since."

Percival wondered whether his son would be in jail with him had he been in the boy's life.

"Five times she made the hour-and-a-half drive to see me in Jackson after she told me you was my pops. And five times I refused her visit. But I read all twenty-six letters she wrote.
All of them were apologetic and all of them explained why she hid the truth. And in her last letters she told me what you've been through this last year. That's jacked up about your wife and son. I wouldn't wish nothin' like that on anyone." He shook his head. "I love my mother, but I ain't sure if I can forgive her for what she done, and I know I damn sho' ain't ever gon' forget it."

"Samuel," Percival put a hand on the young man's shoulder, "your mother loves you. She's in a great deal of pain. What she did, she can't take back. You have to reach deep down into your heart, and find a way to forgive."

Tears welled up in his eyes. "I ain't gotta do nothin' but stay Black and die." He rose to his feet and pointed a finger at Percival. "This is the last thing I'm gon' say about any of this, so listen up, Pops. I'm not gon' say that there is or isn't a God, but if God does exist, he don't give a damn about me. If He did, He wouldn't have let a sixteen-year-old straight A high school junior be charged as an adult and sent away to the pen for life for a murder that they know I couldn't have committed," he said as his voice broke.

Percival got up and took his son in his arms.

"Let me go, Man. Let me go," he said as he tried to struggle and break away.

"No. I promise, I'll never let you go," Percival said as he fought with all his heart and strength to hold onto his son.

"Where was your God my first night in the penitentiary when they threw a blanket over my head, stuffed a pillow in my mouth, and held me down while they took turns raping me? Huh, Pops? Where were you? Where was your God then?"

CHAPTER 26

"Family, open your Bible and turn to Psalm 1:12. Read along with me. Verse one through three," Bishop Money said as he stood behind the One World podium.

"Praise ye the Lord. Blessed is the man that feareth the Lord that delighteth greatly in his commandments." He paused to bob his head. "His seed, hah, I said his seed shall be mighty upon earth. The generation of the upright shall be blessed." He walked to the side of the podium. "Listen, family," he said before continuing, "wealth and riches— hear me now, family, hah, I said wealth and riches shall be in his house. And his righteousness endureth forever.

"Stop right there," he said, extending his arm in a traffic-guard like motion. "I am not the author of this book." He held his Bible in the air as the lights dimmed, while green and yellow spotlights shone on the Bible's brown leather cover. "I didn't write these words. Not Bishop TJ Money, but the Lord said..." he pressed a red button on the remote he'd been holding in his free hand. He smiled as the church members jumped at the sound of thunder erupting in the church, but it was the simulated lightning bolt that had streaked down onto the Bible in the bishop's hand that had the congregation wide-eyed and in awe.

Not missing a beat, several octaves higher, he continued, "I said the Lord said, that the man that feareth Him and enjoys serving him will be rewarded with wealth and riches."

"Hallelujah! Thank ya, Jesus, thank ya Jesus. Yes, Lord. Thank ya, thank ya, thank ya, thank ya, Jesus," Sister Jones stomped, hollered, and waved her hands in the air.

"I see somebody's feeling the spirit this Sunday morning." He pointed as two ushers escorted the hollering, super-sized Sister Jones out into the church vestibule.

He looked up at his Bible. "I didn't know why these verses came to mind when they did. But God had them ringing in my head while I was visiting rural areas outside of the city of Accra in West Africa, a couple of weeks ago. "The conditions these brothers and sisters live under are deplorable. One-hundred-plus-degree heat with no air conditioning. Children forced to drink out of contaminated wells and streams. In these impoverished areas, dysentery, malaria, and yellow fever are as ordinary as the common cold.

"And while I was away ministering to these brothers and sisters and assuring them that I would send food, medicine, and water, the naysayers had a field day casting stones at me, when they themselves live in glass houses."

"Amen to that, Bishop," someone shouted.

He pointed a finger in the air. "But as soon as I got back in the states, Psalm 1:12, verses one through three again came to mind. As I exited the plane a brother handed me the articles. After reading them, it hit me like a turbo-charged bulldozer. It was then that I knew why God had put these verses on my mind. I didn't know what was being said about me but as the naysayers were writing it, God was arming me with verses from the written Word to dismantle their slanderous weapons of mass misinformation."

The congregation burst out laughing.

A minute later he continued, "I was gon' let it go. As the young folk say, I was gon' give them a pass. But I was approached by a One World family member a few days ago. He wanted to know what I had to say about the article in the *Gazette* and the small write-up in the *Constitution*."

"Who was the Judas that questioned you, Bishop?!" someone shouted.

"Yeah, who was he?" another angry voice followed.

"That's neither here nor there. But the person who approached me just made me realize that I had to address this issue."

The church was so quiet, a deaf man sitting in the front row could have heard a baby toe tap in the back of the upstairs balcony.

Bishop Money walked down the platform's stairs and onto the thick red carpet. "The naysayers want to crack jokes about you, family." He pointed. "They ridicule you because you're supporting and trusting a Bishop whose last name is Money. They wanna know how can you?" He again pointed to the One World Family. "How can you follow a man who lives in a secured three-million-dollar estate home and drives a car that costs well into six-figures. They wanna know how you can faithfully come through the castle-like church doors every week where a man is ministering to you one Sunday and is off in his private jet the next."

He looked directly into the camera. He wanted the nation of well-wishers and One Worlders who watched these services on television to hear what he was about to say. He pointed to the camera. "You tell the naysayer to read Psalms 1:12, verses one through three. And before they open their mouths, you tell them this—and I want you to repeat this after me, family—say it with me now." He paused. "Bishop Money."

"Bishop Money," they echoed.

He threw his arms in the air. "Louder!"

"Bishop Money!" they shouted.

"Is leading me to the land of milk and honey. So miss me with that mess because I am too blessed to be stressed."

They applauded as they repeated his words.

"Again, say it with me, family." He slowly repeated, "Bishop Money is leading me to the land of milk and honey. So miss me with that mess because I am too blessed to be stressed."

They gave a standing ovation and kept chanting the Bishop's words. The Bishop believed he'd sent a powerful message to everyone and anyone who thought they could threaten the stronghold that he had over the One World immediate church and the extended television family.

"Before I close today, I want to challenge everyone to give all they can. Give until it hurts. Give your cell phone bill money. Retirees, give your Tuesday night bowling and Wednesday night bingo money."

He reached into his back pocket and pulled out a check. Waving it in the air he said, "This is a check for $150,000. I am giving this and whatever we take in today to those brothers, sisters, mothers, and fathers in West Africa. What we give today will save lives tomorrow. Let us today turn our church hope money into pharmaceutical dope money so that we can cure a nation."

*****

Hours later, TJ was in his church office taking a nap, waiting for the phone call for the final count.

Sister Carter or Deacon Wiley usually called him with the numbers. Not wanting anyone to know how much he received every Sunday, he stayed around just long enough to bundle and shrink wrap his love offerings.

It wasn't anyone's business what he took in weekly. Besides, he didn't want word to get out that he was bringing in twenty to thirty thousand a week, which didn't include the thirty to forty thousand he regularly took in from his television ministry. He would have a special armored service take the love offerings away to Penny Savers Savings and Loan, the small bank he'd acquired at the beginning of the year.

Every Monday after the bank closed, he would sit inside the vault where he sorted and ran the love offerings through a money counter. After he'd put some in the mini vault-sized safety deposit box that he had had custom-built inside the bank vault, he would either deposit the rest in one of his many statewide accounts or wire it to his Swiss bank account in Zurich.

And every Wednesday, Penny Savers would make a withdrawal from one of his business accounts to reimburse Wells Fargo for what they had to use to stock the ATMs on the previous Saturday.

Usually the machines were half full when the Wells Fargo armed guards would come to replenish them.

Yesterday, he had the four machines inside the church and the drive-through ATM stocked with forty thousand each, instead of the usual twenty. In the few months the ATMs had been in, he'd never had a problem.

After service, there were long lines at every machine. In an hour's time, members had started leaving and coming back because all the machines were empty.

While waiting, he set his chair on Shiatsu Massage, and, as it started to recline, the smooth jazz of Boney James was piped in through the office. And in no time he was sound asleep.

*****

There was a tapping sound on the office door window.

He snored as the massage chair's rollers worked magic on his spine.

Suddenly the tapping went to banging.

His eyes popped open. His heart was racing.

More banging.

He turned the chair off, got up, and walked to the door. He opened the door, ready to light into Deacon Wiley, or whoever Wiley had sent with the final count for the day's take.

"Shemika? How did you get back here?" he asked, thinking that he'd locked the church administration building.

"With my two feet. How do you think?"

"What's wrong with you, Woman? You got what you wanted," he said.

She smiled. "But look what I had to go through."

"I've been married twice. I'm forty-four and I've never gotten anyone pregnant. I always use a condom. I'm worth a lot of money, and you pop up telling me you're pregnant, that it's mine and you're having the baby. What do you expect me to think? What did you think I'd do?"

"Pop up? Negro, I didn't just pop up. You've been screwing me almost every day since November. Ain't nobody just popped up. The only reason you marrying me is to save face with your church. I ain't no fool," she said.

"And that's what you wanted. You're the one who insisted we get married, Shemika. You're the one forcing this baby on me."

She was right up in his face. "Forced? Negro, I ain't forced your little thang up in me. I ain't forced you to tell your funky congregation you was marrying me. I ain't forced a damn thing."

Now that the DNA test results had come back, she'd gone from being a lady to the hood rat. He'd always known that she was an undercover hood rat, but as long as she stayed undercover, it was fine.

"I know you wanna hit me. I see the veins in your forehead breathin', fists balled up. But we both know you ain't that crazy."

"One hundred thousand dollars," he said with his teeth clenched.

"What?"

"I'll give you a hundred thousand dollars if you have an abortion, and I'll give you an additional hundred thousand if you leave Georgia for good."

She put her arms around his shoulders and pulled him close to her. Whispering in his ear, she said, "A week ago it was fifty; now you've gone up to two hundred. Baby, I'm going to be your first lady, and I'm going to have this child. So, you will just have to deal with me and all of my baggage for the next eighteen-plus years."

He pulled away from her embrace, then calmly asked, "What is the real reason you're here?"

"I'm going to Houston to celebrate with my girlfriend, Reshonda. Her new book, *Can I Get A Witness*, just came out and debuted at number five on the *New York Times* bestsellers' list."

"Soooooo, what does that have to do with you being here?" he asked.

She held her hand out. "I need some money. I'm broke and I have to take my girl shopping. She has to be ready when Oprah calls."

"I seriously doubt if anyone from *The Oprah Winfrey Show* would be interested in a book like that, unless it was written by a white woman," he said, walking over to his desk.

"Hate is not becoming of you, TJ. Just because my girl is not Toni, Alice, or Maya doesn't mean that Oprah won't give her a call."

As he sat down and opened the top drawer of his desk, he couldn't help but smile, thinking how good it would be if Shemika's plane dropped out of the sky. He still couldn't get over the fact that he'd let himself be duped by a ghetto superstar. For nearly six months, Shemika was so nice, so refined, and she spoke so well. And now that she had TJ between a brick wall and a rattle snake pit, all the alley rat in her came out.

He hoped that she'd stay in Houston for a month, until their scheduled Memorial Day wedding. He fought back a groan as he pulled out his checkbook.

"You need to see about flying ReShonda in to do a book signing at the new church when it opens in September. You know she's big with the Christian fiction readers."

Ignoring her, he handed over a check and hoped she would just leave.

"Twenty-five hundred? What can I do with that? That'll barely cover my hotel and travel."

Without so much as a nod, he wrote out a check for another twenty-five hundred. "Here," he said, balling up the check and throwing it at her.

She pointed a red fingernail at him. "That stank attitude of yours is why you ain't got none since the day before you left for Africa."

He got up from his seat. "Let me tell you something, Babycakes." He smiled, showing all his sparkling white teeth. "If I'm broke, homeless, and hungry, I can always get that." He pointed to her crotch.

"Correction." She pointed a finger toward the window. "You can get them, maybe," she swiveled her wrist and pointed to her crotch, "but you can't get this," she said, unballing the second check and leaving the church office.

He sat down and pulled out his cell phone. He scrolled through his phone book until it landed on Professor's Drake's name. He heard someone knocking at the door again. "What do you want now, Shemika?!" he shouted.

"I'm not Shemika."

He got out of his chair and turned toward the door.

Her hair was pulled back into a ponytail. Her eyes were as red as her lips. Her arms were steady as she pointed the infrared-scoped Glock 9mm at his head.

CHAPTER 27

*E*very single day, sometimes two, three times a day, Percival thanked God for Samuel. It had been six weeks since he'd first laid eyes on his nineteen-year-old son. Since then, they'd spent a lot of one-on-one time together, mostly talking about life, the future, and books they both had read. As long as he didn't speak of God or Carmen around Samuel, they were just fine.

Samuel still wouldn't allow his mother to visit, but he did let Percival introduce him to Deidre' a few weeks back. And since then, they'd been corresponding regularly.

Deidre' would be taking her GED test next week and she seemed to be prepared, according to Samuel. He'd been tutoring her in the visitation booths and over the phone. He was more of a mentor to her than a tutor, or maybe it was the other way around. Whatever the case, he was just excited that they had found one another.

Besides having a lot of pent-up anger inside, Samuel was a natural-born leader. And intelligent was an understatement; the boy was a strategical mastermind, especially when it came to the law. The only missing piece in his puzzle was his acceptance of Jesus. But he didn't fool Percival; the God in Samuel was there. Percival could feel it. And many times he saw it when his son spoke so passionately about revolutionaries, or talked about some book he'd read.

As Poppalove had said on several occasions, all Samuel had to do was turn around and he would see God. Once Samuel had seen God, then he would understand how Jesus was the most revolutionary leader of all time. Percival thought he understood his son's anger. If Percival didn't have Jesus in his life, he figured he'd be as angry as or angrier than Samuel was now.

Samuel had served two and a half years in a maximum security prison for a crime he clearly hadn't committed. After reading and dissecting over four hundred pages of Samuel's trial transcripts, Percival couldn't understand how twelve men and women had found him guilty of murder.

Samuel had stayed behind the wheel. He never stepped foot out of the stolen white Ford Explorer when his two former friends, wearing George Bush masks under black ski caps, robbed The Cathouse strip club.

In the process, owner Prince Charles Williams, a notorious drug dealer, was shot and killed, along with Mia Murray, an eighteen-year-old stripper.

Samuel was six foot four. The club was dark and there weren't any cameras, but a bartender and a dancer testified that the masked men were under six feet.

The assailants wore gloves, alleviating any possible fingerprints. But as Samuel had pointed out to the appeals court, the gloves that were recovered on a side street, not far from the club, and identified as the ones used in the crime, were mediums; Samuel wore double X's.

The saddest part of the whole ordeal was that Samuel's trial attorney didn't think of the glove scenario, although the gloves were the key in O.J. Simpson's acquittal.

Samuels' conviction was solely based on the testimony of the two men who had robbed and killed the people in the exotic club that night. For their cooperation, Samuel's so-called friends received much lighter sentences.

Percival couldn't even begin to imagine how a sixteen-year-old psychologically coped with being charged as an adult and sentenced to life in prison at such a young age for something he hadn't done.

"What's poppin', Pops?" Samuel asked as he entered Percival's cell.

"Nothing much, just worrying about you," he replied.

"What's to worry about? I got this. Remember, if the gloves don't fit, they have to acquit."

"So tell me about your day in court."

"Well, we finished selecting the jury, and me and the states' attorney delivered our opening statements."

"How do you think it went?"

"I think it went well." He pointed to the book Percival was reading. "I see you reading my man George Jackson's book, *Blood In My Eye.* One of the most powerful quotes I ever read came from him."

"Yeah, he was deep. Reading books like this angers and saddens me, Son. In the past, I've heard about racial injustice in the judicial system, but I have never been inspired to take action until I read about men and women such as Mumia Abu Jamal, Assata Shakur, Geronimo Pratt, and," he held up the red, white, and black book, "George Jackson."

Samuel smiled, happy that his father wasn't the man he'd always thought, and happy because his father was getting so connected to the struggle. "When I first came to prison, I felt the same way. Most people go through life without even realizing that they're slaves and victims of oppression. And the ones that do realize it are either too afraid or don't care enough to risk their lives for freedom." Samuel pointed. "In that book, George Jackson states that the most powerful weapon in the hands of the oppressor is the mind of the oppressed.

"How do you do that?" Percival asked.

"Do what?"

"Remember and recite verbatim what you read."

Samuel shrugged. "I don't know. Powerful words just stick to my mind. Especially thoughts by people I can relate to, like George Jackson. My situation is similar to his."

"Yeah," Percival nodded, "I know."

"Pop's, after you finish with George, I'm gon' hip you Emiliano Zapata, Winnie Mandela, Hannibal, and Menelik the Second. They was the rawest revolutionaries in history."

All this revolutionary talk, and you don't realize Jesus was the baddest of them all, Percival wanted to say, but instead he asked, "How many books have you read?"

"I don't know." He shrugged. "A few hundred. I'm always trying to figure things out, and the best way to do that is to read about others who put down they gangsta before you."

"Gangster?" Percival asked.

"Nah, Pops, gangsta with an A, not an E-R. *Gangsta* is fightin' against a system of oppression. Shootin' and killin' for no rhyme or reason, other than money is what a gangs*ter* is. See, Pops, I study man's failures, struggles, and successes." He paused. "Pops, you think I know the law real well, right?"

Percival nodded.

"I don't know half as much as you think. But what I do know is people. I know the way they think, why they believe what they do, and I know what motivates and drives them. And if you understand those things, you can manipulate them. And that is exactly what I'm doing to the jury, the government attorney and, most importantly, the judge."

Switching gears, Samuel said, "By the way, I saw Mom in court today."

"Really?" Percival nervously replied.

"Ah, you knew she was gon' be there. I bet you called her as soon as I left for court this morning."

"Look, Samuel, I know what you said, but I had to call."

"Relax, Pops." He smiled. "It's all good. I was glad to see her."

He took a seat at the foot of the bunk, next to Samuel.

"I've been doing some thinking, and you were right. She is my mother and she would never do anything to intentionally hurt me. I've been a fool."

"Better to be a young fool than an old fool," Percival said, thinking of himself.

"I can't believe I've been so stubborn. I need her and she needs me." Looking up into his father's eyes, he said, "I just wanna thank you for putting up with my craziness. If it's okay, I wanna talk to you about your case after I get off the phone with Momma."

"I haven't given much thought to my situation."

Samuel stood and walked to the door. "That's why we need to talk about me coaching you, so you can represent yourself and get outta here," he said before leaving.

"You're right. I have to come up with a plan. I've been in this place six months and, as Hassan referred to him, my public pretender hasn't even set a trial date."

After Samuel left, Percival stood up and stretched. He was standing over the toilet about to pee when Jackson Riley, the leader of the Chain Gang, walked up. The Chain Gang got their name because they were notorious for beating their victims with bicycle chains before robbing them.

"I was just about to relieve myself. What can I do for you, Brother Jackson?"

"You know they call me Blackjack. Why you wanna disrespect my pimpin', big dog?"

"Your mother named you Jackson, and that's what I'm going to respect."

"You lucky I got love for ya, big dog," the twenty-something-year-old big man said, rocking back and forth, his long arms in the air, his hands grasping the metal ring over the top of the cell door threshold.

Percival smiled, thinking Jackson looked like King Kong on crack.

"It just so happens that my cellie is making bond tomorrow. There'll be an open bunk in my cell. I know your boy is tired of that concrete," Jackson said as he continued rocking.

"You should talk to him," Percival said.

"Not yet. I wanna see if maybe me and you could work a little somethin-somethin' out before I step to him."A twisted smile spread across Brother Jackson's face.

"What do you mean, *work* something out?"

"Every week when commissary is delivered, you ain't never got nothin'. I figured I have my peoples put a five spot on your books and you can help me and Sammy Sam out."

"I don't speak "Street", Jackson. In English, tell me what you're asking."

"A'ight, I'll have five hundred put on your books. All you have to do is talk your boy into taking care of me."

It was like someone had turned the cell into an oven. Instantly, Percival started to perspire. It was difficult, but he remained civil. "I think you should leave. Like I said, I need to relieve myself."

"Come on, big dog. It ain't gotta be like that. I'm comin' to you as a man. I know you know that your boy is a loose booty. And I bet he can suck a beach ball through a water hose."

Beginning to lose it, Percival said, "That's enough, Jackson. I said leave! Now!"

A sharp pain exploded in Percival's head. Everything turned red.

*****

Percival woke up laying face up on the concrete floor of his cell. He had no idea how long or how he'd gotten there. He couldn't move, nor could he open his eyes. He felt as light as a feather.

"Pops! Pops! Oh God," he heard Samuel cry out.

He still couldn't move a muscle.

"God, if you really exist, show me now. Bring my dad back. We just found each other!" he cried.

What is he talking about? Bring me back? I haven't gone anywhere.

"God, please don't take my father from me. Please, God, he's a good man. I had him pegged wrong."

206

"Get him out of here," Percival heard someone say.

"No, he's my dad. I wanna stay," Samuel cried.

"He's not breathing. I can't find a pulse," Percival heard someone else say.

Yes, I am. I hear everything. I'm not dead! Percival screamed in his mind.

"Whew, he stinks."

"What do you expect when they die? Their bowels and bladder release."

CHAPTER 28

"*B*e reasonable?" I don't even see how you fixed your face to say those words." She shook her head. "Been there, done that, didn't work," Carmen said as she continued pointing the gun at the cowering Bishop TJ Money.

"You don't wanna go to prison," he said. He couldn't get a good read on her because her face was emotionless as she stood about five feet away.

"Why not? The two people I love are in prison. One wouldn't be if you had done what we agreed on."

"Carmen, let me explain why PC is not—"

"There's nothing you can explain, Terrell. There isn't one reason why I shouldn't send you to hell. You raped my niece." She took a step closer. "I could've gone to the cops after you choked me, but I didn't. Been there, done that, didn't work, so I'm doing it my way."

"I didn't rape your niece."

Ignoring him, she continued, "She said no." She took another step. "But you didn't listen. And now," Carmen paused, "she's dead."

TJ took a step back, his arms still in the air.

"Move again, and watch how fast you'll fly through that window," she said.

"Why are you doing this? I'm sorry I choked you. I just got a little carried away. Most women like it rough."

"Stop crying." She took another step. "Try to be a man for once. Accept responsibility, Terrell."

Crying openly now, he said, "But I didn't mean to hurt you. I didn't have anything to do with Tracy's death."

"She killed herself because of what you did to her."

"But I didn't rape—"

"Save it!" she shouted.

He flinched.

"Let me get out of here before I end up in jail for murder. No, you're not gon' die today." She paused. "I just want you to see that I can get to you whenever I please."

He let out a long breath. Thank you, Jesus, he silently prayed.

"I'm not threatening you. I'm promising you. If Percival is still in jail come Sunday, you won't see Monday. If you don't believe me just let him be there," she said before turning and walking to the door.

At the door she turned back. "Oh, and by the way," she pointed to the soiled crotch area of his beige slacks, "they make adult diapers for your problem."

Angry, humiliated, and scared were just a few of the emotions he felt. But as the seconds passed after she left, anger swallowed the other emotions.

"I'm not going to let anyone, especially some love-stricken nobody, intimidate me. I am Bishop TJ Money, the Martin Luther King Junior of the new millennium," he said, patting his chest.

After going to the bathroom and cleaning himself up, he threw on a choir robe to mask the stain in his crotch area. As he left the office, he pulled out his cell phone and dialed the number to the phone in the basement. When he got no answer, he dialed Deacon Wiley's cell.

It was bad enough, that these kids forced you to listen to loud rap music before you could leave a message on their cell phone's voice mail, but it was just as bad listening to Dottie Peoples singing *Testify* on Deacon Wiley's cell phone answering service.

He looked at his Rolex. "Six-thirty!" he shouted. "Sweet Jesus!"

It cost him a ton of money to get Wells Fargo to pick up on Sunday. *Lord, please let the big red armored truck be outside.*

Just as he thought, the truck was gone. Deacon Wiley, Maggie Parker, and the other four would just have to spend the night in the basement, he thought as he marched across the street and entered the church. "No one is going anywhere until I can arrange a pickup for tomorrow morning," he said to himself.

A few minutes later, TJ was off the elevator and at the vault-like basement door. He put the first of two keys in the locks; already unlocked, the door creaked as it opened. "What the—" He pushed the four-inch-thick steel door all the way open. "Good God Almighty. Sweet Jesus."

All eight money counters were on the three tables. The shrinkwrap machine was on the concrete floor next to the empty Wells Fargo bank bags—the nylon blue bags that were supposed to be filled with money and checks.

"Help! Somebody, please?" The voice came from a large closet in the back of the room.

After TJ unlocked the door, four deacons and two ushers dragged themselves out like they'd been in the desert sun.

"What in God's name?" Bishop Money said.

"We were robbed," Deacon Wiley said.

"That, I can see, but how in the H-E-double-L did you let that happen?" he asked.

"We have to get her to a hospital?" Deacon Wiley pointed to Sister McMichael.

The bishop looked over next to the closet door where Sister McMichael was on the floor, propped up against the cement wall, coughing, wheezing, and crying.

"Sister Parker and Brother Adams are doing just fine tending to Sister McMichael. Now, I need to know what happened."

"But—"

The bishop interrupted, "No buts."

Deacon Wiley looked over at Sister McMichael and then back at the bishop. He figured the quicker he told Bishop Money what had happened the quicker they could get help for Sister McMichael. And so he began, "As usual, after services, the six of us came down the elevator together. Sister Parker used her key and I used mine to unlock both locks. After rolling the cart in—"

"What cart?"

"We filled five trash bags. It was too much for us to carry, so we rolled the bags in on a trash cart."

TJ was about to be sick. Five garbage bags filled with money and checks. To his knowledge, they'd never filled three bags. "Okay, you rolled the bags in and then you did what?"

"We started emptying the bags on the floor when out of nowhere four women came out of the closet," he pointed to where they'd been locked up, "and told us to put our hands up and back up to the wall."

"And you did?"

"They had guns," Deacon Adams said, still on the floor, seeing to Sister McMichael.

Bishop Money turned and looked down. "I was talking to Deacon Wiley," he said. Turning his attention back to Deacon Wiley, TJ asked, "What did they look like?"

"Like four women wearing black and red Atlanta Falcon warm-up jerseys and matching ski masks."

"Who would rob a church?" Deacon Adams asked.

Someone with access to my church office keys.

*****

It was two in the morning when TJ unlocked the penthouse apartment door with the key she never knew he owned. He didn't turn on any lights as he tip-toed through the apartment with fish line wrapped around his hands.

The bed looked as if it had not been slept in. He went into the bathroom and opened the walk-in, dressing room closet. Her Louis Vuitton luggage was gone.

Three months ago, he would've ruled her out. But after getting pregnant so he'd marry her, he wouldn't put anything past her now.

He climbed into bed, fully dressed, still playing with the fish line. Thoughts of her eyes bulging out of her head as he strangled her played vividly through his mind.

The next morning, he picked up his cell phone. A moment later, he said. "Drake, TJ. I need to meet with you ASAP."

CHAPTER 29

*G*rady Hospital, located in the heart of downtown Atlanta, was the hospital for the homeless, downtrodden, and forgotten—the Atlanta version of St. Elsewhere. It was also the hospital where sick inmates in need of serious medical attention were transported—the hospital where Percival Turner had spent two days fighting the hardest fight he'd ever fought. A fight he had no idea that he was in—one for his life.

At 9:27a.m., the doctor walked into the two-bed hospital room. The loud double beeping of the EKG machine didn't lie, which is how Dr. Martz knew, before he even pulled back the curtain, that Percival was winning the fight.

"Mr. Turner? Mr. Turner, can you hear me?"

Slowly, he opened his eyes but quickly closed them.

Enunciating his words like a third-grade schoolteacher, Dr. Martz said, "Mr. Turner, open your eyes if you understand what I am saying."

In a hoarse whisper Percival said, "The light. Too bright."

After dimming the lights, Dr. Martz re-entered the curtained off area. Back at Percival's bedside he said, "Okay, I dimmed the lights and closed the curtain. Can you try to open your eyes again?"

He did.

Dr. Martz picked up the small Styrofoam cup from the table next to Percival's bed. "Here, drink this." The doctor put the cup to Percival's parched lips.

"Thank you."

The doctor looked down at the clipboard he'd just pick up from the end of the bed. "The swelling in your brain has gone down. I've never seen anything like this. For nearly two minutes, no oxygen went to your brain. And yet you have absolutely no brain damage. All your tests check out fine," the doctor said just as a nurse pulled back the curtain and began preparing to take his blood pressure and check his vitals. "You're one lucky man."

"No. I'm one blessed man," Percival whispered.

"That too."

The nurse pumped the ball connected to the blue nylon sleeve that tightened around Percival's arm.

"How do you feel?" the doctor asked.

Regaining his voice, Percival replied, "I feel good."

"No headache, no tingling sensation anywhere?" the doctor asked.

He slowly shook his head. "No."

"That's weird. Day before yesterday, you had a brain aneurysm, and today it's like nothing ever happened," the doctor said, a perplexed frown on his face, his hand massaging his chin.

Percival closed his eyes and silently prayed that Jackson and his gang wouldn't bother his son.

Percival started to sit up.

"Whoa, whoa." Dr. Martz stuck his arm out. "Not so fast, Mr. Turner," the doctor said.

"Call the guards; I have to get back to the jail. I have to get back now."

"No way, no how, no, sir." Dr. Martz shook his head. "We're keeping you a few more days. More tests have to be run. As I stated, your preliminary tests look fine, and that is completely unheard of for someone who just had an aneurysm."

"Look, Doctor—"

"Martz. Dr. Martz."

Percival rose up. "I'll sign whatever I need to, releasing you and this hospital of all responsibility, but I have to get back to the county jail today."

"If you don't lie back down, I don't want to, but I will have you restrained." Dr. Martz paused while Percival lay back down.

"So, when do I return to the jail?"

"You don't."

"Excuse me?"

"Not only are you lucky and blessed, but," Dr. Martz looked up and smiled, "you have a savior."

Percival was sure Dr. Martz meant well, but he was worried about Samuel and he did not want to play games. All he wanted was to protect his son.

"Did you hear what I just said, Mr. Turner?"

"Yes, I heard you."

"Thought you went off in your own world there for a minute. As I was saying, you should be very grateful to Bishop TJ Money."

Percival closed his eyes and silently said, "Oh Lord".

"That man is one of the good ones. My wife and I are looking forward to attending his church service this Sunday."

He was almost scared to ask, but ask he did, "Why should I be grateful to TJ?"

"Bishop. You mean *Bishop* TJ Money. "Bishop Money posted bond for you and he even made sure that you didn't have to go back to that jail."

You could have driven an eighteen-wheeler right into Percival's mouth.

"I didn't even know who Bishop TJ Money was, until this past Sunday after his church was robbed," Dr. Martz said. "He'd even lost his own money in the robbery. And after all that, the very next day, he posted your bond. I mean, after everything you've done to him, the man came out of his pocket and found the time to help you," he said. Weaving through the curtain again, Dr. Martz left the room.

Percival felt like he was going to be sick. He knew he should've been overjoyed, but there had to be a trick. What it was, Percival didn't know, but he was sure he'd find out soon enough.

Minutes later, a familiar face pulled back the curtain and walked to his bedside.

He pointed. "You're the journalist who bombarded me with those idiotic questions when I bonded out of jail last fall."

The ghostly white, average-size journalist took off the world's ugliest plaid fedora, revealing a thick head of brown stringy hair. "Those were the questions my boss had given me. I was just doing my job, Mr. Turner."

"What do you want, Mr.—"

"Abraham… John Abraham." He stuck his hand out. "I'm with the *Atlanta Journal, Constitution*."

216

Ignoring the man's hand, Percival said, "Mr. Abraham—"

"Call me Skip."

"Okay, Skip, how can I help you?"

"Over the past year, I've been following Bishop TJ Money's sudden rise to prominence in the African-American church. My first story on Bishop Money ran in the paper in July of last year. Since then, I've done a few stories on him and the One World Faith Missionary Baptist Church. You may have seen my latest story, *'Vampire in the Church'*."

The little reporter talked so fast, Percival couldn't get a word in edgewise.

"Back in December, one of my stories on Bishop Money made the local news, *'Cashing In On God'*."

"Yeah, come to think of it, I remember that story," Percival said. "That was the one where you insinuated that Bishop Money used church funds and unethical tactics in acquiring several houses in the West End area of Atlanta for the new West End mall development project."

"Are you saying he didn't?"

"I'm not saying anything," Percival said. He remembered feeling shame and sorrow for those poor homeowners, especially the older woman, Ms. Gertrude Harris. After the story dropped, Carmen had gone and met with the lady. And to his understanding, they became fast friends, sharing a dislike for TJ, for different reasons.

"I'd like to ask you a few questions," Skip said while removing a small tape recorder from the black satchel slung around his shoulder. "I want to do an expose' on you and cover your former relationship with Bishop TJ Money. This is a chance for you to tell the world your side of the story." Skip sat down on the edge of the bed, pad and pen in hand.

"My sources tell me that Bishop TJ Money not only manipulates his church members, but he coerces young women and sometimes underaged young girls into rough, perverted sexual acts." He paused, and as an afterthought he said, "I even got it from a reliable source that the Bishop is bisexual."

"I don't know anything about that."

He looked up at Percival with his thin lips creased in a smile that spread almost entirely across his rectangular face. "Sure you do, Percy."

Percy. No he didn't just call me Percy.

"Bishop Money was accused of sexually assaulting an underaged teenage girl almost twenty years ago. If it weren't for you coming forward, telling the authorities that he was with you at the time of the assault, he would've been charged."

"Look, Skip, I don't think this interview is a good idea."

"I'm confused," he said in a feminine voice. "This man takes your title, takes your church, has you locked up, presses charges against you for attempted murder, and," he pointed a finger in the air," I have it from a reliable source that he arranged for the prostitute and alerted the authorities at the time of your first run-in with the law last fall."

"And, if what you're saying is true, does that mean I have to air his and my dirty laundry through the media?"

"No, you don't. But this is your outlet, your chance to let the world know your side of the story."

"If my side entails me dragging another African-American through media mud, I will do my best to keep my mouth closed. I'm not going to make this thing a media circus. You'll have to find yourself another clown. If you want to start a feud, go to some of those rap artists like you guys always do. If you will please leave—"

"Okay, okay, I'll leave. But you had your chance," Skip said before putting his business card on the tray over Percival's bed. "Give me a call if you change your mind."

*****

"Bishop Turner, wake up. Today is your big day."

He removed the rag from his eyes. "Good morning," he said to the young female orderly.

Dragging her words, she said, "Just barely. It's almost eleven-thirty. You slept most of this bright Sun'ay mornin'."

He'd been in the hospital a week now.

"Here." She handed him a red and white Jordan warm-up suit and a new pair of white Nike Shox running shoes. "Your wife dropped these off."

My wife?

"I know you prob'ly don't 'member me. I'm Patricia Foxx. I used to be a member of One World, 'ack when you were runnin' thangs," she spoke in a slow southern drawl.

He couldn't place the name, but her face was somewhat familiar.

"I'm happy to make your acquaintance, Mrs. Foxx." He extended his arm to shake her hand.

Ignoring his hand, she leaned her small frame over the bed and gave him an akward hug. "It's Miss Foxx, but plea', call me Pat."

He couldn't help but wonder what had happened to her. One side of her face was so alive and the other so dead.

Slowly she continued with a slight speech impediment. "Bishop, I don't belie' none uh what dey said you done. I don' know much, but I do know, ain't no way in Sam-dam-hell a man like you wit' a soul of gol' would use drugs, pick up hookas, or try to kill another human bein'."

"I appreciate that, Miss Foxx, but did I just hear you say that you *were* a member of One World?"

"Yeah. Bu' now, I wouldn't be caught dead in that church. If I was in the middle of the desert, about to die from dehydration, and Bishop Cashflow Tightwad Money walk up to me with a gallon of ice cold Evo'n water I'd tell 'em to take the foot off the clutch and hit da' gas. After the way he did me he could neeeeeeeevvvvvvvvveeeerrrrrr do nothin' for me but die and make the worl' a better place."

"What happened to turn you against TJ and One World?"

"Bishop Money happened. I'm thirty-five and I been a member a' One World since I got saved ei'teen yea' ago in the big red revival tent you used to hold service in."

"I remember those days well," he said smiling. "We all came a long way since then."

"You may see that as comin' a long way but I don't think we went anywhere. We moved into bigga spaces but we, the mem'ers that built One World, are as broke or broker than we were when we praised Jesus in a revival tent."

"What makes you think that?" So much emotion for such a little woman, he thought. She looked like she was fifteen, not thirty-five. He hoped Terrell hadn't tried to bed this angry sister.

"I don't *think* anything. I know. I'm not the only one that turned to the church when I wa' in need. There are lots of us that had the church doors shut in our faces."

"How do you mean?" he asked.

"Well, when I was twen'y-three, I met a single, forty-year-old churchgoin' man. I was in school and he was a tru' driver. We dated for si' months before getting married. Our fir' year together, I got pre'nant and lost my fir' child and I almost died givin' birth to the secon'.

Before I knew it, baby num'er t'ee and fo' came. Oh, but the fi'th one, gave me pure H-E-L-L. I was hospi'lize most of my pre'nancy. During that time my hu'band decided to just up and disappea'.

"Me and the kids depended on him for so much. I hadn't worked in years. I dropped out of college to start havin' his babies. He'd been AWOL for three months by the time my motha' gave her apartment up and moved in my hou' to take care of the kids. I wa' eight month' pre'nant when she came to see me in the ho'pital and handed me a letter from some attorney office. It stated that if I didn't come up with the $9,763.00 I owed by June 1st my hou' was goin' to be foreclose' on June 2nd."

"You didn't know that your mortgage was behind?" Percival asked.

She shook her head. "No, I neve' saw a bill. For the twel' years we been married, all the bill' had gone to his P.O. Box. I just took care of the hou', the kids, and him whenever he came off the road."

"Oh, I see."

"No, you don't, not yet, but you will," she said, dragging out her words. "I had a little over fi'teen thou'an' dollar' from an inheritan' that I been saving, so I wasn't worried about losing our hou'. But when I called my bank, they tol' me that the account had been closed. After I got off the phone, I had a stroke and lost my baby."

"I am so very sorry," he said.

"Don't be. You didn't do anything. Anyway, my motha' didn't have no money or any answers so she went to One World on my behalf.

"My own church turn' me away, because my motha' couldn't prove that I was a tithin' mem'er. I love my motha' but she tends to exaggerate sometimes, so after I recovered and was released from the ho'pital I put on my Sun'ay bes' and hobbled into the church admin'stration building and filled out nine pages of paperwork applying for church assistance.

"Two days later, a church secretary called the Travelodge motel that me, my motha', and the kids were livin' in."

Interrupting her, he asked, "So, you'd lost your house by the time you turned to the church for help?"

"No, but it was fo'closed on by the time I was well enough to ask in person."

He shook his head.

"Anyway, the lady in the church office buildin' tol' me that my application was denied becau' it coul' not be verified that I was a tithing mem'er. She said if I could show proof that I had tithed and was current with my tithes, the church would further review my application."

"That wasn't right." He shook his head. "When did this happen?" he asked.

"Augus' of last year is when I went to the church for assistance. My mother went in May. If you were still there I know you wouldn't have treated me this way."

"No, I wouldn't have."

"Than' God for New Bethel, the church I followed you from. I ain't stepped foot in that church in over eighteen years and dey got me, my motha' and the kids a place to stay. And they hep' me get back in school. Now I work at the ho'pital nights and weekend days while I go to school. Nex' year, I'll be an LPN, and ho'fully my speech will be better." She looked up to see Bishop Money on the television above Percival's bed. "Sorry, Bishop Tu'ner, I have ta' go. I can't look at him," she said before leaving the room.

Curious, Percival hit the volume on the remote.

Wow, was all he could say. One World was already a phenomenal super-structure, but now it looked like the people from the television show 'Pimp My Ride' had teamed up and pimped out the church.

The wooden pews had been replaced with purple and gold stadium fold-up movie seats. The church ceiling looked like the night sky with constellations and shooting stars. The dull red carpet had been replaced with bright red plush new carpet. In the middle of the stainless-steel platform stage was a purple and gold king and queen's throne. It looked like something out of a Julius Caesar movie.

The church orchestra, the choir, the deacons, their wives—everyone wore purple and gold choir robes. Except for TJ.

He walked up to the widest podium that Percival had ever seen. The lone ring he wore looked like the one that Marlon Brando had on his pinky in the Godfather.

TJ wore a tight purple short-sleeved pullover and some loose-fitting, gold slacks. The gold chains around his neck made him look like a pint-sized Mr. T, without the Mohawk haircut.

*****

"Family, I wanna tell you a story this good God morning. A story of love, of friendship, of hope. A story of betrayal," Bishop Money said.

"Tell your story, Bishop!" someone shouted.

"There were two men. They were the best of friends. While one was off on a journey, the other one passed away. The living friend loved his friend so much, that he risked his life traveling back to where his friend had been entombed. The man wept. And afterward, he told his friend to come forth from the tomb of darkness, and the dead man rose from the grave." He paused.

"If this story sounds familiar," he nodded, "it should, family. You may think this is the story of Jesus and Lazarus, but it's not." He shook his head. "No, this is the story of yours truly, Bishop TJ Money, and the former bishop, Percival Cleotis Turner."

He looked around to gauge his audience.

"The words exciting, exuberant, extraordinary, exemplary, and several other exe's could be used to describe our ex-charismatic leader. Unfortunately, our fearless ex-leader died after the loss of his wife and son last year." He paused. "Now, family, I'm not talkin' about no physical death; I'm talkin' about the death of the soul, the death of the mind."

He looked around to again gauge his audience.

"PC, as I called him, was my best friend since our college days at Morehouse. He turned to the bottle, next it was drugs, and finally young ladies of the evening. Now, while he was taking a turn for the worse, I continued on my journey to Jesus. I should've put him in a rehabilitation program. He was my friend, my brother in Christ.

"I won't make any excuses by telling you that I was too busy with the church, or too busy grieving the loss of my own wife. I won't use the excuse of me running what used to be mine and PC's land development company. My best friend was drowning in misery, and the life jacket I threw out to him didn't save him from drowning in a foggy sea of sorrow."

"Sea of sorrow?" Percival laughed while looking up at the 19-inch TV above his hospital bed. "Where are my hip boots?" he said out loud to himself.

TJ dropped his head. "I should've done more."

"You've done enough. If you did any more, I would be standing in front of a firing squad!" Percival shouted at the television screen.

"I loved PC as if he were my own flesh and blood. It doesn't matter that he vandalized God's house. It doesn't matter that he stood in my office and attempted to take my life." TJ shook his head as if he were disappointed.

"Take your life? Vandalized God's house? Did I put Jesus on the cross and drive the nails into His skin, too?" Percival said, as he listened to TJ's sermon.

"PC, if you're watching this broadcast, I want you to know that I forgive you. You tried to take my life; now I'm going to give you life, just as Jesus gave life to Lazarus."

"Please don't. Please let me stay dead. I'll be fine!" he shouted at the television.

"Family, we've lost a lot last week since the robbery. But we still have God, each other, and our health. From my understanding, PC's health is bad. He has no family. If it weren't for prison, he'd probably be somewhere downtown holding a cardboard sign. "No, family," he shook his head, "I can't let that happen. Our brother has suffered enough. I paid his hundred-thousand-dollar bond only because my attorney informed me that, although I dropped the charges, he wouldn't be out of prison for at least another week."

225

"There wouldn't be a bond or a case to drop if you hadn't pressed false charges!" Percival again shouted at the screen.

"I don't want my brother to suffer for one more minute." He bowed his head. "PC, please forgive me. I love you, Brother." He placed a hand over his face. "Forgive me," he cried before turning and walking to the back of the stage and out a back door where two FBI agents awaited.

CHAPTER 30

*H*is nerves were shot to hell. Staying calm while being interrogated for hours by the FBI wasn't an easy task.

If it weren't for his sudden skyrocketing popularity, he was sure that the FBI wouldn't have waited until the popular eleven-thirty service was over. And even then the two brothas blended in with the congregation.

They hadn't said why they needed to speak with him at first, but it was clear by the urgency in their voices that if he refused they wouldn't have hesitated in arresting him in front of the largest crowd that had ever attended One World.

In the most sincere tone he could muster, TJ had told them that they had his full cooperation. The two agents had even allowed him to drive his own car down to the Richard Russell Federal Building.

From four in the afternoon until nine in the evening, TJ sat behind a metal desk while several agents went in and out of the small interrogation room. He must've been asked the same questions in different ways, by different agents, twenty times.

"Do you know this man?" they had asked as they placed a Polaroid of an average-looking, middle-aged, light-skinned black man dressed like a banker in front of him. He'd never seen the man in his life, and he told them as much.

"Did you hire this man to kill Shemika Montrease Brown?" they had asked, pointing to the man in the picture.

"Where were you two nights ago, Friday, May 21st, between the hours of seven and eleven p.m.?" they'd asked.

He couldn't tell them that he was sitting outside Carmen's apartment waiting for her to pull up when he ran into Lexus. So, he told them he was at home preparing for Sunday services.

Finally, after five hours, they had let him go.

"He drove around the city, paranoid and nervous, looking out of his rearview mirror. Satisfied that he wasn't being followed, he pulled over to a pay phone, at a Quik Trip gas station.

Minutes later, he slammed the receiver back down on its cradle. "Damn! Damn! Damn!" He kicked his front tire, angry because he'd called Drake twelve times and had left eight messages.

*****

It was almost midnight. TJ had been drinking coffee and peeing since arriving home. He couldn't stop pacing back and forth from one end of his home office to the other. Exasperated, he threw his hands in the air. "What is taking Drake so long?"

Finally, at the stroke of midnight, TJ's cell phone rang.

"Meet me on the courtyard steps in one hour," Drake said, then ended the call.

*****

With ten minutes to spare, TJ walked at a leisurely pace up the sidewalk toward the Morehouse College psych building. It was a clear night; the moon was bright but not quite full.

Campus security was nowhere in sight. And why should they be? School was out for the summer, and it was almost one in the morning.

The night was quiet, except for the grunting sounds Professor Gardener Drake made as he did stretching exercises on the psych building stairs a few feet away. He wore black speedos, a white muscle shirt, and some black running shoes. If it weren't for his mostly gray and brown hair which, by the way, he still wore in a ponytail, you wouldn't have been able to tell that the man was pushing sixty.

"TJ?"

The psychology building's front steps were called the courtyard because of the often heated social and political Drake Debates that were held on them. They were called Drake Debates because nine times out of ten, Professor Drake was at the center of the discussions.

Drake, the white Malcolm X, as he was called, knew more about the psychology of black folk than anyone on the four college campuses that surrounded Morehouse. And his views on race relations paralleled those of an angry black militant.

The African-American professors hated him for knowing more about the black plight than they did, and the white professors hated him for being an educated black man in white skin.

On the other hand, the students loved him. But besides TJ, no one at Morehouse knew of Drake's double life; he was both a highly paid hit man and a Fuller Calloway tenured psychology professor.

"Have a seat," Drake said, patting a spot on the pavement stairs next to where he was now seated.

TJ reluctantly sat down.

Drake put a hand on TJ's. Looking him deep in the eyes, Drake said, "I've missed you, T."

Jerking his hand away, TJ asked, "What happened? And why did I have to be dragged down to FBI headquarters and questioned before I found out that your man not only didn't complete the job but was arrested in the act."

"Sorry about not bringing you up to speed, but I wanted to wait—"

"Wait for what?"

"For the Fed's to bring you in."

"What?"

"You can't tell them what you don't know. If you were asked to take a polygraph, you'd pass, because you really didn't know what was going on."

TJ turned his head. He didn't like the way Drake was looking at him. "Okay, can you tell me what's going on now?" he asked, staring at the parking lot across the street.

"The man I subcontracted out to do the job was obviously under Uncle Sam's microscope."

"And that's another thing. You know how I feel about my own people. I could've hired a black hitter for a third of

230

what I'm paying you, Drake. But I wanted the best, so I hired you, a white professional, and you still farmed out the hit to a black man."

"In over thirty years of problem solving, I've never had this happen. The man I farmed the contract out to was good at what he did."

"That remains to be seen," TJ said.

"I know, but he really was."

"So, how did he get caught?"

Drake shrugged. "How does anyone get caught?"

"They get careless," TJ offered. "They leave a *t* uncrossed or an *i* undotted. All I wanna know is why I'm not having Shemika's body shipped back to Atlanta as we speak?"

"All I can tell you is that my guy was sitting at a table in the back of the Westin Hotel ballroom when Ms. Brown got up to introduce Mrs. Billingsley to the media and the hundreds of fans that showed up for her book release party. As soon as my guy pulled his gun out, undercovers were all over his ass."

"How did the feds know Shemika was the target?"

"Phone taps, informants." He shrugged. "Who knows?"

"How do you know he won't talk?"

"He can't." Drake smiled. "The guy fell on a knife and died instantly early Saturday morning while being held in protective custody at the Harris County Jail in Houston."

"The Feds didn't tell me that," TJ said.

"Why would they?"

"Well, thank the Lord for unfortunate accidents," TJ jokingly said.

"Because of your popularity and the botched hit, I think you should reconsider the contract," Drake said.

"I already have," TJ replied. "Keep the twenty-five grand deposit. I have another job for you. This time I want you to handle it yourself."

"Who's the job?"

"I don't want to say quite yet, but it's local and I want this person taken out quickly. I'll call you in a few months to place my order," TJ replied. He stood up and began wiping the back of his linen pants off.

"Killing, teaching, and loving is what I do," Drake said as he stood and ran a manicured nail down the middle of TJ's back.

TJ jerked away from Drake's touch.

"TJ, TJ, TJ, my beautiful TJ. Do you ever think about us?"

"No, Drake. I'm the bishop of the second largest black church in the country. I think about God."

"If memory serves me correct, you called out God's name numerous times when we were…" Drake smiled. "You know."

"I was a broke college kid doing what I had to do to make the grade and eat," he said.

"Come on, TJ," his head turned at an angle, "this is old Drake you talkin' to."

Paranoid, TJ turned and surveyed the area before turning back to Drake. "Drake, I-I…"

"I-I my ass," Drake interrupted. "I want you to look me in my eyes and tell me you didn't enjoy walking around my house in high heels, wigs, lipstick, and women's lingerie. I want you to tell me that you didn't enjoy my—"

"No, No, No." TJ put his hands over his ears. I—"

Drake grabbed TJ's arms, lowering his hands. "Don't deny it. You've always denied who you were. Do you think your God would love you any less because you're gay?"

232

"I am not gay. I am…" He shook his head. "I was confused."

"I know," Drake said. "Confused about your manhood. That's why you used to take the money I gave you and spend it on prostitutes and every woman you could get to open her legs. You thought sleeping with different women would rid you of the urge to be with another man. I bet you still sleep with any woman that'll spread her legs?"

"No! No! You're wrong, Drake. I was sick. I was a kid. I love women, not men. I'm not gay. I'm not gay," he repeated. "Homosexuality is an abomination to God."

"Who are you trying to convince?" Drake asked before taking TJ in his arms.

TJ lost himself in Drake's arms, his touch, his lips. "No!" TJ pulled back. "No, Drake. I can't. I won't," he said before running away with a visible bulge in his slacks.

TJ was so upset as he ran to his car, he didn't even see Skip Abraham crouching down in the seat of a green Ford Taurus wearing his signature plaid fedora.

CHAPTER 31

$\mathcal{T}$he sky had a slight overcast, but other than that, it was a sunny, beautiful Memorial Day.

Air couldn't have gotten between Percival and Carmen, as close as they held each other. The small space Carmen and Percival shared while standing a few feet outside the hospital doors was their own private little world. They held each other so tight, their souls kissed.

"I got discouraged, but I never gave up hope," Carmen said, crying in Percival's arms. "You just don't know how many years, days, and nights I stayed up praying and dreaming of the time I'd be able to walk hand in hand with both of my men."

The intoxicating aroma of freedom and love had Percival drunk with happiness. But not so drunk that he didn't catch what she had just insinuated. Breaking their embrace, he took a step back. Looking her in the face, he asked, "Are you saying…"

With a steady stream of tears cascading down her butter-colored, chipmunk cheeks, she nodded yes.

Tears erupted from his soul and exploded from his eyes. "Samuel's coming home?"

Again, she nodded.

*****

They were in Carmen's SUV when she said, "The state dismissed the charges and threw out the conviction two days ago, on Friday."

"I knew it. I just knew it."

Carmen smiled, enjoying Percival's elation.

He reached out and grabbed her free hand. "I prayed so hard, and God has answered my prayers." He smiled. "So, when is my son," he squeezed her hand, "*our* son coming home?"

Her heart melted at the words *our son*. "Could be any day now," she said.

"If he was acquitted, why didn't they release him Friday?" Percival asked.

"They tossed the murder conviction. They're trying to determine whether to retry him for his part in the robbery."

"Oh, okay."

"I'm sorry, Percival. I didn't even ask how you were feeling."

"Me? Woman, please." He brushed her off. "After I get some food in my system, I'll be ready to run the Boston marathon."

She gave him a get-real look.

"Okay, maybe the Playstation Boston marathon."

They both laughed.

"No, seriously, though, other than dying of starvation, the doctors say I'm fine."

"I was gon' stop by the house and surprise Deidre'. You know she has no idea that you're out."

"You didn't tell her?"

"If she has no idea that you're out, what do you think?"

"Okay, Annie Mae, I see I'm gon' have to beat you."

Mimicking Tina Turner, she replied, "Please don't beat me, Ike."

They laughed.

"No, but for real, I wanted to surprise her."

"I'm surprised she doesn't already know, the way your cousin is running his mouth all over the TV," Percival said.

"Nah, that would be your," Carmen pointed, "midget mini-me, soul-brother-number-one-brother-in-Christ. The only cousin TJ has," she nodded, "is the spirit sittin' on Hell's throne"

"Speaking of the devil, I wonder why that fool dropped the charges against me."

"Who knows what tangled web he's weaving now?" Carmen shrugged. "So what do you have a taste for? I guess we could stop off before surprising Deidre'."

"I'd trade you in for some *Geraldine's Fish and Grits*." He smiled. "Ouch, that hurt," he said, rubbing his arm from the shot he just took from Carmen. "Violence doesn't solve anything."

"But it does make me feel good, and it'll teach you to think twice before contemplating trading me in for some talapia and cheese grits."

"But, Carmen, I'm not talking about any ole talapia and grits. I'm talking about *Geraldine's*."

He shrank back as close to the passenger door as he could. "Okay, okay, I'm just jokin," he said as she balled up her fist getting ready to punch him again.

"You'd better be," she said.

For the next ten minutes they rode in silence listening to old school R&B. What had begun as a beautiful sunny day had now turned into a nasty one of spring showers. Percival could care less as he rocked back and forth in the gray leather passenger seat of the Expedition.

"True devotion," he broke out in song with Earth, Wind and Fire, *"blessed are the children."*

The digital clock on the radio read 2:45. *"Deliverance.*

They were pulling into the Kroger grocery store plaza where Geraldine's was located. "We have fifteen minutes before they close," he said.

A few minutes later they were sitting in a corner booth.

Mr. Thomas, Geraldine's husband, had just taken their orders when Percival noticed a somber look on Carmen's face.

"What's with the sad face? Today's a good day."

"I know it is," she replied.

He placed a hand over hers. Looking into her peanut butter eyes, he said, "Carmen, I need to tell you how I feel... about you... about us."

"Before you say anything else, I need to tell you some things." She pulled her hand back and placed it in her lap with the other. "After I finish, I completely understand if you never want to see me again."

"Carmen, I lov—"

"Don't say it." She shook her head. "Don't say it, at least not yet. I want—no, I need you to listen closely to everything that I am about to say to you."

"Bishop, go on and eat before your food gets cold!" Ms. Geraldine shouted from behind the counter.

"Yes, Ma'am," he said.

"I'm gon' lock the door," Mr. Thomas, Geraldine's husband said, as he headed for the glass front door. "Don't rush. You know you can't rush good eatin'. You two are welcome to stay as long as you want. Me and the Missus will be here for a while."

"Is everything alright, Baby?" Ms. Geraldine asked. "Can I get you some hot syrup for your waffle?"

"No, Ma'am. I'm fine. The fish is delicious," Carmen said.

"Well, thank you, Sweetness," Ms. Geraldine said.

"You just give a holla' when you're finished," Mr. Thomas said before following his wife into the kitchen.

Watching the way they still looked at one another after over thirty years of marriage was a testament to true, unconditional love—a love that Percival never thought he'd feel again.

No longer hungry, he looked up at Carmen.

"I've gone over what I am about to say a hundred times, a hundred different ways, and I still don't know where to start."

"The beginning is always good," he joked. "But seriously…" He reached for her hand.

She seemed reluctant, but she placed her left hand over his.

"Just relax."

She exhaled. "Okay, here goes… Percival, you know what TJ did to my niece, but what you didn't know was that after the rape, my niece developed something called Post Traumatic Stress Disorder."

"I've heard of that. As part of my pastoral studies program at Emory University, I took a clinical psychology class and we touched on PTSD."

"Well, then you should know that it is the most common disorder seen in rape and sexual assault victims. Tracy suffered with PTSD for two years. For two years she was afraid of men. She jumped at every sudden noise. And she was on three different prescription meds to help her cope with depression. My sister, Sharon, and I did everything we could. We took Tracy to therapists, rape survival group meetings, extended family vacations, you name it. We did all we could."

He nodded.

"I'll never forget that Wednesday morning." She paused. "I was just about to drop Samuel off at the sitter's and head to work when the phone rang. When I answered, Tracy's fifteen-year-old sister, Meka, was screaming so hysterically that I couldn't understand a word."

"Didn't you live with your sister and her girls?"

"No. By then I'd moved into my own place."

He nodded.

"Well, anyway, I rushed over to my sister's. When I walked into my sister's bedroom I almost fainted. Meka was on my sister's bed, holding Tracy's dead body in her arms."

Percival gasped before closing his eyes. "No! No!" Why didn't you call? Why didn't you tell me?"

In a dry monotone, she said, "What could you have done?"

"But I—"

She squeezed his hand. "Listen, Percival. Just listen, okay?"

He nodded.

"By the time the paramedics and police arrived, I'd just barely managed to pry Meka away from her sister. I'd almost forgotten about my sister, who still stood naked in the bathroom doorway with her mouth open. It wasn't until a week later that Meka was able to tell me what had happened. I don't know if you remember me telling you, but Meka was raped by her father, and she spent two years in a mental hospital after killing him when she was only ten."

"I remember," he said. "Meka must've been extremely traumatized after all she'd seen and been through."

"Very. Meka was the youngest, but she had taken on the big-sister role after," Carmen wiped her eyes, "her big sister was raped. Meka and Tracy were as close as sisters could be."

"When Meka was able to share what had happened, what did she tell you?" Percival asked.

"It seems that, while Sharon was in the shower, Tracy had gone into her mother's bedroom closet, and took Sharon's old .38 special from the hat box. A few minutes later, Meka walked into the bedroom while Tracy was sitting at the edge of the bed with Sharon's comforter over her legs. She told me that Tracy was just sitting on Sharon's bed, cross-legged, rocking back and forth, her eyes squeezed tightly together, and chanting the phrase, *'I am now a woman, so you have to let me be. Get from inside me, TJ Money'*, and then she shot herself."

"I am so, so, so sorry."

Silently crying, Carmen nodded.

Percival let a few seconds pass before he squeezed Carmen's hand and asked, "So, you say Meka didn't see the gun when she walked in?"

"No. The gun was under my sister's comforter, between Tracy's legs, and the barrel was inside of..." She cried, reliving the moment when Meka had told her the story."

"Oh my God," Percival said.

"And to make matters worse, Tracy shot herself on her eighteenth birthday, April 8, 1987."

"Where is your sister now?"

"She died in Georgia Regional Mental institute in February of '91, four years after Tracy shot herself.

"So, where is Meka now?"

"Meka hated Terrell with a driving passion. Her thoughts of revenge are what seemed to keep her sane. And I'd already lost a sister and one niece; I wasn't going to do anything to jeopardize losing Meka."

"So, where is Meka now?" he asked again.

She lowered her head. "Here's where things get really interesting.

CHAPTER 32

*H*e'd done his part. He'd married her. TJ had even given in to ninety percent of Shemika's wedding demands. He was never sold on the idea of spending a hundred thousand dollars on the wedding gown she'd picked out, but he did end up forking out twenty thousand for a white chiffon lace dress with a twenty-foot tail that dragged along the beach. After the Houston fiasco, he had no choice but to give in to some of her outrageous demands.

The biggest and most embarrassing demand he'd given in to was flying forty of her so-called friends to Montego Bay for their barefoot-on-the-beach wedding.

It was eighty degrees. The sun was setting, casting a golden glow over the water. It was Memorial Day, 2005. Pork chop sweat was pouring off every one of Shemika's Pimps Up, Hoes Down players' ball entourage.

TJ remembered smiling at the thought of a big tidal wave coming twenty yards ashore and washing Shemika and her friends out to sea.

The wedding was the only time he'd wished the cameras weren't present. He could imagine the jokes that were being made about the wedding on late night and daytime talk shows.

Aqua blue, passion purple, grass green, blood red, sunkist orange, banana yellow—the entire crayon box had been represented at the wedding. They looked like throwback actors from the movie, *I'm Gonna Get You Sucka.*

As if there weren't enough gold and diamonds represented, one brotha was selling rings, bracelets, and gold chains at the reception, while the man's wife was trying to recruit everybody who would listen, to sign up for *Pre-Paid Legal.*

Bishop Money couldn't have imagined a more ghetto wedding. No one would believe it. He was surprised nobody had fired a shot. But, then again, he wouldn't know because he and Shemika had taken off in a jet chartered for Cancun later that evening.

That was almost a week ago. Now, six days into their seven-day honeymoon, Bishop Money still had a full bottle of Viagra. Sexually frustrated didn't even begin to describe the way he felt standing in front of the wraparound patio window in the presidential suite of the Moon Palace resort. The clear blue ocean waves washing up on the albino sandy shore did nothing to calm his nerves.

"TJ?"

He turned around.

She rubbed her oily naked body. "What do you think? Smooth as a baby's bottom, huh?"

He reached out to touch her shaved area.

She slapped his hand.

"Ouch!" he said, shaking his stinging hand.

"I didn't say you could touch Annie-Poo-Nanny. I just asked what you thought about my Brazilian wax," Shemika said as she flaunted and sauntered her shiny naked body in front of him.

He couldn't take it any more. For six days she had walked around half or completely naked, covered in some type of oil. "Look, Woman," he pointed, "you're my wife. Now, I've put up with your craziness for six days. There's one more day left on this honeymoon from hell and you gon' make love to me."

Her belly was showing, and she looked breathtaking in the sunlight as they stood in the front room of the suite. "You gotta be outta your rabid-ass mind if you think I'm gon' let you hit this."

He took a step forward. "Let? What do you like to say about Slim and None?" he asked, taking another step. "Well, I think Let done ran off with Slim and None." He pointed a finger in her face. "Look here, Woman, you're my wife. You better act like it and start performing your wifely duties."

"Nah, Negro." She shook her head. "What I better do is bite that damn finger off if you don't get it outta my face. That's what I better do. And let me tell your little horny ass another thing." She took a step toward him. Her standing-at-attention, tree-bark brown nipples rubbed against his red silk shirt. "Your eyes may water, and your teeth may grit, but nunna' this poo-nanny is you ever gon' get. And I mean eva' neva', Negro."

"Shemika, that gangster-rapper-Sugar-Knight persona don't faze me. And, Woman, you ain't funny in the least. Annie-Poo Nanny, as you call it... well, it's mine. I own it and I own you."

She took a step back. "Own? Now you have officially gone from a Negro to a Nigga. And, Nigga, I ain't never had a for-sale sign on my ass." She looked him up and down. But you have a trick sign on yours."

He clenched his fists and took a step forward, closing the space between them.

She stood with her hands on her hips, one leg in front of the other. "What? I guess you gon' try to take it now, huh, little man?" You makin' a habit out of ballin' your little fists up. You think you bad? Come on, little man, show me wha'chu got." She threw her hands in the air. "I'm five four, 135 pounds, three and a half months pregnant, barefoot, and naked; but I'll whip your Al Sharpton midget ass, and if for some reason you get the best of me," she ran her hand between her legs, "it'll be cold and dead before you stick your little wee-wee up in me."

"That can be arranged," he quietly said.

"Been there, done that, tried it, and it didn't work, little man."

"How many times do I have to tell you that I didn't have anything to do with that man trying to kill you in Houston?" He smiled. "Although I wish I had and I wish he did."

"I ain't no fool. You of all people should have recognized that by now," she said.

"If you think I had something to do with the attempt on your life, why'd you marry me? Why're you here with me now? And don't tell me it's because you're pregnant!"

She smiled. "The entire eight months I've been dating you was all an act. The proper and prim talk, the attitude, me being a sex-therapist—everything. I played you like the ten-cent trick you are. So self-absorbed, you never questioned my intentions."

"No need, I knew what you were about all along," he said.

"You thought you knew. You so self-absorbed, you think you know everything when you really don't know shit. You thought I was all about money? That's what I wanted you to think. See, little man," she walked over to the kitchen, "everything was carefully planned."

"Plan, what plan?" he asked.

"If you keep quiet long enough, I'll tell you."

Relax, TJ. Relax. Ten, nine, eight, seven...

She poured herself a glass of Chablis. "After I gained your trust, I started taking the condoms off you after sex. You thought I was flushing them down the toilet. Well, I was, after my turkey baster sucked the juice out."

She took a sip.

"It took three months, but thanks to the fertility shots, I finally got pregnant. I knew that was the only way I could get you to marry me."

"You used me?" he said. "You honestly think I'm gon' let you get away with this? You golddiggin' bloodsucker."

"Uhh," she held a finger in the air, "you're a tad bit late." She smiled and kissed at the air. "Sweetie, I've already gotten away with it. And it was never about the money, as I already said. But that's right, you don't listen. No need when your dumb ass knows every damn thing."

Lord, don't give me strength, 'cause if you do... "Okay, if it wasn't about money, then what was it?" he asked through clenched teeth.

"It's about Bishop Terrell Little Man Joseph Money," she said, walking back toward him with the wine glass in her hand. "Sweetie, it's always been about you." She smiled and shook her head. "Ever since you raped my big sister, Tracy."

His eyes grew to the size of small saucers.

"No, I take that back. You didn't become my obsession until Tracy killed herself. I was only fifteen then, but I saw what you did to my family. Now, for the rest of your life, I'm gon' make sure you have the Preacherman blues. This baby I'm carrying," she rubbed her stomach, "is my ticket to your misery."

"You nuttier than that little whore sister of yours. And for the record, I didn't rape her. She owed me. I gave her sixty dollars because of some lame excuse she gave me. After she took the money, she never came back as promised. So, late that evening, I got in my car and drove over to the shack y'all lived in. I waited for the little whore outside your house.

"I didn't have to wait very long. The sun was going down when the whore came out the house with a pair of skates thrown over her shoulders. I waited until she turned the corner on your street before I followed her. When I caught up to her, I offered her whore ass another twenty and she got in. The little tramp wasn't in the car thirty seconds before she unzipped my pants."

"No, you're lying. My sister wasn't a ho!"

He smiled. "Why is that so hard to believe? You and your auntCarmen are whores. Only reason your momma didn't make money on her back was she was way too ugly and too lazy."

"Shut up! Shut up, TJ!" she cried.

"I'm sorry, you're right. I should keep quiet. My mother always used to say if you don't have anything good to say about the dead, then don't say anything at all." He paused. "Your sister Tracy is dead. Good," he said as he walked to the door.

"Fuck you, TJ!" Shemika cried.

"If I wanted to, I would. And just like your whore sister couldn't do anything to stop me, you can't, either," he said, just barely missing getting hit in the head with a wine glass before slamming the door.

CHAPTER 33

*T*he end of June, at seven in the morning, you could already see the Atlanta heat dancing to its own beat.

"So, what's the plan, now that you're a free man, Pops?" Samuel asked as they walked around the neighborhood surrounding Carmen's apartment complex.

You would think that Samuel would've opted to sleep in a soft, warm bed his first night out of prison. Instead, he'd fallen asleep on the floor in his mother's living room, beside Percival, watching *The Cosby Show* marathon on TV 1.

Percival turned to face his son while they continued walking. "I've begun the process of starting up a small ministry. After I'm state approved, I'm going to see about going back into the prisons to minister to the brothers and sisters on lockdown."

"Sounds like a lot of work for one person," Samuel said.

"It is. But I should be able to handle it."

249

"Nah, Pops." Samuel shook his head. "Last time you started up a ministry, look what happened. I think I'd better come along for the ride. You need someone to look out for you. Somebody gotta make sure you don't get taken in by another TJ Money."

Percival turned around and looked at his son. "Why would you do that?" he asked. "You don't even believe in God."

"I never said that. I said *if* He exists. I always said *if*."

"*If* means you weren't convinced."

"I am now," Samuel flatly stated.

Trying his best to mask the joy he felt, Percival asked, "What caused the sudden change?"

"Let's just say I called God out and He answered loud and clear."

"Sooo, do you accept Jesus as your Lord and savior?" Percival asked.

"Most definitely," Samuel answered.

Percival reached out and grabbed Samuel.

"Pops, we in public."

"So? I can't give my son a hug?"

"We in Atlanta. Don't nobody know you my pops. People gon' start thinkin' the rumors TJ put out on you are true."

"I don't care what anyone thinks except you, your mother, and God."

They turned around and started to head back toward the apartment.

"Pops, can I ask you a question?"

"I'm all ears."

"Wha'chu think about a man who takes another man's life?"

"I don't know." He shrugged. "I guess it depends."

"On what?"

"The man's state of mind. If he's remorseful, or if he's just evil." Percival paused. "No one's free from sin. So, I don't believe anyone can truly judge another. Son, it's about what God puts in here." He palmed his chest.

"What would you think of me if I told you that I took another man's life?" Samuel asked.

Percival's pace slowed.

Samuel was looking down at the street with his arms behind his back.

Percival didn't know what to think about a lot of things these days. He'd been on a whirlwind rollercoaster the last fifteen months. He was about to give Samuel a weak answer when someone called out.

"Preacherman?"

At the same time, both men looked to their left.

Poppalove was chewing on a straw, sitting at a bus stop bench, right outside the apartment complex.

"We'll finish this conversation in a second. I'll be right back," Percival said while crossing the street.

Poppalove took the straw out of his mouth, "Nah, Boy, I wasn't 'ferrin ta' you." He pointed. "I'm talking 'bout young buck, the otha' Preacherman."

"Other Preacherman?" Percival frowned up. He turned, looking over at Samuel. "You know him?"

"Yeah. They brought him in the day you had the aneurysm. He's the one that helped me see God," Samuel replied.

"Ah, hell, you might as well come, too!" Poppalove shouted, before putting the straw back in his mouth.

Thank God. Now I know I'm not crazy. Finally, someone else has seen Poppalove, Percival thought.

"Ya'll might as well cop a squat. We might be here a spell," Poppalove said once they walked up. "Have you tole ya' pappy yet?" Poppalove asked Samuel.

"Told me what?" Percival asked.

"I was just about to," Samuel said.

"Told me what?"

Still chewing on a straw, the sun shining on his coal-black bald head, Poppalove said, "Who you is, who he is, and what dat got to do with who I is, and," he pointed a finger in the air, "why I's here."

Confused, Percival slowly asked, "What are you talking about?"

Poppalove waved at Samuel. "Go on; tell him, Boy."

With his hands in his pockets, he looked up. "Pops, I didn't kill Prince Charles, or that stripper I was accused of, but I did set the whole thing up." Samuel exhaled. "And before they were killed, I'd already taken out three other drug kingpins."

Shocked, numb, and confused were just a few emotions Percival felt. It took him a minute to think. And during that minute, the world seemed to pause. Not even the birds chirped. Still bewildered, a minute later he said, "But, you were only sixteen when you went up for murder."

"And I was fifteen the first time I slit a man's throat."

"But why?" he asked.

"Momma got real sick and her insurance wouldn't cover her trip to Cairo, Egypt, where a new treatment was discovered. The FDA in the states hadn't approved the treatment or the medicine to keep her healthy, so it was either me watch my mother die or get up the forty grand it would cost to try and save her. My cousin, Meka, was the only family I had, and she didn't have that kind of money, so I had no choice."

"But what made you take another human being's life? Why couldn't you have just robbed them?" he asked, not believing what he himself was saying.

Chewing on his straw, Poppalove sat quietly on the bus stop bench, watching the exchange between father and son.

"After you rob a kingpin, you don't let him live. I've seen their type of vengeance, and ever since, I've wanted to take out every kingpin in the world; so now I had my chance."

Switching gears, he continued, "Look, Pops." He put a hand on Percival's shoulder. "The apartment complex we live in didn't use to be this laid back. They used to call it little Saigon.

"Back in the early to late '90's, a cat name Black Escobar had these apartments on lock. He had his people running crack and X out of at least three or four apartments like it was legal."

Interrupting, Percival asked, "No one ever called the police?"

"Yeah, a few times. But the time that changed my life was when my childhood babysitter called them." He paused, a look of despair covering his young face. "Black Escobar had lookouts with two-way radios stationed right up there," he pointed across the street from where they were now sitting, "at the entrance, so they could alert his pushers when Five-O rolled down."

He continued, "So, when the Black Cat Dekalb County drug task force rolled through, Black Escobar's workers had already been alerted and the dope was flushed down the toilets inside the trap houses they sold out of. A week after the failed police busts, me and Gina, Ms. Murray's daughter, were sitting on the floor in the living room doing homework while Ms. Murray was talking on the phone in the kitchen.

"Scared half to death, Gina and I screamed as Black Escobar's boys kicked in the front door. Next thing I know, one of the cats grabbed Gina. She was kicking and screaming until one of Black Escobar's boys punched her in the side of the head. Instantly, she went limp in the other guy's arms. I thought she was dead."

Percival shook his head.

"Ms. Murray and I couldn't do a thing to help Gina even if we wanted to. Black Escobar had a gun in both hands one pointed in each of our directions. Before he left, he told Ms. Murray that if she ran her mouth off to the police again, he'd be back for her, me, and her twin baby boys. I'll never forget the smile on his face or his black snake eyes that seemed to stare right through me."

Again Percival interrupted, "What happened to the little girl?"

"Three days later, her left arm was found in front of our apartment building. As far as I know, her body has never been recovered."

"What kind of animal would do something like that to a child?" Percival asked.

"A sadistic drug kingpin trying to send a message to anyone thinking about turning him or his people in to the cops."

"How did he know Ms. Murray called the police in the first place?"

"Come on, Pops. You know half these cops out here are dirty. Black Escobar must've had a pig on his payroll. And whoever that was had to tip him off."

"How old were you when all this happened?" Percival asked.

"Same age as Gina, eleven."

A year ago, Percival wouldn't have believed the type of stuff he was hearing, but after the books and trial transcripts he'd read, and the stories he'd heard, it was easy to believe that the police were so corrupt. "I see," was all he said, before Samuel continued.

"So, a few years later, I got the opportunity to get the money Momma needed and I took it. It wasn't hard slitting a throat or pulling a trigger."

"What do you mean, 'it wasn't hard'?"

"Pops, after what I saw Escobar and his boys do, I no longer saw a drug dealer as human. What I saw was wild animals needing to be put down."

"And the others?" Percival asked.

"Same thing. I didn't know any of 'em, but they were out there poisoning the black community and no telling how many little Ginas that were made to suffer because of the crack they sold. At the time, I didn't see anything wrong with what I was doing. As a matter of fact, I thought I was doing a community service and getting paid in the process."

"And the Cathouse strip club?" Percival asked.

"That was different. Prince Charles always had security around him, and his place was gated and guarded like Fort Knox, so I made the mistake of bringing in a couple of crackheads to do the job."

A teenage boy should be thinking about girls, school, video games, and sports, not killing drug dealers. This didn't make any sense at all, Percival thought.

"I wasn't concerned with money from the strip club. I knew where he kept his stash. I just needed him out of the way to get to it. Unfortunately, an innocent girl got killed in the process."

"Where did your mother think you were getting all this money?"

"She didn't know back then. I gave the money to my cousin, Meka, and she took care of Mom's medical bills."

"So, Shemika knew?"

"Yeah, she knew what was up. At first she tripped, but she knew there was nothing she could do to stop me. My moms was my everything, and I wasn't gon' lose her without a fight. Besides, Meka understood about losing someone you loved."

"Where did Carmen think Shemika got the money?"

"Pops, you'd have to know my cousin to understand. She's always had a way with men. She's a little rough around the edges, but she knows how to make men pay out."

So engrossed was he in Samuel's story, Percival almost forgot that Poppalove was sitting on the other side of him. Turning to face Poppalove, Percival asked, "So what role do you play in all this?"

He stood up, spit the straw from his mouth, and turned to face them. "'Member when I kep' makin' them signs that told you to turn around?"

They both nodded.

Percival turned and looked at Samuel. "I thought you didn't meet him until the day I had the aneurysm?"

"That was the first time I'd actually met the man, but before I got locked up, it seemed like I saw him each time I went out to handle my business. And each time he'd be holding one of those crazy cardboard signs."

"Y'all pay attention now," Poppalove said as they both got quiet and looked up at the mysterious stranger.

"Records say I was birthed October 2, 1800, but they's wrong. If ya knows anything 'bout slavery, when it came to us," he shook his head, "them pilgrims ain't keep no ac'rate records. Truth be told, I was birthed October 1, 1799, in Southampton County, Virginia.

"They calls me Poppalove, but my Christian name is Nathaniel Turner. Only reason my last name be Turner 'cause that's what the pilgrim's name was that owned me. Samuel Turner was what they called him," he looked over at Samuel, "jus' like your name, Boy."

"You sayin' you Nat Turner, the preacher that led the Slave Revolt of 1831, that left fifty-five white folks dead?" Samuel asked.

"What I tell ya' about dem pilgrims and dey records? We sent one hundred and three slave owners, and they kin, ta hell. And it tweren't no forty of us that did it. It was only twenty-two, and half of them were younger than you, Boy." Poppalove paused. "History is just what it is. It's *his story*. Whoever is in control makes whatever history up they want. But it's up to you to turn around and go back for yourself. Study. Learn from yo' dead kinfolks' mistakes."

He took a couple of steps back. "Like mine." Poppalove patted his chest. "What I did was foolish. I killed men instead of their ideas. Just like you, Boy." He looked at Samuel before turning his attention to Percival.

"And you, Percival, let me tell ya' 'bout my congregation. I can't begin ta' tell ya how many I had that listened to what spewed from my mouth on Sundays. But I'll tell ya this: Whatever plantation I was on looked like a slave convention on Sunday mo'nins. Slaves from miles around begged for they massa's ta' give them passes to come hear me spit the Word of God. And look what I did.

"My ancestors, your ancestors, came to me jus' like I don' come to y'all. They didn't bear cardboard signs, but as sho' as pig is pork, they come to me. Problem was, I didn't take heed to the signs I was shown.

"I let my anger and my pride get in the way of my callin'. I let hate consume me to the point of leading not only twenty-two men to their deaths, but hundreds, maybe thousands, of
God-fearin' colored folks, slaves, and free were massacred because of the folks me and my little army killed. And guess what: What I did didn't mean a hill of beans. I died not as an honorable black man, but just anotha' angry, dumb nigga."

He turned his head from left to right. "And as I look around here, I see ain't much changed since the early 1800's. 'Cept back then, we knowed we was slaves. The plantations may have gotten bigga, in this here twenty-first century, and so have the slave shanties, but they still plantations and they still slave shanties.

"Now, you two, y'all flesh of my flesh, blood from my blood," he shook his head, "don't be like me. Don't die like I did. Die with honor, with respect. Die for freedom and, most importantly, live for the Lord and show the world His light and glory."

CHAPTER 34

*B*ishop Money arched his back, stretching, before getting out of the king-size bed. He felt good, refreshed.

"TJ, we need to talk."

Alarmed, he turned to the voice. "Oh my sweet Jesus," he said, remembering where he was and what he'd done. For a moment, he thought he'd be sick.

"TJ?"

Ignoring Drake, he hurriedly put on his boxers and stumbled to the floor trying to put his legs into the white linen pants he'd worn when he boarded the plane in Cancun yesterday. He rushed, trying his hardest to block out the man out who lay on the other side of the bed.

"TJ, did you hear what I said?"

God has tested me and I failed. TJ felt terrible for feeling so good. He couldn't believe he'd been so weak. With his back turned, he replied, "Yes, I heard you. But I have somewhere to be. I really don't have time, Drake," he said, while buttoning his shirt.

"You need to make time. Your life may depend on it," Drake said, sitting up in bed.

The TJ stopped what he was doing. "My life? What do you mean by that?"

Drake grabbed the red silk robe from the floor on his side of the bed. "It's complicated," he said, "but come downstairs and meet me out by the pool and I'll explain everything."

A few minutes later they were sitting out on Drake's Mexican veranda overlooking the thermometer-shaped lap pool in his backyard.

The white, six-foot privacy fence, along with the fifteen-foot palm trees surrounding Drake's manicured backyard provided privacy against anyone trying to look in. And Drake had a surveillance system around his home that rivaled most banks. Too bad he'd been too busy entertaining TJ to monitor it last night and this morning.

"Relax, TJ. I gave the maid the day off. Trust me," a proud smile shrouded his chiseled white face, "no one comes to my home without me knowing," he said, sitting cross-legged, across from TJ, drinking a glass of wine. "You sure you don't want any?" he asked while holding the glass in the air.

TJ shook his head, no.

"You know..." Drake paused. "The life expectancy of men belonging to the Magobi tribe in Argentina is eighty-nine," he said while swirling the red liquid around in the wine glass. "The Magobi men drink a glass of red wine first thing every morning. They say it's the key to their longevity." He took a sip and put the glass on the small round patio table.

"What I'm about to tell you goes against my own principles, and I didn't even consider having this

260

conversation until you called me from the airport in Cancun yesterday. Although I toyed with the idea in my head after you called, I still didn't think I was going to tell you, not even after I picked you up from the airport last night.

"But after what we did last night in the sauna and what you did to me in bed early this morning, some old feelings have resurfaced. And, still, in the wee hours of the morning I lay awake watching you sleep, debating whether to tell you or not."

Would you go ahead and tell me? TJ wanted to scream. But instead he nodded, knowing very well that Drake never rushed anything.

"Do you know a young man by the name of Samuel Lewis?" Drake asked.

"No. Should I?"

"Samuel Lewis is your wife's first cousin."

"Oh, Carmen and PC's boy?"

"He's Carmen Lewis's son." He shook his head. "I don't know anything about him being a son of Percival Turner."

"It's a long story," TJ waved a hand in the air, "but the boy is PC's son."

An amused look crossed Drake's face. "Really now?"

"Really," TJ said. "I did my homework. This kid, Samuel, is in prison serving a life sentence for murder—"

"Was..." Drake said. "His conviction was overturned. Sam was released yesterday."

"Okay, and why should that concern me?" TJ asked.

"Back in 2000, when Sam Lewis was only thirteen, I recruited him."

"You what?"

"The kid was very intelligent. He had no strong male influences in his life; his mother was in and out of the hospital; and he lived in a drug-infested area. He witnessed firsthand the evil power that a major player in the drug underworld wielded."

"So you reached out to him through the Big Brother, Big Sister program you work with?"

"I'm afraid so, and at fifteen, he did his first job. In no time, he became an expert at killing. His only mistake came when he went behind my back and planned a hit on his own."

"But still, thirteen? Wasn't that a little too young?"

"I thought so myself at first. And usually I didn't recruit at such an early age, but Sam was different. He was calculating and very mature for his age. If it weren't for his soft features, you would've thought he was a man. He stood six feet tall at thirteen."

"I'm surprised you let him live after he was arrested."

"In the two years that I trained and interacted with him, he knew me as John Baker. Every time I was around him, my face was disguised. TJ, you're one of the very few people who know who I really am. And when I say I kept my ears open, you better believe I did. At the first sign of John Baker's name being brought up, Samuel would've been a memory."

"I called in some markers, arranging for him to be raped his first night in prison."

"Why?" TJ asked.

Drake took another sip of his wine. "To see if he would break."

"And did he?"

"No. He handled the situation quite admirably. Instead of going to the guards or calling the prosecutor and attempting to turn state's evidence and telling them about me, he bided his time, and within three months of the rape, all four men were dead. They were all killed in different ways. Each kill was clean and no one reported seeing Sam anywhere near the victims before they were found."

With a tinge of panic in his voice, the bishop said, "Drake, you have to get rid of him. Don't worry about the contract on PC; switch that over to Samuel."

Drake looked at TJ as if he were unsure.

"Come on, Drake," he pleaded with his arms out in front of him. "You owe me for Shemika. Because of you, I had to fork out close to a hundred grand for the wedding and honeymoon from hell."

Drake stood up and walked over to where the bishop sat. He bent down and whispered into TJ's ear. "If I take out one of my best killers, I won't owe you." Drake grabbed TJ's chin and turned the man's head so they were face to face. "Contrary to what may be going through your mind," he smiled, "you'll owe me.

Neither Drake nor TJ saw Skip Abraham nestled behind one of Drake's four-foot gardenia shrubs next to one of the fifteen-foot palm trees on the inside the fence.

CHAPTER 35

*I*t was a little nippy outside for an Atlanta October morning. Percival was in his own world, jogging the five-mile trail through and around Piedmont Park. Only the hardcore walkers, joggers, and bike riders were out this particular morning. The light rain falling on top of his gray hooded sweatshirt felt good. Besides, he was too consumed with his thoughts to let a little rain bother him.

As he ran past the lake, Poppalove popped into his head. Whether he believed who Poppalove said he was didn't mean a speck of dirt. What had meant the world to him, was what Poppalove had imparted to Samuel and him back in June. Since then, neither father nor son had spoken of that day.

Less than a month out of jail, Percival had accepted the Christian Chaplain position at the Atlanta Federal Penitentiary. He could tell that Carmen hadn't wanted him to work in the prison because of the hostile environment he would have to go into every day. But, as he had explained to her, that's exactly why he had to take the position.

Over the three-month period during which Percival had been the full-time chaplain, he befriended a young man who went by the name Shabazz. Shabazz was finishing up a five-year bit for identity theft and check and credit card fraud. Shabazz looked like a younger version of Mel Gibson. By looking at him, you'd never know he was Black until he opened his mouth.

Shabazz and Percival had become close. So close that a few weeks after Shabazz's release, he and a sister named Rhythm approached and offered Percival the opportunity to pastor the non-denominational New Dimensions First Church of God, the super-structure under construction near downtown Atlanta. The only catch was that New Dimensions was going to be a megachurch.

Although he'd told Carmen that he wasn't interested in leading another megachurch, he didn't think he'd ever have the opportunity to be a part of the fast-growing, ever-popular One Free movement.

Although Rhythm and her husband Moses "Prophet" One Free, founded the tribal, entrepreneurial, spiritual, hip-hop-like, One Free movement, Bishop Solomon King One Free was its spiritual leader.

New Dimensions wasn't giving people fish; they were teaching brothas and sistas *how* to fish, sending single mothers back to school, and providing free day care in the process. And because the law prevented drug offenders from receiving Pell grants, or any type of financial aid, New Dimensions was providing full scholarships for ex-offenders, upon completion of the *One Free Know Thyself Black Empowerment Program*—this a twenty-week intense cultural awareness reading for understanding class. Many people dropped out but many made it through, and those who did, received full rides to one of the many HBCU's across the country. And after completing college, a significant number of students went back to work for one of the many corporate entities that New Dimensions and the One Free family owned.

Prosperity preaching was a big part of New Dimensions, but it was the type of prosperity preaching from which everyone had the opportunity to benefit.

The One Free family owned record companies, banks, construction companies, stock brokerage firms, schools— you name it, they were into it. Beauty supply stores, nail shops, gas stations, and even schools in the black community were being taken over wherever New Dimensions and the One Free family set up shop.

So for these very reasons, Percival knew he couldn't pass up this honor. He had no doubt that pastoring New Dimensions was the opportunity that Poppalove spoke of.

As he turned the key in the apartment door, he could just imagine Atlanta becoming the Black Mecca that it was touted as being. Percival had nothing against Koreans, Indians, or Middle Easterners; he just thought it would be nice to see Blacks owning the businesses in their own communities.

"I can't believe you were out there running in that rain." Deidre' pointed outside. "Are you nuts? You wanna catch pneumonia? Don't expect me to leave school and come back down here to take care of you when you get sick," she fussed.

"Deidre', calm down. It's just a little rain. I do this all the time," Percival said as he walked in the door to the small apartment that Deidre' had rented for him when he'd gotten out of prison.

He was disappointed that she and Samuel weren't more than friends. But still, words couldn't explain how proud of her he was. Not only did she get her GED, but she'd won an art fellowship grant to NYU and a ten-thousand-dollar cash prize for the picture she'd painted for Percival.

Percival had flown her in from New York for the weekend so they all could celebrate Samuel's acceptance into Percival's alma mater, Morehouse College.

"Rev, I just don't wanna see anything happen to you. You don't know what I went through back when you had that aneurysm.

"I'm sorry, Deidre'. If it'll make you feel better, I won't jog in the rain again."

"Now, you know you lying. You just sayin' that so I'll stop fussin'." She pointed in the direction of his single bedroom. "Go take a shower and leave your wet jogging outfit in the hall. I'll put it in the wash with the rest of your clothes."

"Deidre', you're supposed to be here this weekend to relax and celebrate, not be my maid."

"You should've thought of that before you let your clothes pile up. And besides, I don't mind. I enjoy taking care of you. You're the only father I ever had. Now, go on," she said, shooing him away.

Thirty minutes later, he felt like a new man, and looked like one, too. Finally he'd shaved his Isaac Hayes beard off, trimmed his mustache, and massaged baby oil into his now bald head.

Although he sported the Michael Jordan bald look, he wore his favorite Los Angeles Lakers warm-up outfit. He stood in the mirror smiling. Before Carmen, he wouldn't have been caught dead in a warm-up suit or sneakers. Even in high school he'd been into slacks and dress shoes.

Today was the big day. With the pastoring position he'd accepted, he could finally afford to take care of a wife.

Samuel couldn't hold water, so he hadn't told him his plans. The only reason he had told Deidre' was because Samuel's acceptance into Morehouse wasn't enough to get her to agree to fly back for the weekend. Needless to say, she was ecstatic after he showed her the pearl and platinum ring.

"Deidre', you hungry?!" he shouted from the bedroom. After slapping some smell good on his face, he opened the door. "I know you heard me," he said, closing the bedroom door.

"Me and everyone else in the building. But you weren't speaking to me."

Percival turned around. "Carmen? What are you doing here? I mean, I'm glad to see you, but I thought you were going to be busy last-minute baby shopping with Shemika."

"I was, but things have changed."

"Uh-oh, I don't like the way that sounds." He bent his head sideways. "Where's Deidre'?"

"I let her take my car. She's taking Meka shopping."

He shook his head, "I'm confused. She and I were supposed to do the father-daughter thing today. I wish someone would start telling me these things."

"I'm telling you now."

"You know what I mean, Carmen."

"You're right. I'm sorry, Percival, but I have something important to talk to you about."

"That's fine, Carmen. I just really had my heart set on spending the afternoon with Deidre'. We were even going to drop in on Samuel at the Boys' Club," he said, taking a seat across from her.

"If it will make you feel any better, I saved you a trip."

"What, Samuel's not working today?"

"No. I mean, yes, he's working, but he's busy preparing his group of thirteen to fifteen-year-olds for the Thanksgiving Black History Challenge."

"Oh, yeah." He slapped himself on the forehead. "How could I forget that?"

She got up from the dining room table and went into the kitchen.

"As much as he worries about his kids being ready, I don't know how you forgot. That boy is just like you, Percival, always putting others ahead of himself," she said as she pressed a couple of buttons, bringing the microwave to life.

"I know." Switching the subject, he asked, "So, what do you wanna talk about?"

"Tell you in a second," she said, taking a box out of the microwave.

"My favorite." He rubbed his hands together. "Krispy Kreme donuts," he said, smiling and clapping like a little kid.

After placing a can of diet Coke and four donuts on the table, she took a seat across from him. "Percival," she put a hand over her chest, "I love you more than you will ever know. I fell in love with you outside that police station, and for twenty years I've never stopped loving you."

Interrupting, he said, "I am so in love with—"

"Percival," she extended her arm towards him, "stop right there, please. This is hard enough as it is. So, please, let me finish."

He would've apologized, but he had half a donut stuffed in his mouth, so he just nodded.

"I can't marry you."

He coughed, almost choking on his food. "What? Deidre' told you?"

269

"Don't be upset with her."
"You say you love me. So why not?" he asked.
"I've been living with HIV for seventeen years."

CHAPTER 36

" *H*ello. May I speak with Mr. Money, please?"
"And you are?"

"Are you Mr. Money?" the voice on the other end inquired.

"This is Bishop Money," TJ said.

There was silence.

"Look, I don't have time for games; either you say something or get off my phone."

"This doesn't sound like Mr. Money."

"Because it's not Mr. Money. It's Bishop TJ Money. Who the hell else would be answering my cell phone?"

"Mr. Money, I have some—"

"You either address me properly, as Bishop, or this conversation ends right now. Now who the hell is this on my phone?"

"After you check your mailbox, you'll think I'm a foe, but I assure you I just wanna be your friend," the person on the other end said.

"I don't have time for games. Tell me who you are right now or I'm hanging up this damn phone." He waited.

271

"Hello. Hello." He took the phone away from his ear and looked at the cell phone's display. The person was calling from a blocked number. Probably one of Shemika's ignorant friends playing games, he thought as he pressed the *End* button, reclined in his massage chair and went back to reading the Saturday morning comics.

"Bye," Shemika's irritating voice interrupted his reading.

He put the paper back in the massage chair's newspaper tray. "And where do you think you're going?" he asked.

"To hell if I don't pray."

"Maybe one day soon I can send you," he smiled, "on an all-expense-paid trip."

She stopped at the bedroom double doors. "Just keep threatening me," she said with her hands on her hips.

"You misunderstand me, Babycakes." He smiled. "I'm so sorry if what I said came off as a threat." Continuing with a hand placed over his chest he said, "If something happened to the big black egg with legs that was carrying my seed, I couldn't bear to live with myself."

She pointed a finger at him and shook her head. "You see, TJ, that nasty mouth of yours is why you haven't been able to put it or your little-bitty wee-wee up in this big black egg in, what, seven months now? And guess what, little man? Bush will take over the Nation of Islam, and Farrakhan will become president before you hit this again," she said before turning to leave.

That's what you think, he wanted to say, but instead he spoke in a kinder tone, "Do me a favor, Babycakes. Check the mail before you leave."

"Tell your rotten-tooth, dried out dead momma to check the mail!" she shouted.

He couldn't wait. He absolutely could not wait until after she had that baby. He smiled, thinking that he'd love to stone her to death like they did to unfaithful wives back in biblical days, but his hands around her neck would have to do, he thought as he hit the remote on the chair and switched on the TV security monitor.

"Sweet Jesus!" he jumped out of the chair and shouted. "Stupid whore, they should call you Delirious instead of Delicious!" TJ shouted as he watched her barely miss the big M that he'd had cut into the azalea shrubs at the front gate. And now she was driving across his freshly manicured Bermuda grass. "I'll kill that whore," he said aloud while putting on his robe and running down the stairs barefoot.

By the time he made it outside, Deidre' and Shemika were pulling out of the gates. "Crack head heathen-heifer!" he shouted. Since he was already outside, he decided to walk to the gatehouse to see what that butthole on the phone had put inside his mailbox.

The cobblestone driveway looked good, but it was murder on bare feet. After reaching the gatehouse, he went in and removed a magazine-sized manila envelope from the mail chute.

"Sweet Jesus!" he exploded after opening the envelope. Immediately, he pulled out his cell phone.

*****

After meeting Drake, and giving him the pictures, TJ got back into his Hummer and made some phone calls. An hour later, he had Skip Abraham's cell number. Not long afterwards, TJ arrived home, he parked his vehicle in one of the six garage bays and switched on the voice activated phone inside the Hummer.

"Hello, Sweetheart. Took you long enough, Mr. Money... I mean, Bishop Mr. Money."

"I'm not your sweetheart," TJ said through clenched teeth.

Ignoring him, Skip continued, "You know, it seems that a man as important as you, with so much to lose, would've gotten back with me way before now."

"I didn't have your number."

"You went through all the trouble of getting me fired from the *Constitution*, and I'm sure you're the reason I can't land a decent job with any paper in Atlanta. Now that tells me that you have a lot of pull in this city, and you can get things done. You do all that, ruin a man's life, and you don't even have his number?"

"I don't know what you're talking about. How could I have gotten you fired? I don't even know you," TJ said.

"There you go again. Trying to screw me without as much as a kiss on the cheek. You know damn well who I am. My name is behind every article I've written about you and your church."

"Ohhhhh, you're the clown who called me a vampire in the church?"

"You keep on, and you'll catch a defamation charge along with another rape charge," Skip said.

"Huh?"

"Raping me like you did that young girl all those years ago," he said in a sing-song voice. "My life. My career. And, oh, I forgot, defamation of character," he sang. "Have you heard of freedom of the press?"

"Look," TJ said angrily, "give me the negatives to the pictures you left in my mailbox and I'll help you get your job back—"

Skip interrupted, "Like you helped your friend out of the church? Like you helped Gertrude Harris? No, Sweetheart, I don't think so."

TJ was seething. "Sweet Jesus, let's just get down to it. You have something I want. Now, what do you want?" TJ asked.

"Uhmmm... I'd settle for... let's see... you sitting on a razor-sharp sword doused with battery acid, or... No, no... How about you placing a live grenade up your ass?" He laughed. "But since I don't think you'll listen to reason, I'll settle for half a mil' in small bills."

"I don't know what you're smokin', but whatever it is has made you more insane than you already were."

"Yeah, you're right." Skip paused. "Guess I'll see how insane FOX, CBS, and NBC think I am. You think they'd give me half a mil' for pictures of you and the old professor swapping spit in front of Morehouse? How about the pictures of you and the good ole professor on his patio? A black Baptist gay bishop... Who would've thought?"

"I am not gay," TJ said, seething.

"Could've fooled me." Skip laughed. "No, I've change my mind; you couldn't fool me. At least now you'll be on Oprah. I can see the headlines: *Black Gay Bishop, on the Downlow*. But in your case, it's the lowdown downlow. Or how about, *Get The Lowdown on the Downlow Bishop*."

"Okay, okay," TJ said. "What do you want?"

"Now, I know I speak perfectly good English. Maybe you're a little slow. I mean, in the head. We know you're not slow on foot; you proved that when you ran away from your lover that night at Morehouse."

"It'll take a couple of weeks."

"Not good. Not good at all. It will take three days, and it will be cash, nothing larger than a twenty," Skip sang.

"I can't get that kind of cash that fast," TJ said.

"Now, you must be on drugs if you think I believe that."

TJ heard a knocking sound on Skip's end.

"Call you right back, Sweetboots," Skip said. He pressed *End* but he didn't press it hard enough.

"Gardy, what are you doing here?" TJ heard Skip ask.

"You fucking retard. I told you to be patient. Wait until the time was right. But, nooo, you had to do things your way."

That voice is familiar, TJ thought as he listened in on the conversation.

"Fucking asshole cost me my career. The attorney fees, bills, and child support have all but bankrupted me," TJ heard Skip say.

"It's no one's fault but your own. I told you a long time ago to stop snorting coke. You knew we were dancing with the devil when I gave you the first piece of dirt on him."

Drake! Shit. That double-crosser.

"You warned me about him alright. I wish someone would have warned me about you."

"What's that supposed to mean?"

"You've been screwing him again. Don't deny it."

Drake. I don't get it. Why would Drake set me up?

"I won't deny it," Drake said. "Screwing TJ was just part of the job."

"What job? What are you gon' do with that?" Skip asked.

"What do you think I'm gon' do with it?"

"You wouldn't. You don't have the heart. You're a college psych professor, not a killer."

"That's where you're wrong. You don't know me nearly as well as you think. Being a college professor is just a front. I've been USGIA for three decades."

"USGIA?" Skip asked.

"United States Government intelligence agent. There are hundreds of us masquerading as professors in colleges and universities all around America."

"But why?" Skip asked.

"The three M's," Drake said.

"What?"

"The three M's. My job is to help choose the future leaders in the African-American community and make sure none of them has the potential of becoming a Martin Luther King, Malcolm X or, worse, a Marcus Garvey."

"So, you were going to kill TJ Money?" Skip asked.

Unreal. TJ couldn't believe what he was hearing. He couldn't believe how clear he was hearing it, either.

"No, of course not. TJ's on our side. USGIA made him. We gave him media exposure. We chose him to be a premier leader in the black community, and as long he continues this prosperity ministry, others just like him will rise. Soon, black children all over America will be choosing to go into the ministry for the pay instead of for God."

"I don't understand," Skip said.

"Of course you don't. It was never about TJ. It's always been about Percival Turner. All around the nation, there are secret institutions set up just to study the behavioral patterns of Blacks. Laboratory rats are used to predict how they'll behave when certain obstacles are put in front of them. Greed and envy is what drives Blacks. Money is their

God, and they don't even realize it. But Percival Turner was different. He cares more about his fellow man than he does about money. Combined with his charisma and intelligence, we knew we were in trouble if we didn't take him out."

Skip interrupted, "So, you used me to fuel Money's insecurities?" Skip asked. "Why are you telling me all this?"

"How long have we been seeing each other, John? Eight years, right? You were married to Marna when we first got involved. Since then, I've wanted so badly to tell you, tell anyone, but I couldn't. Out of all the people I've killed, you're the only one who would appreciate this story."

The last thing TJ heard was a hissing sound and then a pop. That's when he pressed the *end* button on his phone. And for the longest time he sat there staring at the red *End* button. Without a shadow of a doubt, he knew that Skip was dead, just as he himself would be if he didn't kill Drake first.

CHAPTER 37

*F*or over four hours, Percival drove around the city aimlessly, contemplating his next move.

He pulled over to the emergency lane on the side of the highway and called Chicago. He'd never met or spoken to him, but he needed to talk to someone he looked up to.

"Hello. This is Percival Turner. May I speak to Bishop Solomon King One Free."

"Brotha Turner, how's life treating you in the ATL?"

"I'm livin'."

"It's hard out there for a righteous brotha tryn'na keep to the right."

"You ain't never lied," Percival said.

"I'm sorry, Brotha, Solomon's in New York meeting with Russell Simmons, Jay Z, Kanye West and a few other hip-hop icons."

"Really?" Percival replied.

"They're trying to find a way to include the church in the next hip-hop summit. I'm sorry, forgive my lack of manners. I'm Moses One Free, Rhythm's husband."

"Prophet, Prophet One Free? Moses Prophet One Free?" Percival asked, sounding like a parrot.

Moses laughed. "That's what some of the younger kings and queens call me, but I'm not a prophet. That's you, King. All you've been through and you're still standing in the light of God. I would say that title fits you a lot better than it does me."

"I'm in awe. I don't know what to say."

"Brotha, I wake up in the morning and put my pants on, one leg at a time, just like you. I'm no different than anyone else," he said.

"Mr. One Free?"

"Moses. Call me Moses."

"Moses, I'm trying to reach the Bishop—"

He interrupted, "Don't let Solomon hear you call him that. He hates that title. Everyone up here just calls him Soul or Solomon."

"Thanks for the advice. Actually, I called for some advice. Now that I'm speaking to you, I'd like to get your take on something," Percival said. "You have a minute?"

"Yeah. Shoot."

Percival took a deep breath as he watched the Saturday afternoon traffic whiz by. "My wife and son passed away nineteen months ago. Since then, a woman I had a brief affair with twenty years ago came back into my life."

"Carmen Lewis?"

"You know?" Percival asked, surprised.

"That's part of my job. You were chosen because of the way you handled yourself through all of the adversity you've faced this past year."

"Okay, I should've known you already knew, with you being a prophet and all."

"Okay." He laughed. "Touché."

"So, Moses, anyway, tonight I was planning to propose, but today Carmen tells me she's HIV positive."

"King, I want you to close your eyes and tell me what you see."

Percival did as he was asked. "I don't see anything."

"Open them."

"Okay."

"Now what do you see?"

"Everything." Percival looked out at the traffic on the highway. "Cars, the road, a bridge," he said.

"Before you two found each other—I'm talking about after your wife and son passed—what would you have seen if I would have told you to close your eyes?"

"Nothing," he said.

"What would you have seen after I told you to open them?"

"Nothing... Oh, wow. That was so simple," Percival said.

"Usually is," he said.

After hanging up, he looked at his watch. It was 6:45. Everyone was meeting for dinner at seven. Percival looked up at the green and white sign ahead. He was one mile from Turner Hill Road in Conyers. The Cheesecake Factory at Perimeter Mall was at least a twenty-five, thirty- minute drive.

Nineteen minutes later, he pulled up at the valet parking area at Perimeter Mall. No one rushed to get his keys. But several young men scrambled to get to everyone else around him. He guessed that they had looked at the old blue dented, beat-up pickup he was driving and thought he'd mistakenly pulled into the valet area. And when he emerged from the truck wearing his purple, gold, and white Lakers outfit, they really ignored him.

Finally, a young Asian kid walked up. "Sir, this is Valet."

"I knew that when I pulled up five minutes ago," he said.

"Uhmmm, it's seven dollars," the kid said.

Percival reached into his back pocket.

"No, Sir, you pay when you leave."

"Then why aren't you parking my truck?"

"I just wanted to be sure you were alright with the fee."

Usually, he wasn't rude, but he snatched the ticket out of the kid's hand and walked off.

As usual, the Cheesecake Factory was packed. He didn't wanna wait on the hostess, so he just barreled his way through the crowd and looked around the restaurant until he spotted them.

"I'm so sorry, everybody. I got caught in traffic," he said, taking a seat. "What? Who died? Why are you all looking at me like that?" Percival asked.

"Pops, you look like the gay abominable snowman in that Lakers' outfit," Samuel said.

"It has purple and gold in it, too," Percival pointed out.

"My point exactly," Samuel said.

Percival had to laugh with the rest of them. The purple was faded.

Deidre' held her hand out. "Carmen, can I get my ten dollars, please. I told you he'd show."

"We didn't think you were coming. We called your cell phone several times," Carmen said, handing Deidre' a ten-dollar bill.

"No," Deidre' pointed at Carmen and Samuel, "you two didn't think he would show."

"Excuse me, Sir," a waitress carrying a tray of food said, trying to pass by Percival.

After turning sideways, letting the waitress pass, Percival took out his phone. The screen revealed seven missed calls. "Sorry, I forgot to take my phone off *Silent.*

Percival looked around. The restaurant was bustling with activity. Not knowing how much time he had before being interrupted by another waiter or waitress, he dropped to his knees. "Carmen Raquel Lewis," he grabbed her hand and put the platinum and cloudy-white pearl ring on her finger.

As if on cue, Luther Vandross's *House is not a Home* played over the restaurant stereo system. Looking deep into her her hazel eyes, he began, "Queen, I can't and won't let another year go by without you being my wife."

Her eyes watered. "What about my—"

He shook his head. "I don't care about any H-I-V or A-I-D. What I do care about is the L-O-V-E that we share for each other." He kissed her hand. "Carmen, I vow to love you yesterday, today, tomorrow, and forever. You are my day, my night, my darkness, my light. Carmen Raquel Lewis, I will proudly love you for life, and in the forever afterlife. Queen," he bowed his head, "please I beg you, please, make me whole, fill the emptiness in my soul, complete my life, be my wife."

Tears streamed down her face. Too choked up to speak, she nodded, yes.

Suddenly, it seemed as if everyone in the restaurant were on their feet applauding.

"I love you so much, Percival," Deidre' cried.

Too choked up for words, Samuel just nodded with his eyes closed.

A few minutes later, after calm was restored in the restaurant, Percival said, "And as for you two, Deidre' and Samuel, I know you're both adults, but I'd be honored if you let me adopt you. On second thought, I guess I just have to legitimize you, Son." He directed his attention at Deidre'. "But you, I have to adopt. It's about time you called me something other than Rev, or Preacherman. And you, Samuel, if you call me Pops one more time, I might have to pop you upside your head."

The two of them turned and looked at each other and then back at Percival. At the same time they said, "We do."

"And Mom does, too, Pop. I mean, Dad."

"Okay, Samuel, you can stick with Pops; you sound like a white kid TV actor."

"Excuse me," Carmen said as she retrieved the phone from her purse. "Hello? Uh-huh. Oh no! No! No! God! Please, no!" Carmen cried.

Percival took the phone out of her hand. "This is Percival Turner," he said. "Okay." Is she going to make it?" He listened carefully. "Uh-huh." He signaled everyone to get up. "We're on our way."

CHAPTER 38

*J*t had been a long time since he'd been able to relax at home on a Saturday by himself. Every Saturday since they'd gotten back from the honeymoon, Shemika had, had something going on at the house—a barbeque, baby shower, card party, something.

All it had taken was for TJ to stay home for one of these functions; she'd never had to worry about him ever being home in the daytime on a Saturday again.

He'd seen most of her circus-clown friends at the wedding, but he had never formally met them until Shemika invited some over for a pool party on a Saturday back in June. Most of the women were named after foreign cars—Mercedes, Porsche, Camry and, TJ's sentimental favorite, Lexus. Most of the guys had double one-syllable names—Bay-Bay, Boo-Boo, Doo-Doo, Ray-Ray, and Jo-Jo. That was enough for him to grab his things and head to the apartment downtown.

He had allowed her to have the Saturday parties because, if he protested, she'd have them anyway, and instead of ending at a decent hour, out of sheer evil, she'd probably make sure they went on well into the wee hours of Sunday morning.

After hanging up from listening to Drake and Skip, TJ went into the bedroom and turned on the TV.

He still couldn't believe that Drake had been playing him all those years. He wouldn't doubt that Drake had set the brotha up who was hired to kill Shemika.

He scrolled through the movie channels. After about three rounds of channel surfing, he settled on *War Of The Roses*. It was a movie about a husband and wife trying to kill each other.

The movie gave him an idea. He knew Shemika would be home soon. She had to get ready for some family dinner at the Cheesecake Factory. So, TJ jammed the elevator before he hurried downstairs, opened the freezer, took out a bag of wings, and put them in the sink. After removing the small deep fryer from under the kitchen grill, he went into the pantry, took out a gallon of vegetable oil, and poured it into the fryer.

Next, he grabbed a screwdriver from a kitchen drawer and loosened up the screw that grounded the fryer's electrical cord. After going up the back stairs, he took the fryer filled with cooking oil into a walk-in guest bedroom closet and waited.

A few minutes passed before he remembered the note— the one he hadn't typed. "Shit," he said after hearing the chirping of a car alarm. He was standing in the middle of the wraparound stairwell. He ran back upstairs and went back into the bedroom closet closest to the stairs.

"TJ? TJ? You home, little man?" he heard her call out.

I have your little man, alright.

"Nah, Girl, I'm fine. Oh, I understand. Yeah, you did the right thing. Carmen, you had to tell him you were HIV positive sooner or later."

Sweet Jesus. Lord, tell me she didn't say what I think she said.

"Percival is a good man. But, Girl, even the best of men wouldn't marry someone they couldn't sleep with. But I think you two will still be best of friends. I can't wait till you give me the word to tell TJ's mini-me ass. Trust, Girl, I will have a gun pointed to his head when I tell him; if not, he'll kill me himself. Yeah, Girl, I know. How many times did you stick his ass with that syringe?" She laughed. "And he thought that was a damn mosquito bite. That was a great idea. Thank God, you didn't have to sleep with his nasty ass. Wait till he finds out he's got HIV."

TJ slumped to the closet floor. He no longer cared about the note. He got up and came out of the closet with the fryer. Just as he peeked around the corner to make sure she couldn't see him, he froze when he heard her next words.

"I'm in the kitchen gettin' some ice. Girl, please tell me you didn't tell Percival about the church robbery. Thank God. I don't know why you feel bad. The nigga ain't shit. Hell, he been robbin' the congregation for years. You needed money for Samuel's and Deidre's tuition. And that poor Ms. Harris, now she can buy herself a nice new home. I know Maggie Parker wouldn't take any, but I still don't feel right not giving her any money."

After he heard the downstairs bathroom door close, he went into the hall and tilted the fryer, spreading a thin layer of cooking oil on three of the hardwood steps.

After he finished with the stairs, he took the fryer back into the guest bedroom, put it in the closet, and ran down the back stairs.

A minute later, he was at his computer.

BABYCAKES:

BE CAREFUL. GONE TO STORE TO GET DEGREASER. ACCIDENTALLY SPILLED COOKING GREASE ON STAIRS CARRYING DEEP FRYER TO WORK ROOM TO FIX A SHORT.

LOVE YOU DEARLY

TJ

As he finished the letter, he heard one of the sweetest sounds he'd ever heard in his life—the anguished shrill screams of Shemika crashing down a long flight of stairs.

While she was screaming, he was going through the key box in the garage. After whimsically studying the six sets of car keys, he chose the Ferarri.

After the garage door went up, he let the convertible top back and pulled out of the garage and up to the front door.

He decided he would give it twenty minutes before going back inside the house. It was hard just sitting there waiting. He wanted so bad to watch her die.

"Shit!" Only five minutes had passed when he heard sirens. No way she'd gotten to a phone or to the alarm console's panic button, he thought.

Immediately he hit the remote, opening the gates, before jumping out of the car and running inside the house.

The sirens were right outside when he taped the note to the bottom stair railing.

Right as the paramedics came in, TJ knelt down by her side.

"You keep trying... but I promise... you'll... die... way before me," she said, before passing out.

CHAPTER 39

"*B*ishop Money, your wife is fine."

"The baby?" Carmen inquired.

The doctor continued, "We had to perform an emergency Caesarean. It's too early to tell, but preliminary tests show that your son is fine and healthy.

"When can I see them?" TJ asked, false enthusiasm in his voice.

The doctor looked a little uncomfortable standing in the emergency waiting room surrounded by Percival, Samuel, Deidre', Carmen, and TJ. "I'm sorry, Bishop Money, but only three people are allowed in the Critical Care Unit at a time." He paused. "Mrs. Money specifically asked for the hospital to keep you out."

"That's ridiculous. I'm her husband. You can't keep me from seeing my wife and son."

"Technically you're correct, but—"

"But nothin'. Doctor Green, is it?"

The doctor nodded.

"You be her doctor; let me worry about the husbanding and parenting part," TJ said.

"There's nothing you can do, Doc? Carmen asked. "Although Shemika specifically said that she doesn't want to see him, he can still go in there?"

The doctor shrugged. "I'm sorry, Ma'am; he is her husband."

"Not as sorry as *he* will be if he takes one step toward those doors," Percival said, pointing toward the Critical Care Unit.

"You haven't had enough yet?" TJ said. "Those six months in jail didn't do you any good, huh, PC?" TJ looked Percival up and down. "Give me a reason to send your black ass back. Just one, that's all I need," TJ said.

"Who you think you talkin' to like that, you little punk-ass weasel?" Samuel pushed Percival aside and stood in front of TJ. "Unlike you, my father is a real man. Let me hear you come out your mouth wrong again. And as for my cousin, I don't have to worry about you goin' in to see her. All I gotta worry about is how I'm gon' beat another murder case if you pass through those Critical Care Unit double doors."

"Look, all of you." TJ took a step back. "I don't want to send anyone to jail. I just want my wife and son home with me. So to keep down confusion, I'll wait out here," he said, retreating to a seat in the packed waiting room.

Samuel took a step toward TJ. "Damn right, you gon' wait out here".

A few minutes later, Samuel, Carmen and Percival were standing over Shemika's bed.

The doctors had said she was fine, but she sure didn't look it. Both of her legs were in stirrups and in casts. She had an IV in her wrist and a bandage wrapped around her head. She had to be in pain. Percival winced. He looked on and silently prayed while she held the little premature sleeping ball of joy in her arms.

"Carmen, I can't do this any more. I want out. I give up," Shemika cried.

"What happened, Cuz?" Samuel asked.

"This time he almost did it. While I was falling down the stairs all I could think of was my baby. I knew that if I let go of my cell phone I would die at the bottom of those stairs. With two broken legs and bleeding like I was, I would have. I hadn't talked to God in a long time, but I thanked him for keeping that phone glued to my hand so I could call 911."

"What, you tripped over something?" Samuel asked.

"No, there was grease on the stairs."

"What was grease doing on the stairs?" Percival asked.

The three of them gave him a you-know-how-it-got-there look.

"As I was being taken out of the house by the paramedics, I heard someone in the background, probably a cop, say something about a note left on the stair railing. It had something to do with the grease that was on the stairs."

"So, Terrell left a note?" Carmen asked.

"No." Shemika shook her head. "There wasn't anything on those stairs."

"Why didn't you take the elevator?" Percival asked.

"I tried. It wouldn't work, but it worked fine this morning," she said.

It was one thing to destroy an adult's life, but to attempt to kill a woman and an unborn baby was the final straw for Percival. He was seething with anger.

An idea started to form in his mind as he walked out of the Critical Care Unit. By the time he walked through the double doors, he knew exactly what he wanted to do. The

how was the problem. He had four Sundays to figure that
one out. He smiled at the possibility of finally being able to
take down the Black George Bush.

*****

"Less than thirty minutes ago, he embarrassed me," TJ
pointed down. "in front of everyone in the emergency
waiting room. I couldn't even go see the whore and my
son".

Drake and TJ were in a hospital restroom on a different
floor of Piedmont Hospital.

"What's the hold up, Man? My life has been threatened.
Why is Sam Lewis still breathing?"

"Timing," Drake said.

"Timing? Drake, it's been months."

"I told you when I agreed to hit him that it would be
done before the end of the year. We still have a month. And
besides, I'm throwing in his father, free of charge," he said.

"Why would you do that?"

"You want me to take out the son and leave the father
alive?"

"No, but..."

"TJ, you know how I feel about you. I'm not taking any
chances on something happening to you," Drake said.

TJ put a hand on his. "Thank you," he said, just as full
of it as Drake was.

"Just be patient. The year is almost over," he said
before turning and wrapping his hand around the door
knob.

CHAPTER 40

*a*utumn was in full bloom. Red, brown, orange, and some green leaves fell everywhere except on the ten-acre, One World Faith grounds. The turf-like grass looked like a golf course that would make Tiger Woods proud. The sun was shining on this particular breezy morning.

As far as a mile in four different directions, police officers ushered the traffic toward the One World Faith mammoth complex. If you wanted a good seat for the most popular 11:30 service, everyone knew you had to be ready to walk in as soon as the nine o'clock service let out.

The sixty-man church orchestra performed as people filed in. By 11:15, the church was packed.

An hour later, Bishop Money was in full swing, remote in hand, when the electronic vestibule church doors parted like the Red Sea. Everyone turned as a cloud of white smoke clouded the rear of the church.

Loud and clear, the words "Jesus walked," rang out from the church's many speakers.

The congregation looked back in awe, thinking that this was one of Bishop Money's church effects, one they hadn't seen.

Bishop Money was the only one who knew that this wasn't of his doing. He repeatedly clicked the remote, trying to get the rear doors to close. Nothing happened.

"Jesus walked," the voice again echoed throughout the church.

The entire ten thousand-plus people in attendance seemed to gasp as Percival emerged wearing all white and holding a microphone to his mouth.

Staring straight at TJ he asked, "Did Jesus ride around town in a diamond-studded, 14-karat gold chariot, trimmed in platinum? Did Jesus have a team of fine horses taking him around to minister to the poor?" He paused. "No!"

The congregation fell deathly silent.

"Jesus walked," Percival said, taking another long stride.

Flustered, TJ's hands moved at a feverish pace trying to get his mike to work. When his attempts failed, he looked over at the blinking light on top of the podium. A couple of weeks ago, the service call really wasn't from the sound system's manufacturer, and the two men in blue THX uniforms that came out to service the system were really there to sabotage it.

"Were the thorns on Jesus' head made of wood, or were they made of gold?" Percival asked, taking yet another step.

Someone brought TJ a bullhorn. "Everyone stay calm," he said. "For those who don't know the man who has interrupted our service," TJ pointed at Percival, "he is the sick and demented former Bishop Percival Cleotis Turner."

"Noooo, One World Family." Percival shook his head. "I'm far from sick and demented. Now," he stuck a finger in the air, "I was sick and demented when I presided over this church. It was just over a year ago when that man," he pointed to TJ, "and I used the Word of God to captivate and control you. I am not solely blaming him for what we did. I was just as responsible for taking your hard-earned tithes and offerings and building our own private businesses, getting rich beyond measure off of your backs."

Again, TJ pointed. "Do you see, family? Look at him. Look at the man who has admitted to misappropriating your hard-earned cash. I was just the associate pastor. He was Pharaoh."

"If I was Pharaoh, then who are you now? Please don't tell us that you're a man of God. A man of God would walk with his people, not ride in three and-four-hundred-thousand-dollar cars while his people have to walk around with holes in the soles of their shoes. If Jesus were here today, do you think he would live lavishly off the money of hardworking people? No, Jesus would walk with his people until they all could ride in cars," Percival said as he took another step forward. "Jesus walked," he said.

As if he were a knight and it were his sword, TJ raised his bible in the air. "Kings 3:13 reads: Moreover, I will give you what you have not asked for—both riches and honor—so that in your lifetime you will have no equal among kings".

Percival lifted his Bible. "Proverbs 22:16: He who oppresses the poor to increase his wealth and he who gives gifts to the rich, both come to poverty." He took a step forward. "Jesus walked," he said.

Samuel got up, walked to the middle aisle, took out a microphone, and said, "Corinthians 2:17: Unlike so many, we do not peddle the Word of God for profit. On the contrary, in Christ we speak before God with sincerity, like men sent from God." Samuel paused. "Jesus walked." And he, too, took a step.

Maggie Parker, Gertrude Harris, Carmen Lewis, and several others in the congregation got up, walked to the middle aisle, and quoted scripture parallel or similar to the ones Samuel and Percival had quoted.

And after everyone had finished, Kanye West's hit song, *Jesus Walked*, burst through the sound system and filled the church. At the same time, a steady stream of white-robed men and women walked through the white smoky church entrance singing the words to the Kanye West hit.

After the song ended, Percival pointed to the entrance before saying, "One Free Family, New Dimensions' Chicago Angels of Mercy choir, and anyone else who wants to see how and wants to know why Jesus walked and still walks, follow us," he said, leading the way out of the building.

The line stretched for three blocks as hundreds, maybe thousands, of the One World Congregation members and the One Free Family walked the four miles to the unfinished New Dimensions First Church of God, singing *Jesus Walked*.

CHAPTER 41

*L*ast month on, Thanksgiving weekend, he felt like Hercules up in One World Faith Missionary Baptist church.

Of course, the media had blown the confrontation all out of proportion, comparing TJ and Percival to deceased rap superstar rivals Tupac Shakur and Christopher "Biggie" Wallace.

"What are you doing up so early?" he asked Samuel, who was entering Percival's bedroom.

"You marryin' my momma today, remember? How I'm s'posed to sleep knowing that after nineteen years I'm no longer going to be the man in her life?" he said, walking up to Percival.

"Nah, I'm just messin' with you. But for real, Pops, I know I haven't told you this, but I love you. No matter what the future holds for us, I just wanna let you know that I'm proud to be your son."

Percival pushed him away. "Ho-hold on, Partna'," he said, looking around the room. "We can't be huggin' like this. We in the ATL. We don't want nobody to think we got a little sugar in our tanks."

Samuel barreled forward and wrapped his arms around his father. "I don't care what anyone thinks. You're my pops and I love you," he said as they laughed and hugged.

Breaking their embrace, Samuel said, "Don't move; I'll be right back." He ran out of the apartment bedroom.

A minute later, Samuel emerged holding a large box wrapped in a brown grocery bag.
"Happy Kwanzaa. Congratulations. All that good stuff," Samuel said, handing Percival the box. Excuse the wrapping paper."

"Ah, Son, you didn't have to get me anything."

He grabbed for the box. "Okay, give it here. I'll take it back."

Percival quickly pulled it out of Samuel's reach. "I said you didn't have to, but since you did..." He peeled the garbage bag away. "Wow, this is too cool," he said, rubbing his hand over the finish.

"Pops, this is 2005. The word *cool* played out in the '80s. The wood-covered African-centered reference Bible you're holding is off the heazy maybe, or off the chain, but not cool."

"Okay, I'll go one better," Percival said. "How 'bout it's off the heazy for sheazy, down right greasy insane in the membrane off the Amtrak train chain."

"You doin' way too much, Reverend Tupac Twista Snoop Dogg Turner," Samuel said.

*****

299

A couple of hours later, Percival and Samuel pulled up to the church that he was going to be presiding over in a couple weeks.

It was 11:30. The service wasn't scheduled to begin until one but, people were already sitting in the pews.

"Dad, where you been?" Deidre' asked.

He smiled. The way she called him *Dad* sounded real good. "Uhhh, home," he said.

"How you gon' show up only an hour and a half early? You was supposed to be here thirty minutes ago."

"Why?"

With her hands on her hips, she continued, "Because that's what we'd planned, remember? We've been rehearsing this for only a month now," she said. "And don't you laugh, Samuel. You just as bad as your father. You know he old and got sometimer's."

"Sometimer's?" Samuel replied.

"Like Alzheimer's, but he forgets things sometimes, you know, when it's convenient." She kept a stern look on her face while Samuel and Percival cracked up. "I don't see anything funny."

"Deidre', did I tell you how beautiful you look in white and brown?"

"It's cream and beige, but don't try to change the subject."

"Where's Carmen? I wanna see my bride."

"Uh, that would be not. You know it's bad luck for the groom to see the bride before she walks down the aisle."

Samuel and Percival walked around greeting the guests and thanking everyone for coming. And before he knew it, the time had come. Percival couldn't be any happier. The organist started playing.

Samuel and Percival started walking down the aisle. A few steps from the altar, Percival stumbled. He was on his way to the floor when Samuel grabbed his arm.

"Pops, you okay?"

Percival turned to his son. And that's when he saw it. Without blinking, Percival dove in front of the red dot on Samuel's chest.

EPILOGUE

a few days before Percival was gunned down, a homeless cripple, wearing an army jacket that looked to have been in every war since the American Revolution, set up his cardboard home near the dumpster on the east side of the new church. Not many paid attention to the new resident. This was because it wasn't uncommon for the homeless to live near a church, especially one so close to downtown, which is where ninety percent of Atlanta's homeless population resides.

For three days, the cripple with the long, gray hair dragged his dead leg and hunched over a shopping cart looking for anything of the smallest value. It was Saturday, Christmas Eve, the best time of year for the homeless, a time when no man ate out of trash cans, and no man went hungry. On this day, he knew he didn't have to leave his new home; food would come to him if he patiently waited for the wedding to end.

Suddenly, what seemed like a happy day went awry. When the first scream and gut- wrenching cry came from the church, the cripple watched a man emerge from a side door. Not five feet away from the black gloved stranger, the cripple calmly called out, "Drake."

Not even a millisecond had gone by before the first silenced gunshot, was released, and immediately thereafter, six more followed, knocking Drake into the church's blond gray brick wall, splattering blood, and brain matter over the stained glass window that depicted a black man pulling another black man out of water.

No one heard the silenced shots, and no one paid attention to the little hunchbacked cripple limping across the street and down the block. The further the cripple walked the less he dragged his leg, and by the time he made it to the alley on 7th and Peachtree, six blocks from the new church, he was walking just fine. He looked around, making sure no one had followed him, before removing and tossing the fake face, wig, and dirty old clothes in the garbage dumpster in front of him. "Sweet Jesus, God is good," TJ said, breathing a sigh of relief.

Too bad he didn't have eyes in the back of his head; if he had, he would've seen Moses One Free's wife, Rhythm, and her niece, Baby Girl, walking past the alley entrance.

While walking out of the alley, Bishop Money said to no one in particular, "In the words of Maya Angelou, And Still I Rise."

PREACHERMAN BLUES II

ARMAGEDDON

**Find out how the saga ends
09/09/09**

STREET LIFE
by JIHAD

RIDING RYTHYM
By JIHAD

*R*iding Rhythm is a love story set in the early 1970's and 80's. Rhythm is a college student in D.C. who learns of Moses King, the man who started the Disciples, a street gang in Chicago. After reading his court case she writes him. The letters start to flow back and forth and Rhythm becomes an attorney to fight the system that has incarcerated the man she falls in love with. Moses' estranged brother,

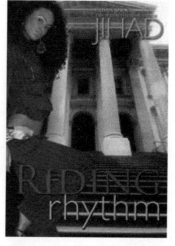

Bishop Solomon King, seems to have his own agenda as he becomes a controversial and popular Baptist minister. Lawrence One Free is Moses' friend and mentor in Atlanta Federal Pen whose guidance causes Moses to change the direction of the Disciples. Pablo "Picasso" Nkrumah was of the 12 kings in the Disciples. When Moses goes down he organizes the Gangsta Gods, a rival gang. The Chicago police and the F.B.I. stay one step ahead of Moses, Picasso, Law, and Solomon, until Rhythm brings them together and teaches what the power of love and unity can accomplish. When Rhythm touches the lives of these men, everything changes and all hell breaks loose. Rhythm's heavenly flow shows hell what love can do.

ENVISIONS PUBLISHING, LLC
P.O. Box 83008, Conyers, GA 30013

Enclosed please find $_____ in check or money order form as payment in full for book(s) ordered. Add $2.00 per book to cover the cost of shipping and handling. Please allow 3-5 days for delivery.

ISBN 978-1893196483 RIDING RYTHYM $9.99

Name_____

Address_____

City_____ State_____ Zip_____

BABYGIRL
By JIHAD

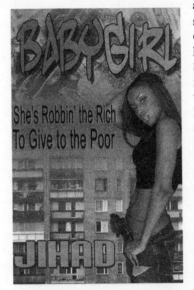

M V P

By JIHAD

MVP is the story of two best friends and business partners. Jonathon Parker and Coltrane Jones have a history. The best friends and business partners have been involved in everything from murder to blackmail, whatever it took to rise they did. Now they're sitting on top of the world, heading up the two most infamous strip clubs in the nation, the duo has the world at their feet. But now they both want out for different reasons. Coltrane is tired of the drug game, He's hoping to settle down with the new woman in his life. Jonathan, now a top sought after criminal attorney, is ready to get out of the game, that's because his eye is set on the Governor's Mansion. With the backing of major political players, he just might get it. There's only one catch. Jonathan has to make a major coup... bring down his best friend, the notorious MVP, Coltrane Jones. As two longtime friends go to war, parallel lives will collide, shocking family secrets will be unveiled and the game won't truly be over until one of them is dead.

ENVISIONS PUBLISHING, LLC
P.O. Box 83008, Conyers, GA 30013

Enclosed please find $_____ in check or money order form as payment in full for book(s) ordered. Add $2.00 per book to cover the cost of shipping and handling. Please allow 3-5 days for delivery.

ISBN 978-1893196483 RIDING RYTHYM $9.99
Name_____
Address_____
City_____ State_____ Zip_____